Steuben's brownshirts planned something big for Chicago

If Bolan couldn't rescue Marilyn Crouder, if he lost it at Coyote Lake, it would be up to Hal Brognola and Stony Man to somehow figure out the target, move in time to head off a catastrophe and clamp a lid on Steuben so that he could do no more damage to society.

Mack Bolan wasn't a fatalist, but he had seen enough of combat firsthand to know that anything could happen at any time. He had prepared himself long ago for the near certainty that he wouldn't die of old age, in bed, surrounded by old friends and family.

And that was fine. He simply didn't want his final hours on earth to be a wasted effort, capped by failure.

The Executioner knew with a certainty that Gerhard Steuben was going down hard.

D0681494

DON PENDLETON's

MACK BOLAN.

DESTINY'S HOUR

THE
TYRANNY
FILES

BOOK I

A GOLD EAGLE BOOK FROM

WORLDWIDE.

TORONTO • NEW YORK • LONDON
AMSTERDAM • PARIS • SYDNEY • HAMBURG
STOCKHOLM • ATHENS • TOKYO • MILAN
MADRID • WARSAW • BUDAPEST • AUCKLAND

First edition May 2001

ISBN 0-373-61478-0

Special thanks and acknowledgment to
Mike Newton for his contribution to this work.

DESTINY'S HOUR

Printed in U.S.A.

How can we arrest racial decay? Shall we form
a select company for the really initiated? An Order,
a brotherhood of Templars around the holy grail
of pure blood?

—Adolf Hitler, 1934

Ten hearts, one beat! One hundred hearts,
one beat! Ten thousand hearts, one beat! We are
born to fight and to die and to continue the flow,
the flow of our people. Onward we will go,
onward to the stars, high above the mud of
yellow, black and brown! Kinsmen, duty calls!
The future is now!

—Robert Jay Matthews, 1984

True evil never dies. It cannot be destroyed.
But it can be contained, its symptoms treated
with a dose of cleansing fire. No victory is
permanent. The war goes on.

—Mack Bolan

For John F. Kennedy, Jr.

PROLOGUE

Wilkes Land, Antarctica

Even with the insulated ski mask beneath the sturdy helmet, the droning of the snowmobile had worked its way inside Joe Statler's head and put down roots between his left eye and his temple, digging in until a dull pain radiated from the spot. Reflections of his headlight from the frozen waste in front of him lanced through his goggles, digging claws into his brain. Statler had found that he could hone the cutting edge of that insistent misery by revving up the engine, letting it unwind, or he could cut back on the pain by slowing, holding the vehicle to a walking pace. The obvious solution was to switch the thing off and take a break, but Statler didn't care for that idea.

Not here. Not now.

Another twelve or thirteen miles, and he could rest to his heart's content at Igloo City. Hot coffee, maybe with a shot of Irish whiskey for the hell of it, space heaters, conversation and companionship, maybe another raunchy movie in the VCR after Malloy had packed it in. It wouldn't do to have her catch him watching Ginger Lynn service a baseball team, with three men on and half a dozen waiting in the dugout.

A sudden diminution of the pain inside his skull snapped Statler back to the here and now. He didn't have to check the snowmobile's speedometer to know that he was slowing—had almost reached the point of stalling out, in fact. And wouldn't *that* have been a bitch, he thought, to kill the engine accidentally in the middle of nowhere, with the mercury standing at seventy-five below.

Getting stuck out here would be the worst bad news imaginable. The protective gear he wore would keep him for a while, but he could never hope to go the distance on a twelve-mile hike across the polar ice cap. Not in the dark, this far from shelter.

Not when he had missed the bear.

Rutledge had sworn that he had seen the bear, a hulking prowler that would dress out around six hundred pounds, maybe more. Rutledge had set a new speed record getting back inside, of course, and Statler wasn't sure he had seen anything at all, much less a hungry polar bear.

Of course, it didn't matter what *he* thought, as long as Neidermeyer called the shots. And Neidermeyer had decreed the maybe-bear a threat to Igloo City, had insisted that ten members of his crew—minus the women, Becker and Malloy—patrol the wasteland on four-hour shifts until they either bagged the animal or satisfied themselves that it was gone.

Meaning they had to satisfy the chief. As far as Statler was concerned, they ought to leave the bear alone—assuming it existed—and relax until such time as it came knocking on the door and asking for a snack.

Unfortunately, Statler didn't call the shots, so here he was, humping the snowmobile with a throbbing headache and the heavy Remington Model 700 strapped across his back. Statler had never actually fired the rifle, but no excuse would get him out of the patrol once Neidermeyer had made up his tiny little mind.

An hour out, two hours cruising through the darkness with a semblance of organization, then an hour back to Igloo City, with the needle on the fuel gauge trembling close to *E*—which stood for "Execute your frigging will if you get stuck out here, too far to walk back in."

He had no fear of getting lost, per se. The GPS uplink took care of that. What Statler feared was getting stuck, and never mind the two-way radio that was supposed to let him summon help at need. An hour out, or maybe more, and damned near anything could happen while he sat around and waited for the cavalry.

Especially if they were sharing territory with a hungry polar bear.

At first he didn't recognize the fire for what it was. Still small and distant, it flickered along the skyline, where the eerie light of a three-quarter moon reflected off the frozen nothingness that was Wilkes Land. A trick of light, perhaps; it could be closer than it looked—or, then again, might not exist at all, beyond the sparking image on his retinas.

Another half mile closer to his destination, and he knew that something had gone seriously awry. The outside lights at Igloo City were high-powered halogens, no flicker to them, and they didn't have this red-orange cast at any range. Statler had followed them across the wasteland far too many times to be deceived.

This was a fire, and not some piddly bonfire, either, by the look of it, from nearly eight miles out. Not just a single building wreathed in flames. No, it looked as if the whole place was burning.

He twisted the throttle with his right hand, headache suddenly forgotten even as the engine screamed. Jolting across the washboard surface of the ice field, Statler searched his mental data banks, trying to think of an occurrence that could send the whole damned settlement—eleven separate buildings—up in flames.

And came up empty.

One thing he was reasonably sure of, though: it hadn't been a polar bear.

So, why did Statler feel a sudden need to clutch the Remington, to work its bolt and slide one of the fat Magnum rounds into the firing chamber?

Two miles out, where he could smell the reek of burning oil and gasoline right through his ski mask, Statler parked the snowmobile and left it idling while he slipped the rifle off its sling, over his head, and worked the bolt. As he moved out again, steering one-handed, Statler held the weapon in his lap, prepared for God knew what as he approached the blazing funeral pyre of Igloo City.

It was incredible, the way the heat waves traveled out to meet him at a hundred yards or more, the first time in eight months that he had actually felt himself perspire. He scanned the compound as he coasted to a halt, but saw no signs of life.

Wait! There was something, over by what used to be the motor pool, before it had imploded. First one human shape, and then another, crooked shadows dancing out in front of them, haloed by firelight from behind.

Statler accelerated toward them, one hand raised in greeting, frozen when it hit him that their black cold-weather gear was unlike anything his fellow sufferers in Igloo City wore or owned.

Another winking flame, this one much smaller than the main bulk of the fire, bright orange, somehow erupting from the shoulder of the nearest black-clad stranger. In the microsecond prior to impact, just before the bullets swept him from the saddle, dumping him behind the snowmobile and letting it go on without him, Statler recognized the muzzle-flash.

And wondered why he suddenly felt deathly cold.

Banks Island, Northwest Territories

SERGEANT ARTHUR DUNLOP, Royal Canadian Mounted Police, braked his Jeep to a halt and reached across the console to retrieve a large-scale topographic map from the passenger seat. The map was folded to the quadrant that he wanted, and it took him only seconds to confirm his own position to a sixteenth of a mile. Relieved—if not especially surprised—that he was still on course, Dunlop replaced the map in the seat to his right, eased off the brake and cautiously accelerated on the winding, unpaved road.

Dunlop wasn't attired in the famous red serge jacket or peaked "Mountie" hat that were reserved, these days, for full-dress ceremonial occasions. He was dressed in forest camouflage, with rugged hiking boots, and a fatigue cap rode low on his forehead, shading his eyes despite the gloomy overcast. There would be rain before the day was out, or maybe snow. His suit of thermal underwear would come in handy in the latter case. He wore a 10 mm Glock automatic pistol in a fast-draw shoulder rig beneath the camo jacket, with two spare magazines in pouches underneath his right armpit. An Ithaca Model 37 riot gun was mounted on the Jeep's dashboard, its muzzle angled toward the ceiling. On the seat behind him, in a zippered nylon case, was his personal favorite weapon, a Heckler & Koch G-3 assault rifle.

Dunlop was hoping that he wouldn't need the guns at all, but he drew comfort from their presence.

His mission was supposed to be routine. The RCMP had complaints on file from several residents about some kind of camp or compound on the island's northeast quadrant, where the folks apparently were fond of shooting guns off, sometimes in the middle of the night. Spotty surveillance from the air had turned up nothing but some photos of a crude stockade with Quonset huts inside, and something that may have been a target range off to the west. Dunlop was to scout the place, perhaps make contact with its occupants, and ascertain what they were doing with themselves.

So far, so good.

Dunlop wasn't especially concerned just yet. He knew there were some strange birds building fortified compounds down in the States, but nothing of the kind had happened yet in Canada. Between the laws proscribing racist speech and publication, and the statutes limiting firearms possession, there was no ''militia'' movement to be found in Canada, no Ku Klux Klan, no major skinhead groups to speak of. You still heard about the violent biker gangs from time to time in Québec, but up here in the Northwest Territories, just a short hop from the Arctic Circle, it was much more likely that a group of poachers was engaged in taking pelts or trophies out of season. That, or else a bunch of city boys who liked to slip away and play at being weekend warriors.

But just in case, he had the Glock, the Ithaca and the G-3.

Dunlop had marked the camp's location on his map, a red dot from a felt-tip marker, and had memorized the photos taken from the RCMP spotter plane. He knew the layout, understood that he would have to pass some kind of gate or checkpoint to gain entry. He was going in without a warrant and would have to turn around if they refused to let him in. In that case, he would drive back to Sachs Harbour, no doubt grumbling all the way, and make a call to headquarters in Ottawa from there. Let someone else decide what happened next, and wait for bloody reinforcements if they had to go back in the hard way.

Right.

By Dunlop's calculations, it should be another six or seven miles before he reached the camp. He could push the Jeep at speed and risk a broken axle on the rugged track, or he could take his time. The choic was obvious, and he was in no hurry, seeing that the job would take all day, whichever way it went.

If it was poachers, he could hand them off to wild-life wardens, forget about the place entirely as long as the wardens had no problem getting in and serving papers on the lot. They wouldn't need the RCMP unless there was trouble of the shooting kind.

Three miles to go.

He checked his two-way radio and got a blast of static, telling him that he was out of range. Too bloody typical. No backup presently within a couple hundred miles, and he was out of touch with that.

The first thing Dunlop noticed, as the stockade came into view, was that the gate stood open. Not entirely, but perhaps halfway. Enough to let the Jeep pass, maybe.

At thirty feet, he stopped and tapped the horn to let them know they had a visitor. When no one had appeared in forty seconds, Dunlop gave a longer blast, immediately followed by two short ones and another long.

Still nothing.

Switching off the engine, swallowing an urge to take the shotgun or the G-3 rifle with him, Dunlop stepped out of the vehicle, took time to lock the driver's door and walked up to the gate, calling aloud as he advanced.

"Hello, the camp! Sergeant Arthur Dunlop, RCMP. Is there anyone home?"

He felt more than a trifle foolish, but it could be worse.

He could be under fire.

When he had reached the gate and still received no

answer, Dunlop poked his head inside, his right hand straying automatically to find the Glock's plastic butt. A sweeping look around the compound, checking out the Quonsets there, revealed no sign of life.

"Hello?" he called again. "Is anybody here at all?"

Nothing.

Dunlop kept calling as he pushed the gate wide open, moved inside and started to check out the huts one by one. If there was anyone about, they had to have heard his calls by now. That could mean trouble, but the place felt empty to him, dead, as if the occupants had pulled up stakes and gone.

Five minutes later, Dunlop found the target range.

They had erected thirteen wooden posts, nailed plywood flats to each and mounted paper targets on the flats. The targets, torn by bullets, stained and crinkled by a recent rainfall, all depicted human beings. Half of them were blacks in caricature, with the swollen lips, buck teeth and bulging eyes like something from a Stepin Fetchit movie in the 1930s, only these were clutching knives and pistols—menacing rather than comical. The other half he took for Jews, although the faces barely qualified as human, with their great hooked noses more like vulture beaks than any human features. Dunlop recognized them by their ringlet sideburns, yarmulkes, the Stars of David worn on long black coats, like badges on a uniform.

"Ah, shit!"

Watching his back, Dunlop retreated to his vehicle at double time, wondering how far he would have to drive before he could make contact with some backup on his radio.

He hoped that it wouldn't be very far.

Hood River County, Oregon

THE ARMORED TRUCK was late. And while that didn't automatically mean trouble, it made Fitzpatrick nervous. He was counting on this score—if not an easy one, at least successful—to secure his place within the Temple and perhaps make his superiors consider a promotion. If he blew it, though, and came back empty-handed...

No way.

It was no great surprise to find the armored truck running a bit behind its schedule. They had clocked it twelve days running, and the shipment had been half an hour late on one occasion, nine to thirteen minutes late three other days. Fitzpatrick reckoned they got caught up now and then at different stops: maybe some hassle with the count, or someone at a certain drop decided they should shoot the breeze a while, the driver too polite or too soft-hearted to just drive away.

No matter.

He would wait all day, if necessary, and the men assigned to him knew better than to give him any shit about it. They were too well-trained and too professional for that.

The truck came out of Portland five days a week, following U.S. Highway 84 due eastward, making drops and pickups at a string of banks and businesses in Bonneville, Hood River, Chenoweth and the Dalles before doubling back. It was never empty, but some days the kitty was fatter than others, and Friday was the fattest—what with paydays for the working stiffs, some outfits wanting extra cash on hand to make change for the weekend trade, while others closed on Saturday and Sunday, wanting what they'd earned all week safe in the vault in Portland. You could almost take your pick, coming or going, and the armored truck should have a couple million dollars in it.

Fitzpatrick had decided they should hit it on the outbound trip, instead of coming back, because the highway traffic at that time of day was lighter, not so many people traveling as in the afternoon, with few commuters on that stretch of U.S. 84. This early in the morning, all the local farmers and their wives were eating breakfast, maybe slopping hogs or milking cows, feeding the chickens, looking forward to another day of drudgery. The Bluebird school bus had passed the ambush site already, only two cars zipping past them since, an average of one car every nineteen minutes.

Perfect.

If they caught a break, they could be finished with the operation in ten minutes, tops, and well away before some pesky witness happened by. If they were interrupted, though, it would be too bad for the interlopers. Ben Fitzpatrick's troops were packing enough heat to deal with the National Guard, much less some transient salesman or a soccer mom.

He checked his watch again and cursed the passing time. The muscles in his thighs and buttocks had begun to cramp from being too long in a crouch, but if he sat, sure as hell, the truck would choose that moment to roll past their lookout, forcing him to scramble for the rocket launcher, maybe fumbling it, losing the perfect shot. To compromise, he straightened, then got down on one knee, reaching for the launcher without turning his head, making sure he could find it by touch alone in a pinch.

The launcher was an 84 mm M-2 Carl Gustav recoilless antitank weapon, originally designed in Sweden, later picked up as the British army's standard infantry weapon for tackling armored vehicles. Unlike the smaller American-made LAW rocket launcher, the Carl Gustav could be rapidly reloaded and wasn't discarded after use. It could penetrate twenty-five inches of armor with one of its HEAT rounds—High Explosive Anti-Tank—that focused the energy of conical hollow charge into a high-speed jet that sliced through armor and into the target vehicle, causing catastrophic damage to crew and equipment.

Not for use against the rear compartment, with the cash, Fitzpatrick thought, and smiled. No problem. They had come prepared for anything, and that included picking up a cutting torch.

The other members of his team were armed with automatic weapons, side arms, antipersonnel grenades—the latter not to be employed unless the worst-case scenario should come to pass, and they were interrupted by police before they bagged the cash and made their getaway.

The walkie-talkie clipped onto his combat harness crackled with static, then a tinny voice announced, "Heads up! It's party time."

Not very military—they would have to talk about that later—but Fitzpatrick felt the warm rush of adrenaline as he picked up the M-2 rocket launcher, swung it to his shoulder, waiting for the armored truck to actually show itself before he pressed his face against the eyepiece of the sight.

And there it was.

The familiar bread-box shape was suddenly before him, coming into view around the curve, accelerating on the straightaway. The loaded launcher weighed in close to thirty-seven pounds, but it seemed feather-light now, as Fitzpatrick pressed the rubber eyepiece flush against his face and watched the armored truck grow even larger, zooming in as if by magic. Lining up the crosshairs on the grille, itself screened by steel mesh that was supposed to save the radiator and the engine from incoming small-arms fire, he counted down the seconds, held his breath and squeezed the trigger.

Whooosh!

They called the piece recoilless, and that was exactly right. The back blast all went out the open tube behind him, scorching tree trunks, limbs and grass back there. He offered up a swift but fervent prayer that the rocket-assisted HEAT round—weighing nearly four pounds, traveling more than one thousand feet per second—wouldn't miss its mark. If he was forced to reload one-handed, aim and fire a second time, chances were that he would be too late, the truck already past him and away.

Fitzpatrick's shot, in fact, didn't impact precisely where he'd aimed. Instead of slamming through the mesh and grille, smashing the radiator, detonating when it struck the engine block, his rocket went in six or seven inches high. It struck the hood, and only then exploded near the firewall.

Close enough.

The armored truck didn't stop dead—momentum saw to that—nor did it vault end-over-end. Instead, it was enveloped in a cloud of thick, dark smoke, erupting from the new vent in the hood, as it began to swerve wildly, losing acceleration, as the driver fought to control his crippled vehicle and keep it upright, staying off the shoulder of the road.

Fitzpatrick snapped into the walkie-talkie's mouthpiece, "On your marks! Be ready!" Setting down the M-2 launcher, he picked up the AK-47 rifle that was lying at his feet.

The armored truck was drifting below him, engine dead. Another second now, and one of the rent-a-cops up front would have the square, dash-mounted microphone in hand, calling for help.

No time to waste, then.

"Go! Go! Go!" Fitzpatrick shouted, plunging down the gentle slope in front of him. He hit the blacktop running, boot heels clomping on asphalt, his Kalashnikov aimed at the truck, though its rounds couldn't penetrate the armored shell.

When he was close enough to see the guards, both ashen-faced behind the flat windshield, Fitzpatrick maintained his right-handed grip on the AK, reaching inside his camo jacket with the left and bringing out the laminated sign that read Use The Radio And Fry. Give Up The Cash, No Harm.

The driver, as expected, had the microphone in hand, but when he spoke, after he read Fitzpatrick's cautionary note, it wasn't to the radio. He half turned in his seat, said something to his partner in the cab. The second, older man said something back and shook his head, flashing a stubborn scowl.

Old bastard wanted to die for someone else's

money, thought Fitzpatrick as he turned and called across one shoulder, "Get the heat up here!"

Bogard was at his elbow in another moment, shoulders slightly hunched beneath the weight of fuel and air tanks for the standard Army-issue flamethrower he carried. Six inches shorter than Fitzpatrick, Bogard was a fireplug, thick and solid from the years of pumping iron.

"Toast them?" he asked.

"Hang on a sec," Fitzpatrick said, and moved closer, holding up the sign where it couldn't be missed, nodding toward Bogard and his weapon. Once again, the driver hesitated, but his gray-haired passenger was tired of waiting, reaching out to snatch the microphone and thumb down the transmitter button.

"Light them up!" Fitzpatrick snapped, stepping out of the way as Bogard raised his weapon. Liquid fire erupted from its muzzle, with a sound like all the gas jets in the world turned on at once. Fire splashed across the hood and windshield of the armored truck and dribbled down its sides like lava, burning bright.

"Try for the gun port," Fitz instructed Bogard, watching as his man played fire across the target's right-hand drawer.

"It's shut," Bogard declared, then splashed a lake of fire beneath the truck to toast them from below. "Hot foot," he said, grinning behind his mask. "It never fails."

Fitzpatrick spoke into his two-way radio. "Bring up the torch."

The acetylene tank on its dolly came crunching and rattling over the blacktop, two men trundling it toward the rear hatch of the armored truck. This was the perfect time for the guard in back to open fire and nail them, maybe blow the tank if he got lucky, but he let it pass. Fitzpatrick didn't know if that was simple cowardice, or if the guy was under orders, but it worked to their advantage either way.

It took time, torching through an armor-plated door. Fitzpatrick had the other troops fan out to guard their flanks, the highway stretching east and west. He had two spotters still in place, so they shouldn't be taken by surprise, but there was still a chance some deputy or traffic cop might happen by and want to rumble, still the possibility his penned-up hostages had managed to broadcast an SOS before the flame-thrower talked them out of it.

He stood and waited with the AK-47 cradled in his arms. There wasn't much else he could do, unless he wanted to start snapping orders for the hell of it, piss off everybody for no good reason. Part of being in command, Fitzpatrick knew, was knowing when to shut your pie hole and let nature take its course. The worst thing sometimes was to micromanage every move your soldiers made, thereby provoking nervous errors or deliberate defiance in the ranks. These men knew what to do, and he had witnessed no mistakes so far.

"Ten seconds!" There was raw excitement in the torch man's voice, clearly a feeling of accomplishment, anticipation.

"Cover them!" Fitzpatrick ordered, glancing backward toward the soldier with the flamethrower. "You got them?"

"They're not going anywhere." There was a smile behind the ski mask, cool and confident.

Five automatic weapons had the rear end of the transport covered as the door was pulled from its still glowing frame. Inside, the third guard raised his hands, advancing slowly toward the exit in a semi-crouch.

Fitzpatrick stopped him with a gesture from the business end of his Kalashnikov. "Your partners. Tell them it's all three or nothing."

Frowning, still not reaching for the pistol on his hip, the guard retreated, muttered something to the intercom that linked his chamber to the cab, listened to some reply, then spoke more sharply, though his words were still inaudible outside the truck.

"Okay," he said, as he returned to stand above the ring of guns. "They're coming out."

Fitzpatrick waited, listening. A moment later, when he heard the first door clank and creak, up front, he said, "Good boy," and shot the rent-a-cop, a short burst to the chest that punched him over backward, dead before he hit the deck. Another *whooosh* from the flamethrower, punctuated by a frantic scream, then he heard the door clang shut again.

"They're done," his fellow executioner announced. "Well done, in fact."

It brought uneasy laughter from a couple of the troops, but Fitzpatrick tried to ignore it. This was business, not some comedy, but he also recognized the need for a release of tension after killing in cold blood.

"We're burning daylight," he announced to no one

in particular. "Let's do it and get out of here before John Law shows up and wants to join the party."

"That's okay," his fire man said. "I cooked enough for everybody."

"Well, then, maybe you should wait around after we're gone," Fitzpatrick answered him, "and handle the buffet."

"No, sir!"

"I didn't think so." His turn, now, to smile behind the mask. "Let's move it, people! Move it!"

CHAPTER ONE

Stony Man Farm, Virginia

No matter how often he made the trip to Stony Man Farm, Mack Bolan never failed to get a feeling somewhere between anticipation and excitement. It wasn't like coming home exactly—"home" had ceased to be a long, long time ago—but it was someplace he could let his guard down, more or less, with friends he trusted.

And it always meant another mission, one more chance to face the Reaper and find out who was better at his job.

He had no clues, this time, as to the subject they would be discussing when they gathered in the War Room, and he didn't try to guess. What was the point? If it was quick and easy, Hal Brognola could have given him the details on the telephone, using a scrambled line. A visit to the Farm meant this was more than just another simple hit-and-git to be wrapped up within an afternoon. More marbles, bigger game.

The plane he'd met in Charlotte, coming off a two-day blitz against some Dixie traffickers in China white supported by the Chinese Triads, was a Beech King Air, the A100 model seating twelve, though Bolan was the only passenger. His pilot was a sturdy African American who greeted him with something close to military courtesy and kept his mouth shut during the remainder of the flight. It was a couple hundred miles, about three-quarters of an hour for the King Air at its standard cruising speed, to reach the Blue Ridge Mountains of Virginia and the hardsite known—to those who knew of it at all—as Stony Man Farm.

Approaching from the south, he spotted Skyline Drive, imagining the Appalachian Trail—which, ironically, wound its way through the Blue Ridge range, on the eastern flank of the Shenandoah Valley, rather than the Appalachians proper, to the west. A glance away, and Bolan would have missed the Farm, but there it was, passing below him, house and outbuildings before the air strip, since his normal route from D.C. and points north had been reversed. They passed the airstrip, then banked to come around for the approach. His pilot would be on the air by now, passing whatever recognition codes were mandatory for this day, this flight.

The Farm was ready to receive them. He had seen that much on the first pass, noting that the single-wide mobile home had been hitched to its tractor and hauled fifty yards from the spot where it normally stood, obstructing both runways. Aside from crash potential, it was still a threat, however, if the pilot muffed his recognition code or tried to land without approval from the ground. In that case, Bolan knew, the "mobile home" would drop its walls, roof flipping over backward when the rear wall went, revealing a matched set of quad-mounted GEC miniguns, each of the eight Gatling-type weapons capable of spewing 7.62 mm armor-piercing and/or incendiary rounds at a cyclic rate of 6,000 per minute. That kind of fire would shred any civilian aircraft, reducing it to smoking scrap before it had a chance to taxi through. And new defenses were operational, as well.

They taxied past the mobile home, blank windows watching them like lifeless eyes, and circled back before the pilot cut the power to his twin turboprops. A moment later, Bolan stepped down into sunshine, picking out the glint of chrome on the approaching Chevy Blazer, which trailed dust on the unpaved road between the airstrip and the house.

The driver was Latino, young, as close to spit-and-polish as he could be in a plaid shirt, blue jeans and desert boots. Though he didn't salute—such military gestures were forbidden at the Farm, in case someone was watching, maybe from a passing satellite—he stiffened to a semblance of attention as he said, "Good morning, sir."

"As you were," Bolan told him. "I'm just passing through."

"Yes, sir. If I may take your bag—"

"It's fine," Bolan said, clinging to the lightweight duffel. "I'll accept a lift, though, if you're heading in my direction."

Bolan's driver blinked at that, not sure how he should take the joke, perhaps not certain that it *was* a joke. At last, he bobbed his head and said, "Yes, sir. Of course. I'll just—"

"I've got it." Bolan was at the door ahead of him,

and opened it himself. The young man, slightly flus-
tered, jogged back to the driver's side and slid behind
the Blazer's steering wheel.

Another moment brought them to the house, where
Barbara Price was waiting for him on the broad front
porch, running fingers through her thick, honey-blond
hair. Bolan got out before the driver had a chance to
run around and hold his door, earning a small, suspicious frown.

"Your boy's gung-ho," Bolan said as he climbed
the three porch steps.

"New man," Barbara replied. "It takes a while to
rub the polish off, and then the service hates it when
we give them back, all rough around the edges."

Bolan smiled at that, imagining some DI having to
review the boot-camp basics with a team of Green
Berets or Navy SEALs. "So, you're a bad influence,
then," he said.

Her smile was bright. "That's what they say."

Their eyes met for a moment, locked and held, before he asked, "Is Hal already here?"

"Downstairs. He's going over slides and what-not
with the Bear."

"I guess we shouldn't keep him waiting, then."

"We'd better not." And then, "I heard you're
staying over, right?"

"Don't know," he said, and shrugged. "I wouldn't
mind."

"So, later, then."

The farmhouse looked entirely normal, if a trifle
large, from the outside. Three floors above ground,
with a normal complement of windows—bulletproof,
with computer-coded recessable steel grating—and

double doors to the garage-workshop to his left as Bolan faced the building. Price had left the front door standing open, which revealed that it was made of armored steel, with coded access limited to members of the team.

On Bolan's right, as he entered, was a den and TV room; off to his left, past stairs ascending to the second floor, security HQ was locked away behind another coded-access door. Above them, on the second floor, were sleeping quarters for the staff and any visitors who were required to spend the night on-site. Above that, the third floor was used for storage and defensive operations as the need arose, with armor-plated garrets that could serve as snipers' nests with a commanding field of fire on every side. Bolan followed Price to a door that opened on another staircase, tucked away beneath the first, and let her lead the way to the basement.

The real heart of the lower level was the War Room. Price led him to its steel door, tapped her access number on the keypad, waiting for a monitor two inches square to scan and recognize her right thumbprint. The double screening process would, at least in theory, bar intruders who had somehow picked up on an access code and cleared the other deadly hurdles to proceed this far.

The door slid open, almost silently, and Price stood aside to let him enter. "After you," she said.

"Into the lion's den?"

"I wouldn't steer you wrong," she said, and winked.

Two men awaited Bolan in the War Room. Both of them were longtime friends, though his relationship with Hal Brognola was the oldest and the most complex. The man from Justice, now in charge of Stony Man and what had once been christened Project Phoenix, had been Bolan's federal adversary in the old days of his one-man war against the Mafia, pursuing Bolan, as he sometimes liked to say, "until the damned guy wound up catching *me*." In time, they had become both friends and allies, with Brognola helping where he could, despite the risk to his career and to his liberty. These days, though their collaboration was legitimized by orders from the White House, it was no less secret than it had been when assisting Bolan had made the big Fed a closet felon in his own right.

The second man, Aaron "the Bear" Kurtzman, was seated in a wheelchair to Brognola's left. A gunshot to the spine, sustained in an assault on Stony Man, had stolen Kurtzman's legs but left his rapier wit intact. He was the Farm's preeminent computer programmer, communications specialist and second in command to Barbara Price, ready and able to take up the slack if anything should happen to Stony Man's mission controller. An athletic standout before the shooting hobbled him for life, Kurtzman still worked out on a near daily basis, maintaining an impressive upper-body strength.

Bolan dropped his duffel in a corner by the door and walked around the table to shake hands with Brognola and Kurtzman. "That was good work down in Charlotte," the big Fed remarked.

"No sweat," Bolan said as he took the empty seat at his old friend's right hand, Price settling to Kurtzman's left, directly opposite. "They weren't all that well organized."

"From where I sat, they sounded pretty damned well organized," Brognola stated. "We earned some brownie points upstairs, the way you closed it down. And put some noses out of joint at DEA, I wouldn't be surprised."

"Whatever gets the job done," Bolan said.

"Speaking of which—" Brognola shifted to the present subject on his plate "—what do you know about the Temple of the Nordic Covenant."

"Based on the name," Bolan replied, "I know I wouldn't want to join."

"Smart choice. It's what the press would call a neo-Nazi group, but this one's tricked out as a church of sorts. You've learned a lot recently about the early Nazi movement."

"More than I cared to," Bolan told him. "I know it's more than just the master-race aspect."

"Yeah. And it didn't just pop up from nowhere after World War I, when Germany got hit with a depression. That's the way most schoolbooks tell it, but they skip the whole first act. Too spooky for them, maybe, or the authors just don't know the story in the first place."

"So, enlighten *me,*" Kurtzman said. "I've never delved into Nazism."

"Barbara?"

"The roots of Nazism go back all the way to 1880," Price told him, taking over on Brognola's signal. "At the time, there was a wide revival of occultism in Germany, much like the spiritualist fad in England and America. They borrowed certain Hindu sacred symbols, like the swastika, threw in some weird translations of Egyptian teachings, mixed it up with anti-Semitism, and it grew from there. You may already know this, but the Aryans they talk so much about weren't originally thought to be a race at all. The term applies to certain Indo-European languages. It got mixed up somehow in the translation with the old fixation that Teutonic tribes must be the chosen people of whatever god you're worshiping this week. By 1884, you've got the German Theosophical Society mixed up with Rosicrucianism, then the Order of New Templars and the Thule Society came right along behind it, making sure the racist element was emphasized. Most of the early Nazis—Hitler included—were Thulists, as you know, before they ever got around to organizing a political party. They picked up gods like Wotan from the ancient Norse mythology, and some of them—Himmler would be a prime example—wandered off into black magic, very similar to Satanism. All of which explains why Catholics and Gypsies had almost as hard a time of it in the Third Reich as Jews."

"How's that?" Bolan asked.

"Early Christians persecuted Wotan's followers before they got around to burning heretics and witches. Call that portion of the Holocaust belated payback time. As for the Gypsies, part of Hitler's hate for them was racial obviously—he regarded them as 'mongrels' and 'subhumans,' even lower than the Slavs—but they were also steeped in magic lore and superstition. Adolf and his buddies didn't like the competition."

Kurtzman frowned. "This sounds like something out of *Indiana Jones.*"

"There was more truth than you might think in that particular fairy tale," Price replied. "During the war, Nazis not only hunted for the Holy Grail, but they also spent a lot of time and money trying to locate a polar entrance to the so-called Inner Earth, where their pure Aryan ancestors supposedly took refuge in prehistoric times. Some reports allege they actually found the Spear of Destiny."

"Which is...?"

"Supposedly," Brognola said, "the Roman spear that pierced the side of Jesus after he was crucified. According to some legends, which the top dogs in the reich apparently believed, whoever holds the spear can never be defeated by a mortal enemy."

"Looks like they didn't read the fine print on the guarantee," Bolan said. "Last I heard, Adolf and company were history."

"If only," Brognola replied. "We may have knocked off the conductor, but the band's been playing steady gigs since 1945 without a break. You name the continent, it's got an active neo-Nazi movement stronger than at any time since VE Day."

"Antarctica?" He dropped the name facetiously, surprised to see the glance exchanged by Brognola and Price.

"It's funny you should mention that," the big Fed said, half turning toward Kurtzman. "Let's do it."

At the touch of some concealed control knob, Bolan saw the lights begin to dim. Off to his right, at the far end of the War Room, a projection screen unspooled from its hiding place in the ceiling, dropping almost to floor level. Instantly, a slide flashed on the screen, depicting burned-out buildings on a field of white. They looked like Quonset huts, scorched black by some terrific heat. Thermite, he guessed, or something similar.

The scene changed, still with snow, but this time it was crimson-spattered, as if someone had drop-kicked a strawberry Sno-Kone. A body lay at center stage, with bullet punctures in the heavy parka, clustered at the center of the dead man's chest. The corpse had frozen prior to being photographed, and Bolan had no trouble making out a carving on the forehead: a circle, perhaps two inches in diameter, with crossed lines in the middle, like the crosshairs of a telescopic sight.

"What's that?" Kurtzman asked, no need to tell the others what he was referring to.

"One of the Hindu power signs," Price replied. "A dedication, maybe."

"Or a message," Brognola suggested.

"This was taken where, again?"

"A U.S. weather research station, down in Wilkes Land. Seven dead, and as you see, the whole facility dismantled."

"Let me guess. That's somewhere in Antarctica?" Bolan stated.

"You win an all-expense-paid ski vacation to the polar ice cap of your choice," Brognola said.

"So, this is what—Nazis on ice? They're killing weathermen at the South Pole for what reason? To make an ill wind blow on Israel?"

"I'd be tickled pink if their activities were limited

to the South Pole,'' Brognola said. ''Unfortunately, they appear to have mobility.''

More slides, this series showing off what could have been an old frontier stockade if color film had been invented in the early nineteenth century. Log buildings chinked with mortar, more logs planted upright to construct the outer wall. The only clinker was the practice firing range, subhuman caricatures shot to hell by someone with an obvious disdain for Jews and African Americans.

''Banks Island,'' Brognola advised him. ''It's a part of Canada—specifically the Northwest Territories. We got these shots from the RCMP.''

''Anything besides the artwork to connect this with the Nordic goons?''

''Ballistics nailed it down,'' Hal said. ''The RCMP never miss a trick. Some of their people cut the slugs out of those poles and ran them all—we're talking two, three hundred rounds—against their files on unsolved crimes. Turns out one of the guns—9 mm, probably an SMG—was used to kill a controversial Jewish talk-show host in Calgary more than a year ago.''

Another slide flashed on the screen. Another corpse, this time stretched out in what appeared to be an underground garage, blood pooled beneath him on the concrete floor. The carving on his forehead was familiar, even with the blur of smeared blood on his face.

''Okay.''

''And this,'' the big Fed stated, ''went down last week in northern Oregon.''

The next few slides were also crime-scene photos,

varied angles of an armored truck that had apparently
been blasted with some kind of rocket or grenade and
scorched by fire, its rear door blown or cut away.
Inside the rear compartment of the truck, where bags
of cash had once reposed, a guard sprawled lifeless
in a bloodied, bullet-ventilated uniform. A close-up
focused on the forehead carving, done in seeming
haste, but clearly meant to match the others Bolan
had already seen. Inside the driver's cab, two other
guards had been incinerated.

"Flamethrower?" Bolan asked.

"Looks that way," Brognola said. "It could've
been some kind of homemade napalm deal, maybe a
plastic jug that melted down without a trace, but from
the scorch marks on the outside of the truck, I'd say
it was a spray job. Either way, they didn't burn the
cash. Best estimate, they walked off with a million
and three that morning, after six or seven minutes'
work."

"They have access to military gear," Bolan observed.

"Officially, it's unconfirmed, but hey, who doesn't
these days? All you need is one or two guys who are
willing to enlist, or find some joker already in uniform
who has a grudge against the world, then convert him,
pay him off, whatever. All else fails, you rob an armory
or log onto the Internet and find the plans to
build your own flamethrowers, mortars—hell,
ICBMs. Why not? We're living in the information
age."

"And this carving is a logo of the Nordic Temple?"

"Once again, it's unofficial," Brognola replied.

"You find it in their literature, but still, it's pretty simple, and it could mean anything. Crosshairs, for instance. There was something like it, forty years ago, on death threats that the Minutemen were mailing out. You find the same thing sketched on letters written by the so-called Zodiac."

"Which one?" Bolan asked.

"Both, although the guy they locked up in Manhattan was most definitely not an Aryan. Also, he was too young to be the California Zodiac—who, incidentally, appeared to have some fairly deep black-magic mojo cooking in his head."

"He got away, as I recall."

"Depends on who you ask. No one was ever charged."

"So, who's the brains behind this freak show?"

Brognola nodded to Kurtzman, and another slide flashed on the screen. This time, it was a classic mug shot, full face and left profile, with a string of numbers racked beneath the subject's chin.

"Meet Gerhard Steuben," Brognola announced. "His mama named him Gary Arthur Stevens, back in 1952, when he was born, but 'Gerhard' likes to play at being German. Fakes the accent when he talks, the whole nine yards. A couple years ago, when he was interviewed by some fringe magazine, he claimed he was 'invested' with the spirit of an SS captain killed at Stalingrad in 1943. If he believes it, I suppose he's crazy. Otherwise, he's just a half-assed con man. Either way, he's got an estimated following of ten to fifteen thousand skinheads, knuckleheads and boneheads spread around the world, including pockets in Germany, Russia and South Africa."

"That many?" Bolan said, surprised.

"I know. It all depends on how you look at it. One way, ten thousand in a population of six billion doesn't even make it as a needle in a haystack. But it took no more than six or seven men to stop that armored car and massacre the crew, then split with a million and change. The FBI says two or three men could have blitzed the weather station. One guy may have taken out the talk-show host in Canada. Sometimes, size really doesn't matter."

"I assume this outfit is domestic," Bolan said.

"Herr Steuben is a native of Topeka, Kansas," Price stated. "The mug shot's from a demonstration in D.C. four years ago. The President was having brunch with some Israeli diplomats, and Adolf Jr. tried to crash the party. All he had was a picket sign, and since he never made it past the fence, he only got six months, the bulk of it suspended after serving thirty days. It cost him, though."

"How's that?"

"Soul brothers in the lockup didn't like his rap about the master race. They worked him over pretty good one night. He lost an eye—the left—and tried to sue the government, but it got bounced. Since then, he alternates between a patch and a glass eye, depending on his mood. One of the marbles has an Iron Cross where the pupil ought to be. I kid you not."

"So, under 'Personality,' I'm thinking we can rule out *sane?*"

"He isn't wrapped too tightly, I'll admit," Brognola ventured, "but he's not some raving lunatic. His speeches all make sense—if you're a fascist out to rule the world for Wotan and his Nordic buds, I mean, and there's no question Steuben has smarts enough to lay the plans for these and other jobs the Nordic Temple is suspected of coordinating. If you listen to him, screen out what he's saying and just listen to the tone, he's got some kind of primitive charisma working for him, too. Word has it that his soldiers are fanatically devoted, not just to the Temple, but to him.''

"Sounds like he needs to have an accident," the Executioner replied.

"We'd like to find out what he's up to first," Brognola said. "There seems to be some kind of plan in motion, but we don't have any focus yet. The Bureau had a couple guys inside the Temple, but they lost them six or seven months ago."

Bolan didn't like the sound of that, but he refrained from asking any details. "If they've got a plan," he said, "somebody must know what it is."

"My thinking," Brognola replied.

"You have locations for me?" Bolan asked.

"A few. These jokers move around some, pull up stakes when they get hinky, like the place in Canada. Our list should get you started, though."

"So, what's the deadline?"

"Hell, I wish I knew. The job in Oregon was certainly their biggest heist, but not the first, we're pretty sure. They only leave the mark, apparently, when someone's killed."

"So, they've got guns and money," Bolan said, "and they've already hit one target that appears to have no practical or monetary motive."

"Right."

"They're turning up the heat," Price stated.

"Suits me," Bolan replied. "I'm always partial to a rolling boil."

"Barbara and Aaron can put you in the picture, then," Brognola said, "as far as where their hangouts are, the secondary players, this and that. I wish we had more for you, but without the Bureau's eyes inside, this bunch leans toward the enigmatic side."

"I'll take a crack," Bolan said. "See what I can find."

"Remember ATF," Price added, addressing Brognola.

"Oh, right! I told you that the Bureau lost its people, but the ATF apparently still has one operative somewhere inside the Temple. Trouble is, they're half-past paranoid, between the G-men disappearing and the criticism going back to Waco. Way I read it, they're afraid to lose their man, and maybe even more afraid of being hit with charges that they're picking on a church, in violation of the First Amendment. Anyway, they claim their source has dried up, more or less. That could be the director, choosing not to share, or maybe someone tagged their man and took him out."

"Where was he when they lost the link?" Bolan asked.

"If they're telling us the truth, he had some kind of job at what the Temple calls its western headquarters, outside Tacoma, Washington."

Bolan considered that. It was a good a place as any to begin, but he would want to see the rest of Price's information first, familiarize himself as much as possible with who was who and what was what inside the Temple of the Nordic Covenant.

"Okay, I'll leave you in Barb's hands, then,"
Brognola declared, already rising from his seat as
Kurtzman switched off the projector and the screen
began to rise. "I've got some congressmen I need to
lobby back in Wonderland. We're getting on toward
budget time."

"Good hunting," Bolan told him.

"Same to you." The handshake, dry and firm,
hung on a moment longer than was absolutely necessary, then Brognola turned and left the War Room,
Kurtzman rolling in his wake.

"You heard the man," he said to Price after the
door had closed. "I'm in your hands."

"I heard," she said. "Your place or mine?"

"I haven't seen my place," he told her with a
smile. "It might not be conducive to the mood."

"Who needs conducive?" Price took his hand in
hers and tugged him toward the door. "Will you
come on, already?"

His place, as it turned out, did just fine.

When they were finished, both spent, they lay together with the rumpled sheets around their ankles,
thankful for the air-conditioning that raised a different
kind of goose bumps in the afterglow.

"I see your point," the soldier said, when he could
catch his breath.

"Which point is that?"

"About the room," he said.

"Told you."

"I hate to break the mood—"

"Then don't," she said, feigning a pout.

"But I was wondering about the next briefing."

"What about it?"

"How long do you figure it might take?" he asked.

She came up on one elbow, offering a stunning view of planes and angles, flats and curves. "You have a date or something?"

"I was thinking more along the lines of instant replay," Bolan said.

"How long have you been psychic?"

"Come again?"

"I mean, you read my mind," she told him. "And I plan to."

"Plan to...?"

"Come again." Her fingers found him, teasing, then demanding. "Say, what's this?"

"Feels like a resurrection," Bolan said.

She smiled at him and murmured, "Praise the Lord!"

CHAPTER TWO

Seattle, Washington

The flight from Richmond, into Sea-Tac International, consumed the better part of seven hours, with a ninety-minute layover in Dallas. Bolan understood the economics of "hub" cities, where commercial airlines were concerned—although it never seemed to lower fares—but there was still something ridiculous about turning a three-thousand-mile direct flight into a 4,100-mile dogleg.

Bolan used the time as best he could, sleeping through most of both long flights. A small deduction from the stash of dirty money he had scored in Charleston let him fly first-class, ensuring leg room and freedom from squalling children who couldn't let ten seconds pass without delivering karate kicks to the seats in front of them. The meals were adequate, the one mixed drink he had on each flight soothing to his nerves, and when he closed his eyes to sleep, he didn't consciously remember any dreams.

A vehicle was waiting for him at the airport. It wasn't a rental, but a year-old Chevy Blazer, dropped off on the rooftop level of the airport's multitiered garage an hour prior to the arrival time scheduled for Bolan's flight. The ride was clean, its gas tank full, and the soldier knew it had been wiped for fingerprints. If anything went wrong from this point on, and he was forced to ditch the Blazer, it wouldn't be traceable to Brognola, to Justice or to any other federal agency.

As for his own prints, Bolan didn't worry. They had been deleted from the NCIC system by Brognola's people years ago.

He placed his duffel in the back seat of the Blazer and spotted the second, near-identical bag that had been left with the wheels. Its padlock was a combination model, and he had the numbers memorized, a parting gift from Barbara Price as she saw him off with a handshake that morning at the Stony Man airstrip. Inside the carbon-copy duffel were the items Bolan hadn't carried with him, checked through in the belly of the 707 from Dallas.

On top, he found the M-4 carbine version of the standard M-16 assault rifle, with a 40 mm M-203 grenade launcher mounted underneath the foregrip. Ammunition for both weapons was included, the rifle's 5.56 mm rounds preloaded into 30-round box magazines, the M-203 rounds slotted into canvas bandoliers, with an even mix of HE, incendiary and fléchettes. Also included in Brognola's CARE package was a Desert Eagle semiauto pistol chambered in .44 Magnum, with holster, belt and a dozen extra 8-round magazines. Another bandolier was filled with Army-issue frag grenades. The second rifle, added almost as an afterthought, was a Beretta Sniper, orthodox bolt action, with a Zeiss Divari six-power scope. Bolan's usual side arm, the selective-fire Beretta 93-R, had been checked through all the way from Richmond, traveling as cargo, while the Executioner had made the trip unarmed.

Those were the most unnerving times for Bolan, even when he knew that no one was expecting him or laying traps to snare him on arrival. He had lived through airport ambushes before, but didn't relish them: emerging from the jetway with civilian non-combatants all around him, weaponless, no place to hide if someone opened fire. Of course, security should bar gunmen from the actual arrival-and-departure lounge, assuming that the guards on duty weren't in league with them or bribed to look the other way, but that still left the concourse and the human zoo where baggage was reclaimed from rumbling carousels. He had to sweat the whole thing out, each time he flew commercial, thinking of the sudden carnage that could turn a modern transportation hub into a slaughterhouse in seconds flat.

But he had made it this time. He was free and clear, no tail in sight as Bolan paid his tab to exit the garage and followed signs that led him to Pacific Highway South.

The sprawling airport was located midway between Seattle and Tacoma, hence its nickname, and some urban planner had decreed that the surrounding neighborhood of restaurants, gas stations and massage parlors should also be named Sea Tac. The small tract houses Bolan passed, southbound, all seemed to cringe each time another big jet screamed past overhead. He wondered idly whether this would be a starter neighborhood for newlyweds still short on cash, just starting out, or a dead end for seniors who were similarly strapped, scrimping to make it through the so-called golden years. Surely, he thought, no one with any better options would deliberately purchase prefab housing with a runway view.

The Sea-Tac Strip—I-5, which linked the state's two most populous cities—was regionally famous as a happy hunting ground for prostitutes who serviced truckers and commuters. For a few years, in the 1980s, it had been world-famous for the stalker who had picked off nearly fifty working girls, dumping their strangled corpses in the nearby woods and rivers, but the predator had seemingly retired, and horror had a short shelf life.

Western headquarters for the Temple of the Nordic Covenant received its mail at a post office box in Tacoma, but the actual facility, according to his after-hours briefing, was located in rural Pierce County, southeast of Fort Lewis and McChord Air Force Base. A woodland setting, from the aerial photographs Price had shown him, and Bolan noted now that in addition to the privacy, its location was also convenient for delivery of any hardware stolen by members or paid accomplices from the nearby military reservations. Fort Lewis and McChord AFB would both be well stocked with small arms and ammunition, perhaps heavier weapons, explosives and such peripheral items as commo gear, body armor and night-vision goggles. With a clever man or two inside, each base would be transformed into a lethal shopping mall.

Bolan found a relatively cheap motel in Spanaway, south of Tacoma, a town of fifteen thousand that apparently survived by catering primarily to soldiers, airmen and tourists en route to Mt. Rainier National Park, some thirty miles due east. He had a look around the room but left his two bags in the Blazer, pausing only long enough to call the cutout number that would update Stony Man on his arrival and location. He wasn't expecting any calls, and knew that Price wouldn't leave a message with the aging drunk who managed the motel, but she might check in and leave a number if she picked up any information that could help him.

Back in the car, he checked the time and found that it was still two hours, minimum, before the sun went down. Despite the tedious duration of his flight, Bolan had gained three hours as he traveled westward, thereby touching down at Sea-Tac International—in theory, at least—barely two hours after he had lifted off from Dallas. Jet lag wasn't a problem yet, but he was left with daylight hours to kill before he made his trip into the countryside.

His first stop was a steakhouse, where at least three-quarters of the customers appeared to be off-duty military personnel. You couldn't always tell, of course, some Boy Scouts looked more military than the soldiers who had come along since Bolan's day, a whole new breed recruited by TV commercials promising adventure, education, travel and a chance to Be All You Can Be.

Bolan put away a twelve-ounce porterhouse with baked potato and a large tossed salad on the side. He finished the meal with coffee—four cups, black and strong—before he drove another block and dropped in at a bookstore. It was large, one of the major chains, with ranks of chin-high shelves that radiated from a central checkout counter in a kind of starburst pattern. Bolan browsed through the history section, noting that books on Vietnam—a fair percentage of them penned by veterans—had come into their own, after a long, long period when nothing but left-wing complaints about the war were seen as fit to print. He moved on to true crime, thumbed through some recent volumes on the Mafia and frowned to see his own name in a couple of the indexes, along with names of mobsters he had killed.

Times changed, he thought. And the more they stayed the same.

His war was much the same today as in those early years when he had fought alone against the odds. Today, of course, he had allies, vastly improved technology, and while the Mafia was still around, it rarely merited attention from the Executioner. Most of the Families had withered from attrition—death or prosecution and imprisonment—with new blood for the monster hard to find in many areas where capos once controlled the underworld. Now, with street gangs, motorcycle gangs and foreign syndicates distributing at least three-fourths of the illegal drugs sold in America, with sundry forms of gambling legalized in roughly half the states of the U.S., with hard-core porn and sex toys readily available wherever VCRs and batteries were sold, the old-line Mafia had fallen and couldn't get up. Its passing had been dutifully recorded—if somewhat exaggerated—in the media, from *60 Minutes* to the pages of *Newsweek* and *USA Today*.

There was a time when Bolan had looked forward

to that moment, hoping he could work himself out of a job, but he had long since recognized the folly of that hope. The predators kept coming, and a look behind the widely varied nationalities and pigments, accents and agendas, showed that they were all the same, down where it mattered, in their morbid, rotting hearts.

The Executioner would never work himself out of a job.

He would be riding his crusade into the grave.

But not, he hoped, this night.

Full dark outside, and while the bookstore would be open for another ninety minutes, Bolan had more-pressing business elsewhere.

Driving south from Spanaway on Highway 7, following the eastern border of the Air Force base, he clocked twelve miles before another road—162—branched off and took him eastward. Once he cleared Kapowsin, Bolan started looking for the unpaved access road that would convey him to a point within a mile or two of where the neo-Nazi "temple" had its western headquarters. As usual with such extremist groups, the place was said to be a fortified compound, perhaps a hundred full-time occupants, though they could host ten times that number on occasion, when a rally of the Temple and its various cooperating fascist cliques was organized. Among the not so happy campers who were regulars, roughly three-quarters were male, between the ages of sixteen and fifty-six. They all shared certain strange beliefs about the origins of man, and what it meant to be a patriot.

And all of them were armed.

He killed his headlights once he left the highway,

navigating by the moon, which would be full in two more days. The washed-out light reminded him of other night patrols, though he had always been on foot for those—and would be soon again. He dared not drive the Blazer any closer to the Nordic Temple compound than a mile for fear of being spotted by outlying sentries, maybe having some remote security device pick out the Blazer's noise or engine heat. For all he knew, the compound's outer guards might be equipped with FLIR guns—forward-looking infrared—or Starlite scopes and parabolic microphones. When you had access to the latest military gear, it greatly simplified the task of self-defense.

Or maybe not.

There was a decent chance his adversaries had no such equipment in their stockpile, or that such sophisticated gear wouldn't be regularly used around the compound, if no imminent threat was expected. Then again, he knew from personal experience that haters of the fringe, both right and left, existed in a state of constant paranoia, constantly suspecting that some enemy—competitors, extremist opposition or the state—was plotting overtime to thwart their dreams and frustrate or destroy them.

Mostly, they were right.

Because fanatics feed on hatred, malice and suspicion, even those who seem to be allies are frequently at odds with one another. In the 1920s, vicious infighting had destroyed the Ku Klux Klan, reducing it from a mass movement of five million members that dominated politics in several states, to a ragged remnant of societal pariahs. Ten years later, the same fate—helped along by covert agitation and extensive infiltration from the FBI—had doomed the American Communist Party. Same for the Black Panthers in the 1970s. In the 1980s and 1990s, internecine power struggles had done as much to weaken the ailing Mafia as had state and federal prosecutions.

To Bolan's mind, it was a kind of natural balance, a built-in means of thinning out the predators. He didn't seek to undermine the process, but rather to assist it, cranking up the volume on the paranoia that his adversaries lived and breathed until it brought them crashing down.

He found a place to leave the car, four-wheeling for a distance off the narrow road, until the vehicle was concealed by shrubbery and trees from any casual observers passing by. He took a moment to strip to his Jockey shorts and pulled on his blacksuit. With the addition of a lightweight Kevlar vest, his combat webbing, pistol belt and bandoliers, the tourist rapidly transformed himself into a man of war. Special combat cosmetics blacked his face and hands against reflecting moonlight, and he slung the M-4 carbine by its strap from one shoulder.

All good to go.

It is impossible for any human being to move silently through virgin forest if he plans to cover any real expanse of ground at all. The forest floor is covered wall-to-wall with rocks and twigs, with logs and fallen branches, with dead leaves and dried needles shed by evergreens. With every step, there is a frond or sapling to be brushed against, a root or thorny tendril to be snagged and gently disengaged. Few animals are truly silent in the forest—even mice and insects rustle through the undergrowth as they go on about their tiny lives.

The trick was not to eliminate any sound—a task admittedly impossible—but rather to moderate and control sound, producing noises that *belonged* in a particular wild setting. There was a world of difference between a native tribesman stalking game in the Ituri Forest or the Amazon and some "white hunter" thrashing at the undergrowth with his machete, slapping the mosquitoes that were drawn to sweat and blood.

Bolan had learned to use the forest, jungle, desert—any battleground, in fact—to his advantage, in the dark or in broad daylight. He could pass unnoticed without passing silently, and when he had to freeze, he was immovable as any outcropping, waiting days, if need be, for the moment when prey came within range and he could make the kill. The sounds he made were covered by the forest and its native sounds—its breezes, bird calls, chirping frogs and insects, slinking reptiles, scuttling rodents, dripping rain and chuckling streams.

Bolan had no intention of making contact with his enemies on this probe if he could avoid it. It was pure reconnaissance, but he was still prepared to fight his way clear of a trap if he should find one waiting for him. By the same token, if an irresistible opportunity for mischief presented itself, he was prepared to take advantage of it and advance the schedule of his own campaign.

A savvy warrior kept his options open, kept it flexible and used that flexibility to keep himself alive.

He smelled the camp before he heard it, picked up

sounds of human habitation well before the compound came in view by moonlight. Humans in groups made noise; there was no way around it, one more law of nature, as immutable as gravity. If they remained in one place any length of time, then they had to feed, relieve themselves, do all the things that cast their scent adrift, so wildly different from the way a forest or a desert ought to smell. Except when wildfires were on the loose, no forest in the world produced the aroma of roast meat, and there had never been a forest fire that smelled like Tex-Mex chili cooking in a cast-iron kettle. Mother Nature never played Germanic war songs on a boom box, intercut with snatches of a dead fanatic's too familiar voice, ranting to listeners, themselves long dead, who chanted back at him, *"Sieg heil! Sieg heil!"*

The camp wasn't well lit from the outside, perhaps because their huffing generators had a limit to their output, possibly because the men in charge didn't see fit to put their compound on display. They had been forced to hack a clearing from the forest. The land was bought up at auction, on the cheap, with Gary Stevens and his storm troopers favored by a stroke of fortune when their competition—a Seattle lumber company—was razed by fire and had to pull its bid, investing in repairs before new forest acreage. The upshot was a hundred-acre tract of forest, purchased free and clear for settlement by members of the Temple of the Nordic Covenant, with only minor interference by inspectors from Pierce County, who had certified their homes were up to code. The rest was history…or mystery, depending on your point of view.

Seen from outside, the log stockade reminded Bolan of something from an ancient John Wayne
movie—maybe *Fort Apache,* or *She Wore a Yellow
Ribbon.* He could almost picture men in coonskin
caps and buckskin, bearing flintlock rifles as they
paced the catwalks, watching out for any sign of hostile movement in the darkened woods beyond the par-
apets. At any moment, they might hear the sound of
war whoops, arrows hissing through the night to find
their targets with a slap of flint-invading flesh.

Except there seemed to be no guards atop the wall
this night. In place of them, he saw closed-circuit television cameras, mounted every sixty feet or so, revolving slowly on their pedestals, positioned so that
each arc overlapped and covered the entire perimeter.

Or did they?

Bolan spent three-quarters of an hour circling the
stockade, looking for a blind spot, and he found it at
the northeast corner of the compound. There, a kind
of culvert had been cut beneath the wall of logs, and
from it spilled a brook, rippling along a steep-walled
bed of stones and clay that sloped away downhill to
the northeast, amid a tangled mass of brush and ferns.

The compound dwellers had been clever, building
on a site where they had running water piped in from
the earth itself, but they had been a tad too clever in
deciding not to dam it up inside the walls and risk
stagnation. Rather than controlling the terrain and nar-
rowing the stream's bed to a trickle where he passed
beneath the wall, they had erected their stockade
across a gully cut by Mother Nature on her own. It
wasn't much, from Bolan's point of view, and they
might well have rigged some means to close it off if

they were under siege, but at the moment, he could see no obstacle to climbing the gully, squeezing underneath the wall and trying for a look inside.

There was a heightened risk, of course. The spillway would be recognized for what it was, a weak point, by the men who built the stockade and by those who occupied it. When they thought about security— and Bolan knew that paranoid fanatics thought of little else, until they made time for the planning of attack—it would be only logical for them take some measure that would block potential enemies from creeping underneath the wall. The spillway might be covered by a grate, for instance, which he couldn't see from where he stood. It might be booby-trapped in some way, though he frankly doubted whether an explosive charge would have been mounted underneath the wall.

And then again, it could be something simple. All they had to do was post a sentry on the inside of the wall, to watch the spillway through the night. One soldier with a pistol could prevent a hundred men from coming in that way, simply by standing off to left or right and gunning down each creeping adversary as he showed himself.

Still, he decided it was worth a try. If there was some kind of a stationary hatch or grate in place, he would retreat, with nothing lost but time. As for a trap, the narrow confines of the spillway would allow him to examine it for trip wires, weighted levers and the like before he was committed to the final stage of his ascent. A posted sentry was his greatest danger, and since he couldn't imagine any surefire way to guard against it, Bolan simply made his mind up to be careful, take his time, withdraw the moment he sensed any watchful presence on the inside of the wall.

Risk was a part of life. A soldier who was frightened of it ought to find himself another trade, before his fear betrayed him and it was too late.

To beat the high wall-mounted cameras, he melted back into the forest, sought the brook out by its sound and followed it one slow step at a time, back up the slope toward the stockade. Its nonstop rippling over stones concealed whatever sounds he made along the way, and Bolan exercised due caution, making certain that he didn't slip and fall or make any unexpected splashing noises that might serve to put an unseen lookout on alert. He kept his carbine slung and used both empty hands to keep his balance, shifting this and that way as the slope began to steepen, digging in the thick toes of his jungle boots and making sure the clay was firm enough to hold his weight before he pushed off for another step.

It took him all of twenty minutes, but at last he reached the final stage of the ascent. From that point onward, he would have to climb the spillway on his hands and knees, cold water rushing over hands that soon were nearly numb and soaking through the blacksuit from his knees to his ankles. This was where he stood to lose it, on his own, without the help of booby traps or lurking guards. It really took no more than simple gravity, a shifting stone or twisted ankle, fingers that couldn't dig deep enough or hold the grip that they had found.

But Bolan knew his limitations, even as he recognized his talents. Had he thought the climb impossible or suicidal, he wouldn't have tackled it—at least, without a more compelling motive than a simple look around inside the camp. He was prepared to face the risks and fairly confident they could be overcome, as long as he didn't grow overconfident.

Inside the open mouth of the spillway, Bolan had room to nearly stand erect. His feet were braced to either side, knees slightly flexed, and he took time to rinse his hands of mud, then dry them on a portion of his blacksuit that wasn't already soaked, to keep any weapons from slipping or fouling. Peering upward, with his head bent at an angle that sparked pain from muscles in his neck and shoulders, Bolan was a bit surprised to find no grate across the spillway's opening.

Next, he had to check for traps.

He had a small penlight but dared not use it, even with the lights. One flash, however brief, would put a watcher on alert...assuming that there was a watcher, and that he wasn't already poised to strike, his weapon sighted on the spillway's mouth.

Bolan bit the bullet and wormed his way up through the spillway, hesitating for another heartbeat at the point where he would either have to show himself or call it off. He took it slowly, easing up enough until he had a slug's-eye view in all directions and had satisfied himself, incredibly, that there was no guard on the single glaring weak point of the camp.

His estimation of his adversaries dropped a notch right then and there. It was a foolish error, and it made no difference that their compound stood on land they owned, that they had never been attacked before or even seriously threatened. If this had been an exercise in combat tactics for military officers, the candidates responsible would find themselves policing toilets for a month of Sundays.

As it was, though, Bolan meant to take advantage of their glaring oversight.

He double-checked to make sure that he wasn't zeroed in from some emplacement on the wall, and having verified that he was all alone, he hauled himself into the camp, pushing with knees and feet to supplement the power of his grip on smooth-packed soil.

Inside, the camp seemed roomier than Bolan would have guessed from simply scouting the exterior. In large part, that was due to placement of the buildings, leaving space for a fair-sized parade ground on the east side of the camp. He guessed that it would double for PT and training in the art of unarmed combat. From the northern sector of the compound, he heard muffled noises from a generator, which undoubtedly powered the handful of lights he could see, perhaps also providing juice to the communications center, readily identified by its small roof-forest of antennae, dim light spilling from the single window he could see.

Bolan ignored the buildings that were obviously living quarters, memorizing the location of the commo hut and fixing the direction of the generator, though he couldn't see it yet.

There had to be vehicles inside the wall, some kind of motor pool, for there were none outside, and he couldn't imagine even the most dedicated Nazis hiking back and forth to Spanaway for their supplies. The cleared parade ground could have doubled as a helipad, if they had access to a chopper, and it might well serve the same function for raiders, if and when the law came calling with assorted warrants.

Bolan worked the semidarkness, stayed close to the wall, melded with shadows where he could and kept a sharp lookout for any roving guards. Most of the storm troopers in residence were tucked in for the night, or else had better things to do than stroll around the compound, working on their goose-step. The soldier had completed something like one-quarter of the circuit, had just spied the motor pool when he was suddenly distracted by a spill of light that marked a newly opened doorway.

He had turned in that direction, had the doorway covered with his M-4 carbine when a woman stumbled through it, nearly falling, two men close behind her, dressed in camouflage fatigues. One of the men was carrying a pistol in his right hand, muzzle pointed toward the ground. The other held what could have been a billy club, some two feet long, with which he prodded at the woman's back.

From her reaction—twitching, gasping out a cry of pain that seemed excessive in reaction to a fairly gentle nudge—Bolan reassessed the nature of the weapon in the second man's hand. A cattle prod perhaps?

The woman's denim shirttails had come loose—assuming they were ever tucked in to begin with—and its buttons were undone or maybe torn away, some halfway from the collar to her waist. With all that light behind her, Bolan couldn't see her visage well enough to tell if she was bruised or bloodied, but her movements told him she was hurting.

And the words, the mocking laughter of her escorts,

told him she was in for something worse before the night was through.

"Keep moving, bitch!" the stick man said, prodding her again, an inch or two above the waistline, both men laughing as she jerked and stumbled.

"Got a nervous tic there, Mary?" asked the pistolero. Adding, "Hey, no sweat. It's not that far, and you can rest a good long time."

"Hell," Stick Man offered, "you can rest forever."

They were heading for the gates, a little stroll into the woods, and Bolan understood that one of them wouldn't be coming back.

He also understood that his soft probe was now officially a rescue mission.

Great. Just what he needed, he thought, falling into step behind the mismatched trio, closing up the gap.

CHAPTER THREE

The first, most pressing question, now was whether he should try to follow them outside and take them in the woods, or risk an incident inside the compound that could blow up in his face and leave him trapped, cut off, completely screwed. The woods were clearly preferable, but he had a problem when it came to following the two goons and their female captive through the compound's gate.

First and most obvious, a rifleman was posted at the gate, the first guard Bolan had observed inside the camp so far. A little closer, and he made that "rifle boy," but age and field experience were immaterial when it came down to spotting an intruder in the open, following a trio cleared to leave the camp. If he could count to four, the jig was up—and even if he couldn't, there was still the matter of the Executioner's unorthodox attire, his war paint, the self-evident conclusion that he wasn't playing for the home team.

He would have to try before they reached the gate, then, and he was already running out of time.

The thought barely had time to form in Bolan's mind before he drew the powerful Beretta 93-R from its shoulder holster, counting on the custom sound suppressor to serve him well. He needed a diversion, though, and sidestepped into the midnight shadow of a structure he had taken for a barracks, calling out to the retreating threesome, "Mary, hey! What's going on?"

All three stopped dead, the woman glancing back across her shoulder in the general direction of his voice, a slightly dazed expression on her face. And livid bruises. Her escorts also turned, Stick Man stepping forward, cocky and belligerent.

"None of your business, soldier," he replied to someone he couldn't identify, had yet to see. "And show yourself!"

Bolan obliged him, stepping from the shadow, giving Stick Man a glimpse of Death before the 93-R coughed and opened up a keyhole in his forehead, just above the hooked bridge of his nose. The guy was dead before he knew it, folding at the knees, then flopping over backward with his legs bent underneath him, in a pose that would have hurt like hell if he were still alive to feel it.

The Executioner took the shooter next, a clean shot to the heart that stopped his rising pistol halfway to the point of target acquisition. Even so, the guy had strength or will enough jerk the trigger of his double-action autoloader twice as he was toppling toward a crude collision with the earth. Both shots were wasted, missing Bolan by at least a yard, but that wasn't his problem. It was noise that mattered, and his dying adversary's weapon had no suppressor attached.

In fact, the piece was as loud as hell.

The sentry on the gate forgot his military discipline and blurted, "What the fuck was that?" He didn't charge in the direction of the noise, though, rather dropping to one knee, hunched over what appeared to be an M-16 or the civilian semiauto version, waiting for a target to reveal itself.

Bolan was at the woman's side a heartbeat later, gripping her right arm in his left hand. She didn't try to pull away immediately, squinting at his blackened face, striving for recognition, as she asked him, "Who the hell are you?"

"Let's save the introductions," Bolan said. "It's time to go, unless you want somebody else to pick up where these two left off."

"You killed them," she remarked, as if the revelation might surprise him.

Bolan had no idea who this woman was or what her beef was with the Temple of the Nordic Covenant. Saving her life had been an impulse, and he wondered if it was about to blow up in his face, the way police would sometimes interrupt domestic brawls and find the two combatants suddenly united in attacking the outsiders who had interfered.

"I owe you one," she said, then added, "did Archer send you?"

"Somebody!" cried the kneeling sentry by the gate before he finally remembered the prescribed routine and bawled out, "Sergeant of the guard!"

The summons was unnecessary, as the pistol shots had roused almost everyone in camp. Bolan couldn't see many of them yet, but he could hear them coming, boot heels tramping dirt and gravel, startled voices calling out questions or directives.

"This way," Bolan grated, and pulled the woman back toward the spillway exit from the compound. She didn't resist him, though she seemed a bit unsteady on her feet, either from shock or the result of her apparent injuries. There had been no time for him to assess the damage, and he had none, now. If she couldn't keep up…

Rounding the corner of a barracks built from logs, Bolan nearly collided with a pair of soldiers who had clearly been in bed, or getting ready to retire, when they were routed from their quarters by the sounds of shouts and gunfire. One of them was bare chested, a large black swastika tattoo emblazoned on the left side of his chest; the other wore a white T-shirt that showed off well-developed delts and abs. Both carried automatic rifles, one a Ruger Mini-14, while the other had a folding-stock Kalashnikov.

The sudden confrontation startled Bolan's adversaries into fleeting immobility. He took advantage of the moment while it lasted, pressing on instead of backing off. He swung the weight of the Beretta's muzzle in a short, tight arc against the topless Nazi's nose and heard the cartilage give way with an explosive crack. The other took a short hop backward, bringing his Kalashnikov to bear, but Bolan got there first and slammed a silenced round between his eyes.

A second round ended the anguished groaning of the Nazi with the broken nose. As Bolan raised his eyes from that kill, it was his turn to be surprised. The woman—Mary—had scooped up the fallen AK, and with what appeared to be an expert's moves, confirmed the presence of a live round in the firing chamber.

Bolan braced himself, prepared to fire if she drew down on him, but all she turned in his direction was a slightly crooked smile.

"That's better," she announced. "We're heading for the spillway, I suppose?"

"We were," he said, impressed, "unless you know a better way to shake this place."

"I don't much like our chances on the gate," she said. "Let's do it your way if they haven't cut us off."

And saying that, she turned from Bolan and took the lead, jogging back toward the point where he had crept into the compound. He was puzzled, but the curiosity would have to wait.

Until he found out if they had a future.

Just now, questions were one of many luxuries the Executioner couldn't afford.

THE COMRADES CALLED her Mary Krause, and she had worn the name so long that sometimes it was difficult remembering her own, recalling who she really was—or had been, in the days before she joined the Temple of the Nordic Covenant.

Short moments earlier, she had been certain that she was about to die. The night had yawned before her like an open grave, with her name on the tombstone. There had been no out, no exit hatch. She was as good as dead.

Until the stranger came from out of nowhere, interrupted Vince and Tommy, stopped them dead before they got her to the gate, marched her into the woods, on to some random point that was supposed to be the last place she would ever see on Earth.

It was a kick, sometimes, how things could turn around so suddenly. Fortune's reversals, like the movie title said—the one about some rich freak who had tried to kill his wife with insulin. One minute you were riding high, top of your game, and then, before you knew it, you were facedown in the dirt. What tipped them off? And did it even really matter, once you knew that you were well and truly screwed?

So, then you started wondering what it was like to die. Not take a beating or a flesh wound, as before, but getting ready for the Big Ride, baby, wondering if there was anything but everlasting darkness on the other side. Then, bam! Some paint-it-black commando type was standing over corpses that had been your would-be executioners a moment earlier, and he was telling you to kindly get your shit together if you didn't mind, and run like hell.

The woman lately known as Mary Krause had seen men die before—had dropped the hammer once, herself, and no sincere regrets—but there was something cold and almost casual about the way this black-clad savior did his work. As if he brought so much more power to the game than his competitors, he barely had to think about it. Will translated into action, in the time it took to twitch a trigger finger. Four men down, and he had yet to break a sweat as far as she could tell.

The folding-stock Kalashnikov felt good in her hands. It was an AK-74, chambered in 5.56 mm like the M-16, and consequently lighter than the AK-47 by a good pound and a half, even before they ditched the standard wooden stock.

She knew where they were going—had considered

slipping out that way herself, in fact, before the roof fell in—but this would be a different sort of exit, with the whole camp on alert. There was a world of difference between a sneak play and a banzai charge, with fifty pissed-off Nazis standing in your way.

She hoped they would collect around the gate, maybe pick over the bodies for a while, trying to figure out what had happened. It wouldn't take long for Fletcher to command a search, but Mary and her savior didn't need *that* long. A few more minutes, just enough to slip out of the compound, get themselves a fair head start before the hunt began.

Once they were in the woods, well, they should have a fighting chance, at least. The darkness there would aid them, make their enemies more obvious when they came prowling through the trees with lights and walkie-talkies crackling.

"Slow down!" the man in black whispered, and Mary realized that they had nearly reached the spillway. It was just around the corner or the barracks that was hiding them from view of those collected in the middle of the compound. Just a few more steps, and they would see—

Four troopers stood guard around the only exit from the camp that offered any hope at all.

She knew all four of them, of course. You couldn't live in proximity to fifty, sixty people for eight months and thirteen days without at least becoming casual acquaintances. This foursome—Gary, Mike, Eddie, and Carl—hung out together any time they weren't on duty, drinking beer and cleaning weapons, working on their unarmed combat, telling Jew jokes to amuse themselves.

"What now?" she asked her nameless sidekick.

"Either this way, or the gate," he said, stating the obvious.

"I'd rather go this way."

"Same here. Can you use that thing?"

"Just try me."

"Right. On three," he told her. "One...two..."
Three!

They came around the corner, firing, Mary thankful now that she had picked up the AK-74, no recoil to speak of from the 5.56 mm rounds. She put a short burst into Gary's chest from twenty-five or thirty feet away, conserving ammunition, checking the amazed expression on his face before he toppled over, like a falling target in a shooting gallery.

Eddie was bringing up the 12-gauge pump he favored over rifles, since a person didn't need great skill to nail his or her target with a shotgun. Eddie favored triple-aught buckshot, and Mary knew that while a blast at this range might not kill her instantly, it would be powerful enough to disembowel her, leave her writhing in the dirt until somebody had the simple grace to finish it.

She hit him with a rising burst that kicked the pump gun from his shattered hands, the last three or four rounds ripping into his chest, throat and face. He went down in a heap, and by the time she swung around to help the stranger with Mike and Carl, the both of them were down and out, not even twitching on the deck.

She heard a storm of angry voices blowing toward them from the general direction of the gate and the CP. "You want to do the honors?" Mary asked the stranger, nodding toward the spillway as she voiced the question.

"Ladies first," he said.

"A gentleman. Terrific."

Mary used the spillway like a children's slide. The smooth stones bruised her backside, cold stream water soaking through her blue jeans, but she had been wet and bruised before. It wouldn't kill her, and the risk of hypothermia was so remote, with psyched-up killers racing after her and all, that she didn't even think about it.

At the bottom of the spillway, where the streambed leveled out, she scrambled to her feet and kept on going for another forty yards or so, then stopped to see if Mr. X was keeping up. She saw him in the moonlight, like an animated shadow, watching as he paused, maybe halfway between her own position and the camp, and turned back toward the spillway.

She recognized the *pop* of the grenade launcher and braced herself against the detonation of a high-explosive round. It was precisely placed, inside the spillway, underneath the stockade wall, its shock wave ripping several logs from their foundation, dropping them into the cut, while clay and gravel pattered back to earth.

Not bad.

It slammed the door and gave the hunters something new to think about, maybe a little extra taste of fear to slow them. It wouldn't stop them, though. Mary knew that much, also, from experience.

Determined not to let the bastards get their hands on her again, she turned and ran into the night.

SEAN FLETCHER'S rage was legendary, but he kept it on a leash, used it the way a canine cop used his dog. To lash out blindly, mindlessly, was a pathetic waste, no matter how inviting it might be to simply take the nearest face and pound it into dog food. If he couldn't channel rage and use it, rage became his master.

This much he knew: the woman known to them as Mary Krause—though that was almost certainly a pseudonym—had managed to escape from custody, the troops assigned to smoke her being smoked themselves with what appeared to be a silencer-equipped side arm, or maybe a 9 mm SMG. Either way, he now had eight dead soldiers, altogether: two more taken out with the 9 mm whisper gun, the last four sprayed with automatic fire around the spillway, where they had been standing guard. As for the streambed cutting underneath the wall, of course, someone had blown that shut, presumably after they fled the camp, slamming the back door rudely in his face.

The trick now was to figure out how many "someones" he was dealing with and what they had in mind. Until the HE blast, he had allowed the possibility, however slim, that Mary could have done the wet work by herself. She got a pistol from somewhere—there were certainly enough of them in camp, some of them fitted with suppressors—and she dropped her escorts. Vince and Tommy weren't the brightest bulbs in anybody's chandelier. Fletcher could see it happening, particularly if they got distracted, thinking they might have some fun with Mary in the woods before they took her out.

Okay. She dropped the first two, and before she

made it to the spillway, she ran into Blaine and
Mickey. They were surprised to see her, hadn't got
the word about her treason to the Temple—Fletcher's
fault on that one, since he had tried to keep it quiet—
and she took them out before they noticed that she
was packing. It was feasible, if stretching credibility.
Then Mary grabbed Mickey's Kalashnikov and kept
on going, met the sentries watching her escape hatch,
and she hosed them with automatic fire.

Still possible, he thought. The brass around the
spillway was all 5.56 mm, which fit the missing
AK-74. Granted, he could have sworn there were two
weapons firing for a second there, one of them lacking
the Kalashnikov's distinctive sound, but it was tricky
sometimes, judging sounds like that.

Until the spillway blew. There was no way in hell
that Fletcher could believe Mary had managed to pick
up explosives, certainly not in the time elapsed between her break from Vince and Tommy and the blast
that shut the spillway down, preventing an immediate
pursuit.

Meaning the bitch had help.

Next problem—Fletcher had to figure out if the assistance came from someone in the camp or if someone from outside had come to rescue Mary from her
fate. The two alternatives were almost equally disturbing. On the one hand, it was bad enough to think
about the Temple's western headquarters being pen-
etrated by one spy, much less multiple traitors; on the
other hand, if help had come from the outside, how
had the interlopers known that they were needed?
How had they gained access to the compound? Was

the whole damned place under surveillance constantly?

Job one, after recapturing the runner, was to find out whether anyone was unaccounted for. Fletcher had picked eight men—his best—and sent them out on trail bikes, roaring through the woods behind their wobbling headlight beams, to catch up with their enemies and bring them back dead or alive. As for the rest of those who should have been inside the compound, Fletcher called them all together, lined them up on the parade field—corpses off to one side, under tarp—and started counting noses. After he had done it twice, and factored in the hunting party, only Mary Krause was gone.

Which meant that someone from the world outside had come to fetch her home. If Vince and Tommy had obtained the answers Fletcher needed—whom she worked for, what her mission in the camp had been, how much she had disclosed already to the Temple's enemies—the poor, dumb bastards were beyond revealing what they knew. Fletcher had trusted them to do a job he should have done himself, and it had come around to bite him on the ass.

It all came down to his selected hunters now. If they caught up to Mary and her little helpers, they could finish off the job that Vince and Tommy started. He didn't expect the quarry to be caught alive, so there would be no further questioning, no second chance for him to do it properly. He might learn something from the corpses, though, before he had them taken out and burned.

One thing was clear: if Fletcher's unknown enemies were close enough and slick enough to penetrate the compound when they felt like it, and snatch a hostage out from underneath his very nose, then it was time to split. Get the hell out of Dodge before something worse happened, and Fletcher wound up with an even greater problem than embarrassment.

Like sudden death, for instance.

When he thought about it that way, he wondered if perhaps some unsuspected intuition had prevailed upon him to choose Vince and Tommy for the job. If he had been a member of the execution team, his lifeless body could be one of those stretched out beneath the tarps. It made the short hairs bristle on his nape, and Fletcher clenched his teeth against the sudden chill.

No time to think about it now. The Reaper had already passed him by, and he had work to do.

"All right," he barked at the assemblage, "pack up your things as rapidly as possible and fall in by the motor pool. We're getting out of here!"

WHEN BOLAN HEARD the motorcycles coming after them, he knew that they would never reach the car without a fight. He paused, turned back and counted headlights, marking four and noting from their speed that there was no way normal infantry could keep up with the off-road bikes. If he could stop the cycles, then, do it both quickly and efficiently enough, it ought to buy some time.

He didn't want to think about the possibility that other vehicles were fanning out along established roads, that one of them might find his car before they got there, silent snipers waiting in among the trees.

One problem at a time.

"What are you waiting for?" the woman asked him in a sharp stage whisper.

"Motorcycles," Bolan answered, hoping that would say it all.

"I see them," she replied. "Believe me, you don't want to meet the drivers."

"Better on my terms," he told her, "than to have them overtake us, running in the dark."

"How much farther to your wheels?" she asked.

"Too far. Almost a mile."

Bolan could almost hear her thinking. "We could hide," she said. "The way they're driving, they're not spending any time on marking trails."

"They won't give up," he said. "They'll go for speed and distance first, and if they don't catch up to us that way, they'll backtrack. In the meantime, others may be coming up behind them."

"Shit! So what's the plan?"

"Same plan as always," Bolan said. "Take care of business."

Noting that the bikes had fanned out on a front some forty yards across, flanking the stream and doubtless seeking out the paths of least resistance through the trees, he found a spot that placed him roughly in the center of their skirmish line.

"What should I do?" the woman asked.

"You're staying?"

"Staying? Where the hell am I supposed to go?"

He shrugged in the darkness, pointed to a stout oak several paces to his left. "Take cover over there," he said, "and wait for me to start the party. Once you open up, do what you can with what you've got."

"That's it?"

"You should have fifteen, maybe twenty rounds left in that magazine, assuming it was fully loaded to begin with. Try to make them count and don't get killed. That's it."

She muttered something Bolan didn't copy as she moved off toward the oak, and the soldier did his best to put her out of mind. She was a fair hand with the AK, had already proved herself in that respect, but there was all the difference in the world between a moving target in the darkness, maybe shooting back, and careless men caught with their guard down, standing in the open. They would simply have to wait to see what happened next.

He had already primed the M-203 launcher with another HE round, and that would be his leadoff when the action started. Left or right? He knew that taking out a biker on the left might help the woman stay alive, but since he hadn't warned her in advance, there was an equal—maybe greater—chance that it would startle her and spoil her aim, thereby precipitating her into some even greater jeopardy.

Make it the right, then. Near or far?

Bolan had an advantage on his targets from the start, because the M-203 launcher had no muzzle-flash, and with their engines revving, maybe helmets covering their ears, they likely wouldn't hear the launcher's muted pop, no warning of the death about to burst upon them until it was happening.

So, near or far?

He chose the nearest of the motorcycles, since the driver—and his passenger, if they were riding double—were more dangerous to Bolan by the simple virtue of proximity. The farthest hunter to his right would have a choice to make once the explosion came: he could retreat and try to save himself, or else veer toward the blast and find out what was going on. In either case, Bolan would have a few more seconds to correct his aim, sight on the headlight, make his shot.

He waited with M-4's stock against his cheek and shoulder, counting down the seconds, knowing that the range of an approaching light in utter darkness was notoriously difficult to estimate. On top of that, he had to lead the cycle, dared not waste the high-explosive round by overshooting, dropping it behind them in the forest, where its impact would do little more than speed them on their way.

"Steady," he told the woman, speaking normally, no fear of being overheard at this point by the trackers on their racing bikes. "Hold on and wait for me."

"I'm waiting, dammit!"

She was spunky, this one. Gung-ho all the way. He wondered, for a fleeting moment, whether saving her would be cause for regret once she was finally identified.

He found his mark, squeezed off and felt the weapon lurch against his shoulder, precious little recoil in relation to the 40 mm gun's destructive capability. He couldn't track the HE round through darkness, but he saw it hit, the red-orange flash that left spots dancing on his retinas, immediately followed by a thunderclap of sound.

Before the fireball flickered out and died, he saw the trail bike vaulting through a crazy somersault, two bodies tumbling through the smoky haze. So they were riding double, probably a shooter on the pillion of each bike to deal with any running targets spooked from cover by the lights and noise. Two down—or stunned, at least—and that left six to go.

Before the echoes of the HE blast had died away, he heard the woman firing, short bursts, taking care with it. He didn't look in her direction, concentrating on the far bike to his right, its headlight weaving through the trees as if the driver had to brake and think about his next move, then proceeding rapidly toward Bolan, in the general direction of the blast.

Come and get it, Bolan thought.

He didn't use the launcher this time. Instead he waited, sighting down the M-4's barrel at a point above and just behind the trail bike's headlight. Inadvertently, the bike was headed nearly straight at Bolan, so the lead wasn't a problem. Holding steady on the mark, he stroked the trigger lightly for a short burst and watched the bike veer sharply to the left before colliding head-on with a tree.

There was a chance, he knew, that one burst could have tagged both passengers, but Bolan wasn't counting on it. Glancing briefly toward the woman, he was just in time to see her take down another motorcycle, the high-revved engine stalling as it slid through mulch and leaves for several yards before it came to rest. One of the bikers didn't move, but number two was up and running in a flash, the woman tracking him and squeezing off another burst that dropped him in midstride.

Content that she could handle her end of the fight, Bolan broke cover, dodging in and out among the trees, proceeding toward the point where his second target's headlight still burned through the night. He

paused to listen, halfway there, and heard a thrashing
in the underbrush, tracking it with his weapon. When
the limping man-shape lurched erect and moved
across the skyward-canted headlight beam, Bolan was
ready, squeezing off another burst that slammed the
shooter over backward, out of frame.

He walked back toward the place where he had left
the woman, calling out to her when he was nearly
there, "It's me."

"Who's 'me'?" her voice came back to him.

"Belasko," Bolan answered as he kept on walking.
"Mike Belasko. And you are…?"

She blinked at him, stray moonlight showing him
a stark expression of surprise. "You mean you don't
know who I am?"

He frowned at that. "Is there some reason why I
should?"

"I thought…I mean…. So, you weren't sent to pull
me out of there?"

"'Fraid not," he told her. "Welcome to the wild
and wacky world of pure coincidence."

"Well, damn! I thought for sure Archer sent you
after me."

"I've never met the man…or woman, as the case
may be," the Executioner replied. "And since I don't
know who *you* are…"

"Oh, right." She stuck a hand out, gripping his
with strength that somehow didn't startle Bolan now.
"Marilyn Crouder, Federal Bureau of Alcohol, Tobacco and Firearms."

CHAPTER FOUR

"So, ATF."

They had returned to Bolan's rented room in Spanaway. Although it might not qualify as neutral ground, it was the best available in lieu of cruising aimlessly around Tacoma and environs while they talked.

Upon first glance at the motel room, Bolan's unexpected guest had frowned and said, "This isn't you."

"It isn't anyone," he said. "It's twenty-seven bucks a night."

"Does that include a sleepover?" she asked.

"Who says you're staying?"

"Ah. So chivalry *is* dead." She flashed the crooked smile again. "Mind if I use your shower, at least, before you kick me out to meet my fate?"

"Feel free."

He heard her lock the bathroom door behind her, switched the television on and ran through half a dozen local channels, nothing on that caught his fancy at that hour of the night. He wondered briefly what the scene was like, just then, back at the Temple compound. Would survivors of the raid be scrambling to pack their gear and flee? Were they already gone? Or would they reason that the prowler who had wreaked such havoc in their midst couldn't be an official caller, from the way he had appeared and vanished, without the usual accompaniment of flashing lights and sirens, badges, warrants, bullhorns and a retinue of TV cameras?

Would they decide to stay? Bury their dead and tough it out, perhaps, to see what happened next?

Bolan was only vaguely conscious of the shower's noise until it stopped. Assorted rustling sounds behind the bathroom door evoked unbidden flashes of his visitor and bath towels. He switched on the television again and found the channel had reset itself, as many motel systems were designed to do, displaying a selection of the porn films available on pay-per-view.

"We going to the movies, soldier?"

Bolan switched off the TV and turned to face her. Marilyn had put her jeans and denim shirt back on, the tails tucked in this time, but she looked better: freshly scrubbed, revitalized after a fashion, blond hair damp and plastered to her skull.

"Sorry," she said. "I didn't bring a change of clothes."

"It's not a fashion show," Bolan replied.

"You want to tidy up?" she asked. "I promise not to read your diary while you're in the shower."

"It'll keep," he said. "We need to talk."

"I was afraid of that." She found one of the room's two wooden chairs and settled into it, keeping her distance from the bed where Bolan sat, at least as far as the restrictive quarters would allow.

"So, ATF."

The lady nodded. "And you're not. So, who the hell are you?"

"I told you. Mike—"

"Belasko, right," she interrupted him. "But, then again, what's in a name? We both know what I'm asking you."

"Who do you think I am?"

"Hey, neat! A guessing game. Let's see...are you my knight in shining Kevlar? No? I think Prince Charming's out. Maybe a hit man with a soft spot for the damsel in distress?"

"You meet a lot of those?" he asked her.

"Who?"

"Hit men with soft spots."

"You'd be number one," she told him. "With a bullet, so to speak. Look, can we just please cut the crap and talk?"

"Sounds fair," he said. "Let's say I'm on your side, at least in general terms. I don't represent any competing fascist groups, Klans, cults, what have you. I'm official, more or less. The rest is strictly need-to-know."

"And I don't need?"

"Bingo."

"Well, anyway, you saved my ass, so thanks for that."

"It seemed worth saving," Bolan said.

That smile again. She cocked her head in the direction of the bathroom, asking him, "You wouldn't have a some kind of *Candid Camera* rig in there, by any chance?"

"I would have," Bolan answered, smiling back, "except I wasn't counting on the company."

"Oh, well. Your loss."

"You're listed MIA," he said, relieved to change the subject.

"Yeah? It figures. Since we went to ground at Freedom Home, there hasn't been a lot of opportunity for me to phone in my weeklies."

"What's Freedom Home?" he asked.

"The love nest you just pulled me out of. Western HQ for the Temple. Were you briefed, or what?"

"Nicknames were optional," he said. "I didn't want to spend the extra quarter. From the way it looked to me, you were about to be evicted."

"That's about the size of it."

"What happened?" Bolan asked.

"You know, I really do appreciate the bacon-saving gig and all, but since we're not related job-wise, and I'm still way short of understanding just exactly who the hell you are, I'm not sure I should spill my guts, you know?"

"I'll show you mine," he said.

"We talking information now?" the lady asked. "Or are you asking me to join you for some kinky R&R?"

"The FBI had two moles in the Temple," Bolan said. "They're both dead now. When you went MIA, it looked like Stevens and his goons were three for three."

"Don't let Herr Steuben hear you call him that," she said. "It ticks him off big time. So, where do you come in, if everybody else has bought the farm?"

"You might say that I work for a collection agency," he said. "The Temple's debt is overdue."

"Friend, you don't know the half of it," she said.

"Meaning?"

The woman considered her response and her responsibilities for several silent moments. When she spoke again, preceded by a shrug, it was apparent that she had decided it was time to share.

"I don't know how much you've heard about the Temple of the Nordic Covenant," she said, "but they're not just another bunch of Nazis looking for a synagogue to vandalize. The *temple* part of it is deadly serious, as far as I can tell. They honestly believe they're on some kind of cosmic mission for the ancient gods to cleanse the world and make it ready for replanting the Aryan seed. Most of it's Viking voodoo bullshit, and you have to be a headcase to believe it, but—"

"Headcases are a dime a dozen?" he suggested.

"So it seems. The thing is, that for all their talk of carving out a new white bastion in the northwest part of the United States, they're really shooting for the whole damned ball of wax. 'Tomorrow the world,' you know? They don't expect to do it all at once, but they've got timetables and scheduled trigger incidents, the whole nine yards. Along the way, they're hoping they may find some artifacts to amplify their power."

"Artifacts?"

"The Holy Grail, Ark of the Covenant, the Spear of Destiny," she said. "You know—the usual."

"Somebody sat through one too many reels of *Indiana Jones*," Bolan replied.

"You'd think so, right? Except the legends came before the movies, and the first-string Nazis under Adolf had the same bug up their butts. Some say the witchy stuff was finally what cost them World War II.''

''That and insane devotion to a raving lunatic,'' he said.

''Raving or not, he left his mark. The Temple isn't just another cash cow for some tin-pot führer scamming every penny he can milk out of the troops. Steuben believes in what he's doing, from the master-race thing, on through the religious mumbo-jumbo, right down to the quest for Inner Earth. Of course, he tries to keep it practical. The gods can't come again until he's finished cleaning house to make things ready for them. That's where the blood comes in.''

''You mentioned a timetable,'' Bolan prompted.

''So I did. You know your history?''

''The basics,'' he replied.

''Then, you know Hitler's gig was the reunion of the Nordic people, all the so-called Aryans, under his leadership. 'One race, one reich, one leader.'''

''Sounds familiar.''

''Steuben's working on the same idea,'' she said. ''He's networked all around the world. You'd be surprised how many different places his theology has put down roots, and if the Temple doesn't have a chapter in a given area, the odds are they've got other neofascists whose beliefs are similar enough to let them play along. We're not just talking Oklahoma City here,'' she said. ''We're talking a total obliteration of races.''

''If he could pull it off, you mean,'' Bolan said.

''If he doesn't,'' Crouder replied, ''it sure as hell won't be from lack of trying. And it won't be from a lack of hardware, either. He's got access to all kinds of shit, from small arms up to the big bang.''

"Your people know about this?"

"Bits and pieces. I've been MIA, remember?"

"And when they hear?"

"I guess some of it has to go to State and Justice," she said. "Maybe the CIA. We've got no brief to operate on foreign territory, though it's not unheard of, when we rig some kind of sting. A thing on this scale, though… I shouldn't say this, but I don't think ATF can handle it."

"About that timetable…"

"Uh-uh," she said. "You've seen enough of mine. I haven't had a peek at yours, so far."

He thought about it for a moment, wondering how much it would be safe to tell this total stranger. He would never speak to her of Stony Man, of course, but if he didn't give her something, it was clear that her cooperation would evaporate.

"I tend to operate in those gray areas where rules are more a hindrance than a help," he said.

"The pesky crap like warrants, rules on use of deadly force, that kind of thing?" she said.

"For starters."

"And I'm guessing, maybe, you could cut through some of the red tape at Justice, if someone asked you nicely."

"I'd prefer a total bypass," Bolan said.

"As in, what they don't know won't hurt them?"

"More like, what they don't know may not rock the boat and get me killed."

"Which makes you…what? Some kind of global vigilante with a license?"

"Just a troubleshooter," Bolan said. "Like you."

"You obviously haven't seen the book of federal regulations, rules and guidelines recently," she answered back. "It makes a nifty doorstop."

"I could get you off the hook with some of that," Bolan suggested. "Brief me on what's doing with the Temple, and I'll carry it from there. You can get back to a routine where cattle prods aren't an issue."

"Never happen," Crouder replied. "At least, it won't without a thumbs-up from my boss. I'd have to make a call, and he'll need more specifics than this 'troubleshooter' line."

Bolan considered it. There were procedures for a situation such as this, though they were very rarely needed, and more rarely used. "I've got a number for your boss to call," he said at last. "If he's not satisfied with what he hears—" a shrug, more casual than Bolan felt "—I guess we go our separate ways."

"Mind if I use your phone?" she asked. "I'll need some privacy."

"No problem," Bolan said. "I have some calls to make myself. I'll use the pay phone by the ice machine."

And the fun was just starting, he thought as he got up and went to spread the word.

CLINT ARCHER WAS asleep when Marilyn Crouder phoned him at home, in Woodstock, Maryland, a few miles west of Baltimore.

"Hello." No gravel in his voice, no hesitancy to suggest that he had been snatched back to Woodstock from a sunny South Pacific beach where clothing was distinctly frowned upon.

"It's Viper," said a female voice.

He blinked at that, surprise colliding with relief. "Is this line secure?" he asked.

"Not sure," she said. "I think so, but I wouldn't take it to the bank."

"Hang on a sec," he said, rising from bed as quietly as possible. The phone was cordless, and he took it with him, moving toward the bathroom. Halfway there, he was arrested by the sound of Susan's sleepy voice.

"What is it, Clint?"

"Just business, hon. Go back to sleep."

He closed the bathroom door behind him, sat on the cool edge of the tub and killed the light. Some things were best discussed in darkness, if you had to speak of them at all.

"Where are you, Viper?"

"Some motel," she said, wisely omitting any mention of locality. "I had to bail."

"What happened?"

"Caught with my hand in the cookie jar," she summarized, as economical as ever with her words. "It looked like premature retirement for a minute there, until I caught a break."

"Which was…?"

"Some guy dropped in and gave me an alternative. I'm at his place right now, if you want to call it that."

"Some guy? What guy?"

"I've had some problems working that one out. He says he's one of ours, but not specifically—you follow me?"

"Okay." Not ATF, she meant. But who, then? FBI? The U.S. Marshal's Service? How would either agency know where to find his missing operative? Why would they move to pull her out, danger or no, without informing Archer first?

"I'm still not sure exactly what his deal is, but he's no desk jockey, boss. He takes life seriously."

So there had been casualties. "Are you all right?" he asked belatedly.

"Nothing a good makeover wouldn't fix," Crouder replied. "The thing about this guy, it seems like he's on more or less the same track we are, but without the speed limits. He seems to think it might be to our mutual advantage if I handed off the ball and let him run with it."

"Is that right?"

Archer knew the name of that tune well enough, from years of playing office politics and watching out to make sure that some sneaky bastard didn't stab him in the back. In his view, it was a disgrace how law-enforcement agents competed with each other, often jeopardizing major cases, letting stone-cold psycho killers walk because they simply couldn't curb their feuding over who got credit for a bust, whose wire-taps and informants took priority, which television network was entitled to exclusive coverage of this or that event. If Archer had been paid a dollar for each time some petty personal concern had interfered with his performance on the job, be could have purchased beachfront acreage on that island from his dreams.

"I blew him off, of course," Crouder said. "More or less."

"Meaning?"

"Meaning, he knows I'm a team player, not a free agent. I've got a number that he gave me, for the D.C.

area. He says that if you call his people up, maybe you can work something out.''

''Who *are* his people?'' Archer asked.

''You know what I know, boss.''

Which was exactly squat. ''Okay,'' he said, ''give me the number.''

Crouder read off ten digits, starting with area code for the District of Columbia. Archer repeated it aloud and banked it in his memory, where it would stay until he had no further use for it. Damned foolishness, but he should thank whoever was responsible for rescuing his agent in the field, and he couldn't do that without first learning who would be on the receiving end of all that gratitude. As far as some collaborative effort went...well, that would simply have to wait.

''Got it,'' he told her when he had the number memorized. ''Let's talk about that cookie jar.''

''It's deeper than we thought. More like a variety pack, you might say. An international flavor, with something for everyone.''

''Specifics?'' Archer prodded.

''Well, besides your basic corn pone, there was quite a bit of strudel and a few surprises. Some piroshki, this and that. Can't remember much more on an open line.''

Piroshki? What the hell was that? Was it—?

Oh, shit!

''We obviously need to talk in more detail,'' he said. ''How soon can you come in?''

''Um, sir, about this other thing...''

''You're recommending that I make the call?''

''It's your decision. From what I've seen so far, it couldn't hurt.''

"You remember that we have procedures? Guide-lines."

"Absolutely, sir. I also heard about the Bureau's people. That was almost me."

"You have a number there where I can call you back?"

She read it off. Archer repeated it aloud and filed it with the other one. "Okay," he said. "Stay there. By which I mean, don't go out for a walk, don't hit the coffee shop, nothing. We clear?"

"Crystal."

"All right. I'll be in touch."

He broke the link, was reaching for the bathroom light switch, then withdrew his hand. The darkness helped him think sometimes.

The phone number his field agent had given him didn't strike any chords of memory, but there was no good reason why it should. All federal agencies had private lines, and some habitually used cutouts, elevating caution to the level of a fetish. What he needed to decide right now was whether he would make the call or not.

Someone was dead. He knew that much already, from the little Viper had told him. And it had not been a line-of-duty killing, in the strict sense, or she would have been calling from a police station somewhere, asking for verification of her link to ATF. As far as who had done the killing, Archer only had her brief description of the man who had apparently rescued Viper, after she was caught with her hand in the Temple's "cookie jar."

He takes life seriously.

A shooter, then, but what of it? The act meant nothing, in itself. Members of every law-enforcement agency found themselves in killing situations at one time or another. Archer was more concerned with the approach—specifically, the total lack of any official response to the incident. Granted, he had made no attempt to follow up on it yet, but it was obvious that Viper wouldn't have been calling him from "some motel," address unknown, if she were in the middle of a bust against the Temple of the Nordic Covenant.

So, what to do?

He thought about it for another moment, then switched on the bathroom light and started tapping digits on his cordless phone. It was a crazy hour to be calling anyone, but what the hell?

If he couldn't sleep, he thought, nobody would sleep.

PERHAPS A MINUTE after Archer fumbled for the bedside telephone, wrenched from his dream of sundrenched tropic sands, a similar event woke Hal Brognola in the bedroom of his Arlington, Virginia, home. Older and more experienced than Archer, still he didn't snap immediately to attention, but his waking mind was clear enough to recognize the muted chirping of his private line.

There weren't a dozen people in the world who knew that number, and a wake-up call from any of them in the middle of the night was ominous, to say the least. He grabbed the handset on the third chirp, silencing its soft insectile noise, and he could hear the echo of his elevated heartbeat in his ears before he spoke.

"Hello."

"It's me," Mack Bolan said.

"So, how's Tacoma? Is it raining?"

"Spooks and moles," the Executioner replied.

"Sounds messy. Don't forget to wear your rubbers."

"I know it's late, Hal, but it's not *The Late Show*. How's the line?"

"It's clean on my end. Do you want to scramble?"

"No can do. I'm on a pay phone, and I haven't got the right equipment with me."

"Where's the phone?" Brognola asked.

"Outside of a motel."

"You're getting rest, then. This is good."

"Not lately," Bolan said. "I dropped in on those folks we talked about out here, and ran into a cousin no one's seen or heard from in a while."

Brognola blinked at that. Unless there was a player in the game he didn't know about, this "cousin" had to be the ATF agent whose operation and reports were being kept securely under wraps.

"Really. And how's he doing?"

"Well, for one thing, he's a she," Bolan replied. "From what I saw, she'd just about worn out her welcome when I got there. You know how reunions are. They wanted me to stick around, but I decided we should split."

Translation—he had saved a female agent of the ATF before she got her ticket punched, and they had fled the Temple's compound, probably with bodies strewed in Bolan's wake. Hal made a mental note to phone out west, once Bolan cleared the line, and see if there were any rumbles on the grapevine about bloody doings at the camp.

"So, have you had a chance to get acquainted?"

"We've been working on it, but she doesn't like to tell tales out of school."

"Smart girl," Brognola said.

"I've tried to get around that by suggesting that her uncle gets in touch with you. That outside line, you know?"

"I'll check it when we're done."

"No rush," said Bolan. "They're just talking now. I've got one thing to pass along, but it's a little vague."

"Let's hear it. I can work with vague."

"From what I'm getting here, the stuff we talked about before may only be a warmup for these people. If our cousin's not mistaken, they have bigger plans in mind."

"Bigger than what?" Hal asked.

"Try going global."

"That would fit with what we have," Brognola said. "We've got them on four continents already, if you count the polar gig."

"Tip of the iceberg," Bolan said. "No pun intended."

"Right. This from a guy who has the nerve to criticize *my* jokes? So, what's the rundown?"

"I don't have the details," Bolan said. "Our cousin doesn't want to share until she's cleared it through her uncle, but she dropped some hints. It sounds a lot like chaos theory. Trigger incidents at crucial stress points, with a follow-up where feasible. She also used the *N*-word."

"You're surprised, the crowd she hangs around with?"

"I was thinking of the other *N*-word."

Brognola was frowning when it hit him. *Nuclear?* "You don't mean Nagasaki?" he asked Bolan.

"Close enough."

"That puts a whole new slant on things."

"It's not confirmed, but this one seems to know her business."

"Any take on motive?"

"Only what you know already," Bolan said. "The whole religious thing, wrapped up in race and politics. Apparently, these folks think Armageddon is a ticket to white Christmas everlasting. I'm not saying they can pull it off—"

"But even if they don't," Brognola finished for him, "cleaning up the mess could take forever."

"That's what I'm thinking."

"Fair enough. So, what's the plan?"

"First thing, I try to find out if we're cleared for a collaborative effort. If that doesn't fly, I'll have to root around and find someone who feels like talking."

Brognola wouldn't have traded places with that someone if he had been offered all the bullion in Fort Knox. How would he spend it, when the Executioner was done with him? How could a truckload or a trainload of the richest ore on Earth change Bolan's mind, once it was fixed upon a course of action?

No damned way at all.

For just a second, the big Fed felt sorry for the members of the Temple, but it passed almost before he had a chance to recognize the feeling. Right behind the pity came concern, Brognola wondering, as he so often did, if he had matched his oldest living friend against the overwhelming odds that would destroy him this time.

No.

He might be short on details for the latest scheme hatched by the Temple of the Nordic Covenant, but Hal Brognola knew exactly what Bolan was capable of doing when he set his mind to it. He wasn't Superman, of course, but he would do until Clark Kent stopped playing hard to get.

"I'll see if I can find out where the major players are, in case you want to look them up," Hal said. "*Der Führer* likes to take it on the road, from what I understand. Stay in one place too long, he has to figure someone's coming for him."

"Just because he's crazy, doesn't mean he's always wrong," Bolan said.

"Like the broken clock," Brognola added.

"How's that?"

"It gets the time right twice a day, regardless."

"Ah."

"Don't say it. I'm not giving up the day job."

"Well—"

"I'd better get a start on waking people up," Brognola said. "They may not like it, but that's why they get the big bucks, right?"

"If you say so."

"I don't know when I may have something, but I've got the pager number. Want to give me one for the motel?"

"I won't be here," Bolan replied.

"Your cousin?"

"Up to her. The only thing I want is information. I'm not looking for a sidekick or a back seat driver."

"This one's not too swift, I take it?"

"Just the opposite," Bolan said. "She's got plenty on the ball and knows her way around an AK when the chips are down."

"Sounds terrible. You wouldn't want her getting in the way."

"Enough with the reverse psychology, okay? You know I don't play well with strangers. Even if she pulls her weight, I still don't like it."

"So, she's pretty, too?"

"Irrelevant," Bolan replied. "This isn't *Love Connection,* and last I heard, our brief didn't include involving personnel from other agencies unless it's unavoidable."

"I wouldn't go that far," Brognola said. "If she can help you out—"

"My take," Bolan interrupted him, "is that she's true blue to her people, and they play it strictly by the book. I don't need someone second-guessing every move I make and passing gripes upstairs. It's not a good idea for anyone concerned."

"No sweat," Brognola said. "Her people probably won't call me, anyway. They've had so much bad ink the past few years, my take is that they're gun shy. Which is pretty odd, considering—"

"I get it," Bolan cut him off again. "Gun shy. The ATF. I'm going now."

"You've been a lousy audience," Brognola groused. "Next time, there'll be a cover charge."

"Next time, I'll call collect. Stay frosty there."

"You, too."

The line went dead, and as he cradled the receiver, the big Fed was conscious of his wife's deep breathing. She was sound asleep, God bless her. All these years, and she had learned to screen the wake-up calls, the same way he had been conditioned to respond on cue. She didn't even need the second pillow for a muffler anymore.

To spare her dreams, regardless, Brognola eased out of bed and pulled on a robe as he left the bedroom, skulking toward his office through the dark and silent house. His private line rang through in there, as well, and he could make his calls without disturbing anyone who wasn't paid to be awake and worried at this hour of the morning. Also, if he got a call from ATF and it was routed to him through the cutout number Bolan had supplied to his unwanted guest, Brognola would feel better talking from his desk, instead of from his bed.

He had mixed feelings toward the thought of a collaborative effort with the ATF. Despite some headline-grabbing screwups and the occasional lapse of what he considered basic common sense in certain leadership positions, Treasury's Bureau of Alcohol, Tobacco and Firearms still did an above-average job of enforcing federal laws that fell within its jurisdiction. That did *not* mean he was ready to broadcast the secrets of his covert operation to another agency, and he suspected Bolan was correct about ATF's commitment to play by the established rules. It didn't take that many public spankings for a gang of bureaucrats to figure out that they should concentrate on dotting i's and crossing t's, instead of making waves.

It shouldn't be an issue, then. But if it was...

Then he would leave the field decisions to his soldier on the firing line, and let the chips fall where they may.

That was the nice part of a strictly covert war. You didn't always have to tie the loose ends up into a stylish bow.

By the same token, though, you had to make damned sure those loose ends didn't make a noose—or, if they did, that it was wrapped around somebody else's neck.

CHAPTER FIVE

Gerhard Steuben was accustomed to bad news. It was the only kind he ever got when he was Gary Stevens, in the bad old days before he found himself, his destiny. It still persisted, since the world at large—meaning the Jews, mud people, Communists and all their stinking allies—hated him and what he stood for, but the bad news didn't seem to bother him as much these days.

That was the major benefit of prophecy. You didn't sweat the little things—or big things, either, for that matter—if you absolutely, positively knew that you were destined to succeed.

Careful!

He caught himself, remembering that even destiny could be diverted from its course in the short run by an unworthy prophet. If he rested on his laurels, took too much for granted, then the gods might punish him for his conceit, use him as an example for some future generation of the pitfalls to avoid.

He had to stay strong and persevere, be confident but never overconfident. The worst sin that a holy warrior could commit was underestimating those he faced in battle.

So.

The news from Washington was bad, all right, but it could still have been much worse. A traitor had been found within the ranks at Freedom Home, duly condemned, but at the very hour of her execution, someone else had crept into the sanctuary of his faith and carried her away, killing nearly a score of Steuben's men in the process. It was blasphemous and unforgivable.

It was a royal pain in the ass.

Steuben hadn't been startled when the Judas in his fold turned out to be a Jezebel this time. Women were naturally duplicitous, if not tightly controlled. His own late mother was a perfect case in point, giving herself with lecherous abandon to a filthy Jew after her husband—Gerhard's proud white father—died in military service, one of Red Jack Kennedy's first Green Beret advisers on the firing line against the godless Communists in Vietnam. He had distrusted women from that day, when he was barely ten years old, and while he knew their sex was vital to perpetuation and expansion of the master race, Steuben denied them all his essence, understanding that a legend sometimes left no heir of flesh and blood behind.

He had been furious at first when Fletcher called to tell him of the raid on Freedom Home, but Sean had taken all the necessary steps to compensate, and they were still on schedule for the next phase of their plan. The sword hadn't been blunted; its descent upon the stretched necks of their enemies wouldn't be even momentarily delayed.

What troubled Steuben most wasn't the fact that Washington and ZOG had sent another infiltrator to destroy his movement from within. That was expected; he had weeded out others before, and doubtless would again before the final smoke of battle cleared. Nor was he startled that the pigs would have a backup plan to save their Jezebel if she was threatened.

No, what worried Steuben was the way in which the rescue had been carried out—covertly, with ruthlessness and an almost surgical precision, as well as a silence that was absolutely foreign to the enemies whom he had dealt with in the past.

The Jews were capable of subtlety, he realized—witness the death grip they maintained on Hollywood, on Wall Street and on Washington, suspected only by a relative handful of patriots—but when they dealt a blow to what their propagandists liked to call "hate groups" or the "lunatic fringe," they preferred to do so with a fanfare of publicity, heaping scorn and ridicule on those they persecuted, sometimes hounded to untimely graves. It was unprecedented for the Zionist assassins to behave this way outside the Middle East and parts of Europe, where they had been killing Israel's enemies covertly for the better part of half a century.

Such stealth, applied in the United States, told Steuben that his mortal threat to ZOG had finally been recognized by those who called the shots. No longer would he be dismissed in sneering media reports as a fanatic and a mental case, beneath contempt; no longer would he and his soldiers be harassed with nuisance litigation in the courts. From this point on, he understood, the gloves were off.

His enemies were out for blood.

It was a fitting change, all things considered. Granted, he had hoped to make a bit more progress before the final "coming out" in an apocalyptic blaze of glory, but the shift couldn't be helped. Looked at another way, he saw it as a golden opportunity, almost a blessing, coming when it did. With no holds barred, his soldiers would be even more inspired from that day forward, to the moment when they claimed their final victory. They now had murdered comrades to avenge, aside from all the other wrongs that Jews and mud people had perpetrated from the beginnings of recorded history.

The target he had chosen for the next strike was a fitting one, Steuben believed. Both symbolic and practical, it would provide his adversaries—and the world at large—with a token of his resolve. They hadn't as yet seen his wrath full-blown, but when they did, it would be awesome to behold. Some of the fawning race traitors and sycophants who served the common enemy today might well experience a change of heart and join the holy cause before it was too late to save themselves.

As for the rest, Steuben himself would strike the match when it was time for them to burn.

Meanwhile, he had a little ethnic cleansing to conduct.

Scattered around the dining table inside the aging Winnebago that transported him from place to place—incognito and certainly more economical than any of the Jew-owned airlines—were magazines and newspapers containing articles about his long crusade. Some of the magazines and newspapers were old and dog-eared. Many of the reporters failed to understand what they were seeing, even when they got the raw facts straight. The strike at Wilkes Land was a perfect case in point, widely attributed to certain unnamed ecoterrorists, perhaps some bid to further publicize the threat of global warning or destruction of the Amazon rain forest.

Idiots.

Even when Steuben signed his work, they were too blind to read his signature.

Or were they?

It was possible, he thought, that ZOG had chosen to obscure his role in certain incidents deliberately, thus simultaneously robbing Steuben and the Nordic Temple of publicity and the potential for increased recruiting, while the blind and stupid masses dwelled in ignorance of the impending revolution. He wouldn't have been surprised to see the outings by his soldiers advertised as ''solved,'' some patsies hustled off to prison while the Hollywood machine cranked out another movie of the week, bearing the message that all was well.

But all was *not* well in the empire of his enemies. Whether they knew it yet or not, the wheels of retribution had begun to turn, gears meshing, grinding flesh and bone to pulp and powder. There would be no stopping that machine once it began to gather speed, and Gerhard Steuben had his foot on the accelerator. He was in the driver's seat.

Or close enough.

Up front, a couple of his young disciples listened to an all-news channel on the radio and spoke in muted tones, one piloting the Winnebago while the other kept him company and helped him watch for cops. Nevada had increased its freeway speed limit as soon as federal law had yielded that small power to the states, but it was still a far cry from the good old days of "safe and prudent," when a man could barrel through the wasteland at a hundred miles per hour if he felt like it, and no one but the jackrabbits who had to dodge his guided missile gave a damn.

One more small freedom stripped away, because no one had seen it coming, or they were too damned preoccupied with self to even care.

All that would change, and soon.

Steuben could smell the great change coming.

Its aroma smelled deliciously of smoke and death.

Washington

THE TAKEOUT breakfast came from one of those fast-food restaurants that nearly always botched orders at the drive-through window. Bolan took his time and doubled-checked each item, while the hungry motorists behind him fumed and muttered, none of them quite brave enough to try his horn.

It was a short drive back to the motel, nothing in Spanaway located very far from anything else. On the approach, Bolan scouted the neighborhood for watchers, anyone or anything that struck him as unusual, and while he spotted license tags from half a dozen states, there was no reason for alarm that he could put a finger on.

It had occurred to him that he might return and find the woman gone. She hadn't balked at Bolan's offer to stay over, and the two of them had shared the double bed, both fully dressed, Bolan atop the covers, waking with a stiff neck and the sense that he may well have been more comfortable sleeping on the floor. They had agreed on breakfast as a concept, although the menu had been unpredictable, and Crouder was shower bound when Bolan left to see what he could find. Now, as he pulled into the motel parking lot, he thought again that it was possible she would be gone, seizing the opportunity to break away from him and get back to her people with a minimum of hassle.

And for just a moment, Bolan wished it would be so.

Despite the fact that she had proved herself in combat, more or less, despite the fact that he harbored no doubts about a woman's capability in crisis situations and despite her inside knowledge of the Temple of the Nordic Covenant, the two of them were strangers. The day before a blitz was no time to be breaking in recruits, especially when they were from different services, with very different sets of rules.

Parking the Blazer, Bolan stacked the cardboard containers, breathing the aroma of the scrambled eggs, hash browns, pancakes, biscuits and gravy—a little something for every taste—and reached back for the cardboard tray that held paper coffee cups, plus plastic "glasses" of orange juice. He had the room key in his hand, the other items balanced, braced against his chest, before he reached the door. It would have been the time to take him, someone coming up behind him with a pistol, maybe sniping from across the street, but nothing happened, and another moment saw the door swing shut behind him, Bolan safe inside.

With Crouder just hanging up the phone.

"Room service," Bolan announced, and though he offered something in the nature of a smile, his eyes were on the telephone, her fingertips still resting on the handset.

"That was Archer calling back," she said. "I let him have the number here, so he could reach me when he got done talking to your people in D.C."

"Which means that ATF could have this place staked out right now."

"Which means," she answered, turning it around on him, "that if they had a move in mind, they would have come last night. Relax, already. Archer doesn't want you. He was calling back just now to tell me I should give you full cooperation…to a point."

"What's that supposed to mean?" Bolan asked.

"Look, he understands about last night, okay? Shit happens in a crunch, and he says thanks for helping me. As for the rest, well, he was tight on details as to what he and your people talked about, a lot of cloak-and-dagger mystery, but ATF still has a brief, subject to oversight, and Archer isn't authorized to write blank checks. He can't just say, 'Go on and do whatever's necessary,' right? So, I'm supposed to touch base with him twice a day, at least, and blow the bridge if I see anything that could reflect adversely on the bureau."

Bolan's smile was genuine this time; at least, it felt that way, as he began to lay out containers on the small round table near the window. "Well," he told her, "you can have some breakfast, anyway, before you leave."

"Say what?"

"Will they send someone out to pick you up, or should I drop you in Tacoma? Maybe at the Amtrak station?"

"Earth to Mike! Were you not listening? I told you, I've been cleared to go ahead with this."

"And bail if you see anything that could 'reflect adversely' on the ATF," he added, pulling up a chair and stripping shrink-wrap from one of the odd plastic utensils known as sporks, a tiny spoon with jagged teeth.

"Well, hey—"

"Your breakfast's getting cold," he said.

"I lost my appetite."

A shrug from Bolan, as he pried the plastic lid off of his coffee cup.

"So, what's your problem, anyway?" she challenged him.

"I haven't got a problem," Bolan said. "You do. From what you've told me, you're approved to feed me information—and presumably to tag along—until such time as you have reason to believe I've thrown the book away. Is that about the size of it?"

"That's it."

"So, let me spare you the embarrassment of getting on the bus, then having to hop off again, before it leaves the curb. You won't like anything you see from this point on, and frankly, I don't need to be distracted by concerns that you're about to rat me out at every turn and drop a SWAT team on my back."

"Emergency response team," she corrected him. "We don't use 'SWAT.'"

"You didn't answer me."

"What was the question?"

"Will they send someone to pick you up, or—"

"Dammit! I'm not going anywhere!" she snapped.

"Okay. The room's paid up until tomorrow, noon. As far as transportation goes, you're on your own."

"Who are you, really? What are you?"

"You must have picked up something from the brass," he said.

"I told you, cloak-and-dagger stuff. Top secret this, top secret that."

"Which leads you to conclude…?"

"That someone's crossed the line," she answered, pulling up the other chair and sitting down. "I think… Is that French toast?"

"Don't think," he said. "Don't ask, and I certainly won't tell. If we go one from here, you'll see adverse reflections everywhere you look."

"I spent more than a year inside the Nordic Temple, building up a case. Do you know what that means to me?"

"So prosecute," he told her. "That's the job description, right?"

"We still don't have enough to do it right. It's not enough to net the small-fry in the States and let the sharks swim off to snack on someone else."

"It's a dilemma, I admit," he said. "You've reached your limit of authority, the line you're not allowed to cross."

"So, I just walk away? Pretend none of it ever happened?"

"That's your call," Bolan said. "I can't make it for you, but if you've got conscience problems making that decision, then you definitely don't belong with me. That's not an insult, by the way. It's just an observation.''

"You don't think I can pull my weight?"

"I don't think you can pull *my* weight," he said. "And there's no reason you should try."

She spent a moment picking at the wrapper on her spork before she said, "You're bringing down the Temple, right?"

"I'm giving it a shot."

"Okay. There are some things you ought to know."

California

THE CHEAP HOTEL Sean Fletcher had selected was on Third Street in Los Angeles, a short walk south of Little Tokyo. He liked to have the enemy close by, for inspiration, even though the Japanese weren't his target this time. He was aiming higher on the radical-subversive ladder, moving toward a master stroke that would leave Jew-run la-la land in shock, but it revitalized him sometimes, getting out among his adversaries, brushing past them on the streets that they monopolized, seeing the gibberish on their signs and placards, filling his ears with their alien, singsong jabber.

He had considered looking for a hotel on the edge of Watts, but decided that the proximity of all those jiving mud people would be an undue distraction for his men. The last thing Fletcher needed, at the moment, was some well-intentioned soldier going off half-cocked and shooting up some soul-food palace for the hell of it, before they had a chance to make their move.

The target chosen by his Führer would, in its destruction, cause more anguish to the enemy than any slaughter of their stupid drones in Watts or East L.A. Mud people were expendable, deliberately so. There was, so far, an endlessly renewable supply of muggers, rapists, gangbangers and terrorists available to those who called the shots and pulled the strings. That, too, would change in time, as warriors of the Nordic Temple moved toward the eventual, predestined checkmate in a game of global domination, but for now, the enemy had hard-line Aryans outnumbered, and a series of attacks upon their livestock would be tantamount to wasting precious time and energy, playing into the hands of ZOG.

No, thank you very much.

Herr Steuben's choice of targets was inspired, no matter that it called for Fletcher's team to strike within a half mile of police headquarters and the Hall of Justice. Sheer audacity could compensate for numbers in the short run, and if all went well, there would be various diversions for the little piggies to pursue, while Fletcher and his men slipped in to do their work.

He had eleven men to help him do the job—the "Dirty Dozen," as they called themselves, though Fletcher failed to see the humor in comparing the strike force to a group of fictional felons that had included a black, an Indian, and several drooling deviates. Three would be detailed to provide distractions in advance of H hour, while Fletcher led the eight-man team against their primary objective.

He was looking forward to it, as he had anticipated nothing else in years.

Time for a hardware check. Spread out in front of him, across the smallish, boxlike bed, Fletcher had carefully arranged the gear his men had brought in from the vans in OD duffel bags. A dozen kilo bricks of C-4 plastic explosive, close to thirty pounds in all, was well separated from the blasting caps and detonators. The hit team was equipped with Uzi submachine guns, with Galil sniper rifles for long-distance work, delicious irony in the selection of Israeli-manufactured hardware for the strike against these tools of Tel Aviv. The side arms were Berettas liberated from an Air Force base in Colorado, no one the wiser once some cash changed hands. The weapons had been tested on the firing range at Freedom Home, then fieldstripped, cleaned and reassembled on arrival in Los Angeles, their magazines loaded by those who would depend upon their flawless function for survival when the jump-off order came.

Fletcher was satisfied with his equipment and the handpicked members of his team. There were no cherries on the squad. Each soldier had been blooded since enlisting with the Temple of the Nordic Covenant; each had displayed the necessary willingness to take life and to risk his own in defense of the master race. Fletcher wasn't concerned that they would let him down when the strike was under way.

He was concerned, however, that the scheming bitch who had escaped her rightful punishment at Freedom Home would try to ruin the plan before he had an opportunity to score against the Jews. Exactly how she might accomplish that was still unclear to

Fletcher, but he wouldn't sell her short by underestimating her resourcefulness.

If she could find a way to screw the Temple, Fletcher had no doubt that Mary Krause would follow through.

That wouldn't be her name, of course. What was it, really? Fletcher wondered. Magda Krebbs, perhaps? Mahalia Kravitz? Mazel Kroskie?

Never mind.

The wheels were turning, trying to determine who she was and whom she worked for, which of ZOG's diverse and deadly tentacles was probing for a death grip on the Temple of the Nordic Covenant. You knew a group of patriots was making progress, gaining ground, when the subversive scum in Washington decided it was time to infiltrate, disrupt and persecute the Aryans involved. The Klan had been destroyed, for all intents and purposes, by lawsuits, prosecutions and a nonstop stream of ridicule from the media. George Lincoln Rockwell had been murdered by a traitor in his own inner circle, J. B. Stoner neutralized by trumped-up charges in a thirty-year-old bombing case, Bob Matthews murdered by the FBI, Connie Lynch hounded to an alleged heart attack by federal harassment. David Duke had felt compelled to go mainstream, complete with plastic surgery, and look where it had gotten him: a footnote in the textbooks under "neo-Nazi runs for President and gets his ass kicked at the polls."

So much for working with the system.

It was time for revolution, and the Temple of the Nordic Covenant was on the cutting edge, Sean

Fletcher in the vanguard. In a little less than twenty-four more hours, he was going to make history.

And he could hardly wait.

Washington

"ARE YOU FAMILIAR with the Eli Sturnman Center, in Los Angeles?"

Bolan washed down the last bite of his breakfast with coffee prior to answering. "It sounds familiar," he replied. "Is it some kind of Holocaust memorial?"

"That's part of it." Now that she had begun to tell the story, Marilyn Crouder felt almost liberated, and that feeling, in its turn, made her uneasy, as if the temptation to discard her ethics might be so compelling, so alluring, that she had no power to resist. "They have a Holocaust museum, though it's much smaller than the one in Washington, D.C. The center's namesake, Eli Sturnman, was a German Jew who got packed off to Dachau in the spring of 1939. Two years later, he was transferred to Auschwitz, but he managed to survive the war and made his way back home—if you can call it that. He watched the war-crimes trials and saw how many Nazis weren't indicted, much less prosecuted. Some of them were back in government, from beat cops and judges to the chancellor's office before you could say, *'Sieg heil.'* The CIA was hiring them to spy on Russia, and the folks at NASA couldn't get enough of German rocket scientists who spent the war years firing V-2s into London."

"That's old news," Bolan said.

"It wasn't back in 1948," she said, "and not to

camp survivors who had watched their families and friends go up in smoke. Sturnman decided to do what he could to keep the pressure on the Germans and Americans by tracking Nazi fugitives from justice. He helped Israel pin the tail on Adolf Eichmann, and he chased Dr. Mengele around South America for twenty years, until the crazy bastard drowned himself in Paraguay, or wherever the hell it was.''

''Sounds like a fighter.''

''Up until the day he died, in 1993. The center is a showcase for his work. It also carries on where he left off—investigating Third Reich fugitives who've managed to survive this long, particularly if they're hiding in the States or Canada, and filling annual reports on neo-Nazi hate groups, lobbying for legislation to control their paramilitary exercises, things like that.''

''In other words,'' Bolan said, ''it's not the Nordic Temple's favorite charity.''

The smile surprised her with how easily it came. ''You've got it,'' she replied. ''In fact, Herr Stevens and his bully boys have talked about destroying it for years. According to the plans I stumbled on to back at Freedom Home, they've reached a point where they're prepared to go beyond the talking stage.''

''Specifics?''

''That's the bad news,'' Crouder informed him. ''If your little rescue operation doesn't throw them off, a hit team is supposed to move against the center at precisely noon tomorrow, L.A. time.''

''You've told your people this?''

''Of course.''

''And their response was...?''

"They can't move against the principals until they find out who and where they are. Since they've got nothing but my word to verify the plot, they may have trouble getting John Doe warrants, and they couldn't serve them, anyway, until they track the hit team down. By that time, it could be too late."

"They're tipping off LAPD?"

Her shoulders slumped. "You'd think so, wouldn't you?"

"That's not a yes."

"You know the way it works, all right? How many times have local cops complained about the FBI ignoring boundaries and hogging headlines for itself? After the heat they took from Ruby Ridge and Waco, my guys try to play it cool whenever possible, and most particularly when they're dealing with a so-called church. The oversight committees have been spanking us with First Amendment issues for the past eight years. Nobody wants to cry wolf in the media, much less come out and say the sky is falling."

"But you mentioned grabbing headlines. Will they mount some kind of operation on the sly?"

"I wouldn't count on it," she said, and felt the angry color rising in her cheeks. "The last thing Archer told me on the telephone was that I ought to 'see what my new friend can do about this little problem.' What a sweetheart, huh?"

"It works for me," Bolan said.

"You're serious?"

"Why not? You've got a date, a time, an address. If your information's good—"

"I've told you what they're planning," Crouder responded, conscious of the anger in her voice, unable to control it. "I can't promise you they'll go ahead, after last night."

"There's one way I can think of to find out," Bolan stated, draining his coffee cup.

"You think your guys would cover it?" she asked him.

"I was thinking I would."

"Just like that?"

"No harm in trying, right?"

"We're sitting in Tacoma—"

"Spanaway."

"Whatever. We're in Washington, and you decide to bust an operation going down in Los Angeles, in—" she paused to check her watch "—a little under twenty-seven hours? That's what, twelve hundred miles away? The straight-through drive alone will take us twenty hours, minimum, and we'll be wasted when we get there."

"Transportation's not a problem," he replied. "I know a guy who knows a guy."

"Does this magician have a time machine?"

"He has jet planes," Bolan said.

"Okay, the next-best thing." She hesitated, almost losing steam before the next objection reared its ugly head. "Did I forget to mention the diversions?"

"I believe you did." An edge of frost had crept into his tone, and Crouder was startled to discover that she found it more unnerving than rewarding.

"Sorry. What it is, their target being more or less downtown, the hit team plans to keep the cops distracted, draw them to other areas, just long enough to make their move and clear the scene."

"Won't work," Bolan said. "LAPD is broken

down into something like half a dozen regional divisions. Officers from Hollywood don't roll on calls from East L.A., for instance, and the crowd at Parker Center won't be traipsing off to see what's happening in Wilshire or Van Nuys. You'll get a uniformed response, no matter what."

"Maybe," she said, "but simple logic tells me that the size and speed of that response may be affected by peripheral events, depending on how serious they are. Remember Rodney King? The Simi Valley trial? How many cops do you suppose were hanging out around headquarters then?"

"You said 'diversion,' not 'disaster.'"

"What's in a name? These goons preach racial holy war, okay? They'd start a riot for the hell of it, to see how many will wind up DOA. You think they'd hesitate to do it in pursuance of a holy cause?"

"So, what's the plan? Dress up like cops and kick some butt on live TV?"

"Strategic marks," she said. "L.A. is full of activists and spokesmen for minority communities—Latino, African American, you name it. Think about a well-placed bomb or bullet, multiplied by half a dozen, with some suitable graffiti, maybe pamphlets 'accidentally' discarded at the scene. Time it to play an hour or two before the main event, and you could have a fair approximation of a three-ring circus by the time the hit goes down."

"About these other targets…"

"Sorry. There were no specifics I could find, before they bagged me."

"Fair enough," Bolan said. "We'll run with what we have."

"About this guy with the jet planes…"

"I think you know him," Bolan replied. "His friends all call him Uncle Sam."

CHAPTER SIX

Hal Brognola pulled some strings to arrange the air lift from McChord AFB, outside Tacoma, to Camp Pendleton Marine Corps Base, some fifty miles south of Los Angeles. No fighter plane available would seat three passengers, together with the hardware Bolan carried, so Marilyn Crouder was consigned to a Gulfstream C-21A, the military version of a Learjet business aircraft, normally employed for VIP transport or as reconnaissance and special-purpose aircraft.

Bolan calculated that the "special-purpose" label covered his assignment pretty well. In any case, the flight shaved roughly eighteen hours off his estimated drive time, putting him on the ground at Pendleton fairly refreshed, ready to fight.

The immediate problem was he still had seventeen hours and change left to kill.

Another car was waiting for them at the base, this one a four-door Ford with California tags and plenty of room in the trunk for Bolan's duffel bags. He had worn the Beretta 93-R in a shoulder rig all the way from Tacoma, no pesky metal detectors or other devices invented to delay, frustrate and annoy travelers. He thus arrived fully armed, found the ride fully gassed and took a leisurely three-quarters of an hour driving north to L.A.

On entering the city that was familiar to him from previous campaigns, Bolan asked his navigator to show him the target before they got down to selecting hotels. The Eli Sturnman Center was on Olive Street, perhaps a half mile from the teeming anthill of downtown Los Angeles, close enough that a good marksman with the right weapon could have hit it from the rooftop of police headquarters—if it weren't for all the sky-scraping giants that stood in the way. The center stood six stories tall, a relative pygmy in that company of behemoths, and boasted its own parking lot, as well as what appeared to be some kind of planted area out back.

"That's the memory garden," Crouder told him, as they passed the place at something close to walking speed. "It's part of the museum. The rest is all inside."

A quick pass turned up nothing in the way of lurkers checking out the place, but Bolan had expected nothing of the kind. Between pedestrians and vehicular traffic, it would have been difficult to spot watchers in the open, much less pick out observers who had made an effort to conceal themselves. Besides, the raiders would have cased their target in advance, would have made sketches or taken photographs to help them plan their strike. They had been planning it for months, if not for years. If they weren't ready now, they never would be.

Fifteen hours later, at his post across the street, the Executioner wasn't so sure. He had begun to question whether they were coming, to consider once again the possibility that Crouder's escape might have compelled them to revise or scuttle plans, for fear of being intercepted. He was just about to check his watch, consider shifting to another vantage point for the variety, when muted static crackled from the tiny earpiece that he wore.

"It's started," the lady ATF agent said. "We've got a shooting down in Watts. Some minister involved in politics. He's critical. The shooter was apparently a white man, and he got away. They've got reports of scattered incidents already, and the cops are rolling out."

Bolan couldn't reply without appearing to be caught up in a conversation with himself, and he already felt exposed enough by loitering, without inviting stares.

"Hold on a second," Crouder said. "They've got something…damn! A bomb, it sounds like. East L.A. Some high school. Christ, it's really going down!"

Or was it? Bolan wondered. And if so, exactly what was going down? What was there to prevent the Nordic Temple's goons from writing off their primary target, dismissing it as too risky with Crouder alive, at large and maybe talking to authorities? Why not proceed with the diversions as distinct and separate missions on their own? They might not target Jews this time, but Hispanics and blacks ranked high on the Temple's list of enemies, condemned as subhuman "mud people" and the source of most crime in America. Who was to say the fascists might not cut their losses this time, and be satisfied to stir up violence in the ghetto and the barrio, with wider potential for loss of life once the police became involved?

"Heads up!" Crouder said. "They're here!"

He couldn't see her, had left her to pick the vantage point that suited her the best, with an agreement that she would make no attempt to join in any combat that took place. Her role was to observe the layout and alert him to the presence of familiar faces if she had an opportunity to do so. Bolan, meanwhile, made a show of window-shopping, counting on the movement and deliberate aloofness of pedestrians to cover for the fact that he had browsed past only four shops in the past three-quarters of an hour.

Now, he checked the street's reflection in the nearest plate-glass window, made his turn casual, perspiring inside the sport coat that was cut a size too large, specifically to cover the Beretta slung beneath his left arm and the Spectre submachine gun hanging on a sling beneath his right.

"You're looking for a van, dark blue," his spotter told him. "No one showing but the driver. He's a guy I've seen at Freedom Home."

The words had barely registered when Bolan saw the van, a full-sized G10 Chevy with no windows at the back or sides, no logo, nothing to distinguish it from any other of its make in town. The plates were from Nevada, which meant less than squat. The driver was a burly skinhead type, midtwenties, wearing mirrored shades and what appeared to be a denim shirt or coveralls. As Bolan watched, the driver wheeled the van in to the yellow-painted curb before the Eli Sturnman Center, filling up the loading zone. The driver left the engine running, swiveled in his seat, said something to invisible companions in the rear compartment of the van.

"Stand by," Crouder stated.

The G10 Chevy van had sliding cargo doors on either side, and double doors in back, its overall appearance reminiscent of a paddy wagon or an old-style military ambulance. From where he was, across the street, Bolan couldn't observe the cargo door as it slid open on the starboard side, but he had registered the rocking motion of the van, as unseen passengers climbed out. A moment later, and he got a fix on four men, all in faded denim coveralls, mounting the low steps to the entrance of the Sturnman Center. Each of them wore a watch cap that could just as easily be a rolled-up ski mask, waiting to be yanked down into place. Each man was carrying a metal toolbox in his left hand, freeing up the right.

"Three more in back," Crouder told him, "one of them staying in the car."

A flanking move.

Okay.

The Executioner stepped out into traffic, dodging vehicles that barely slowed, as if the drivers either didn't see him, or they simply didn't give a damn. His right hand slipped inside his open jacket as he zigzagged toward the idling van.

THEY HAD DRAWN LOTS to see who would go in the front door, who would take the back. Fletcher had chosen to allow that much democracy, because it gave his men a sense of being more than simple pawns or cannon fodder. In such fashion, Fletcher had been relegated to the backup team, and while he could have pulled rank at that moment, or refrained from joining in the lottery, he chose to let it go.

One reason for his seeming pliability was that he felt his men were all well trained enough to handle either end of the assault without him breathing down their necks and second-guessing every move they made. The other was that Fletcher understood how frightened minds worked, and he knew the staff and any visitors inside the Eli Sturnman Center, once they heard the first few gunshots coming from the lobby area, would try to slip out through the back.

And find him waiting for them there.

The prospect brought a hungry smile to Fletcher's narrow face. The rolled-up ski mask made his forehead itch, but he could live with it. Another moment, and it would be time to pull down the mask, covering his face. He hoped that the precaution proved to be unnecessary, that they would leave no survivors, but such things could never be predicted with assurance. Even with the Uzis and C-4, there was a chance some Jew would wriggle through the net and make it out alive.

So be it.

If the Führer, with his thousands of devoted servants, couldn't wipe the slate clean in a dozen years, no one could logically expect Sean Fletcher and his tiny band of soldiers to achieve perfection in a single afternoon. But they would do their best, and if they missed a straggler or two, it only meant that they would have some free publicity among the Jews, the tale of panic and annihilation spread by word of mouth among the Temple's enemies.

"Get ready," Fletcher said, and Jerry Biehl responded with a grunt as he reached up to pull down his ski mask. A heartbeat, when the world went black in front of Fletcher's eyes, and then the wool was snug against his face.

The back door to the Sturnman Center was always locked, but Fletcher had the key. He had obtained it from the night custodian, mere hours earlier. The old man had resisted stubbornly until the thumb and fingers on his left hand had been broken, one by one, and they were ready to get started on the right. Dumb bastard thought that giving in would save his life, apparently, and that had been his last mistake. No one at work would miss him for a day, at least, in the chaotic aftermath of the attack, and by the time they found his body with the rune carved deep into his wrinkled forehead, it would be too late for his demise to serve as any kind of warning to the Jews he served.

The latex gloves Fletcher wore were thin enough that he had pulled on a second pair, remembering an article he'd read about some test the FBI had recently invented that could sometimes pick up latent prints, or even DNA, from residual amino acids that a single layer of latex didn't block. It made him all the more suspicious of the condom advertisements that he saw on television and in magazines, but for the present mission, he'd decided double-gloving with a layer of talcum powder ought to do the trick. His troops were likewise covered, and unless they ran into security, unless one of them spilled his blood inside the center, they shouldn't be leaving anything behind except printless spent brass and the pall of death.

The key turned effortlessly, silencing last-minute fears that the old man might have deceived them, toughed it out and handed over the wrong key. It would have elevated him in Fletcher's estimation, but it didn't prove to be the case. Another moment, and they were inside a storage area, with cardboard boxes of the kind that normally held books or printed fliers stacked on either side.

"Hold up," he said, and Biehl stopped on a dime, using the moment to remove his Uzi from the toolbox. Fletcher did likewise, the weapon cocked and locked, nothing for him to do but thumb off the safety and curl his index finger through the trigger guard.

No sounds of battle yet, and he wasn't about to jump the gun. The front-door team was scheduled to begin the party; he and Biehl were there to plug the exit hatch.

Fletcher had waited for this moment for the best part of a year. A few more seconds made no difference, either way, except to those he was about to kill.

MARILYN CROUDER WAS about to break her word. It was some kind of sin to lie, of course, but she believed the man upstairs—assuming he existed—was prepared to make allowances for certain special circumstances.

Like the fact that Mike Belasko was about to get his ass shot off, for instance.

She had seen him work, and he was good, all right, but she had also seen the storm troops of the Nordic Temple when their blood was up and they were on the hunt. The fact that she had managed to escape their clutches, due in large part to Belasko's help, killing a number of them in the process, had resulted—in her view, at least—as much from luck as skill. And that defeat would make *this* hit team all the more determined to succeed, whether the men involved had been at Freedom Home the previous night or not.

One thing she had to say about the Temple of the Nordic Covenant: for good or ill, it was a brotherhood, its rank and file fanatically committed to their officers, the brass as mindlessly devoted to their Führer as if Gary Stevens really did possess the spirit of some Nazi "hero" killed in World War II. They weren't the kind to passively surrender, even in the face of overwhelming force, much less one man who tried to tackle eight of them at once.

That morning, prior to staking out the Sturnman Center, her companion had reluctantly supplied her with some 5.56 mm ammunition to reload the plastic magazine of her liberated AK-74. He had watched her stash the rifle in a canvas shopping bag, a veto perched on the tip of his tongue, finally permitting her to bring the piece along when she had vowed to hang back from the action no matter what happened, stay out of the way, and to use the rifle only if, by some freak accident, the raiders found her vantage point and threatened her directly. Otherwise, she had committed to a strictly noncombatant role as his observer.

And she had been lying through her teeth.

Not consciously, of course...at least, she told herself that she had meant it when she spoke the words. Her grave misgivings had developed only moments later—five or six, at the outside—when she had started out by wondering if Belasko could handle all the raiders by himself, and wound up positive that he most certainly could not. From that point on, with the decision made, there was no looking back.

Archer would bust a gut if he could see her now, emerging from the stairwell that had been her lookout's nest, dodging through traffic on the yellow light, the AK in its tote bag slapping heavily against her hip. She made it to the far side of the street and jogged along the sidewalk, just in time to catch Sean Fletcher's profile as he tugged down his ski mask and pushed his way in through the back door of the Sturnman Center.

Now what?

If she followed them inside, she knew there was a chance she could surprise them, cut off their retreat, but any confrontation she provoked or joined within the building magnified the chances that her own rounds might strike some third party, cause the very damage and destruction she was trying to prevent. Still, waiting on the street outside struck her as cowardly, defeating her intended purpose of assisting Belasko when he faced their common enemy.

Okay. Inside it was.

But was the back door still unlocked? Would her approach alert the driver who remained behind the wheel of Fletcher's vehicle? And if the door *was* locked, how would she ever make her way inside in time to be of any use?

She was some ten or fifteen paces from the backup vehicle before she saw the driver's face and bit her lip to keep the curses trapped behind her teeth. She knew him from the compound. Billy Thatcher, twenty-two or -three years old, as mean as a snake when he was drunk and not much better when he wasn't. For a moment, Crouder was hopeful that her dark sunglasses and the scarf she wore over her hair would mix him up enough to let her pass, but then she saw his mouth drop open, showing yellow teeth. There was a beat of hesitation, Thatcher making sure before his door swung open and he stepped out of the car.

She shrugged the cloth bag's strap off her shoulder, with her hand already deep inside and wrapped around the AK's pistol grip. The bag slid free and brushed against her leg as it was falling, Thatcher just about to call her name—or maybe call her something else—before he saw the muzzle of her weapon rising to the level of his chest.

He had a piece, as well, she saw, just coming into view around the straight edge of the open driver's door. An Uzi, and she knew that she was out of time. Her finger tightened on the AK's trigger, and the rifle hammered out a 5- or 6-round burst.

At least three of the slugs ripped into Thatcher's chest, their impact slamming him against the car and wiping any readily identifiable expression from his face. He dropped the Uzi, but the built-in safety in its grip prevented it from firing when it hit the pavement, the gunner folding at the knees and going down on top of it a second later. There was blood smeared on the car behind him, hence no Kevlar, and if Thatcher wasn't dead, she figured he was on his way.

One down.

Surprised to feel nothing but glacial calm inside, despite the beads of perspiration sprouting on her face, she turned and sprinted for the back door of the Sturnman Center, where Sean Fletcher and the other goon had disappeared.

BOLAN HAD COME UP on the driver's blind side, caught him glancing in the mirror, swiveling around too late, and shot him at close range. The silenced round from his Beretta drilled through the skinhead's temple, battering him over sideways in his seat. An instant later, Bolan had the pistol tucked away and out of sight, mounting the stairs to reach the tall, ornate doors of the Eli Sturnman Center.

Going in, he had the Spectre out and ready. Its unique closed-bolt design made it essentially a double-action weapon on the first shot, safe enough to carry with a live round in the chamber and the safety off, as long as nothing snagged the trigger accidentally. Its streamlined 50-round box magazine also provided nearly twice the firepower of any other SMG, though it was under fourteen inches long and weighed about the same as an Ingram MAC-10 machine pistol.

Bolan heard the first explosive sounds of automatic gunfire as he shouldered through the door, screams echoing along behind the sharp reports. The entryway was lined with photographs, blown up to poster size, of haunting scenes and faces from the Nazi death camps, skeletal and hollow eyed. Somehow, it almost seemed that *they* were screaming, giving voice to horrors that, for most of them, had been the substance of their final months on Earth.

A fleeting sense of unreality enveloped Bolan, shattered by another burst of automatic fire, and someone shouting, "Get the goddamned charges down!"

He passed beneath the ghostly visages of martyrs to a madman's nightmare, following the voices and the sounds of gunfire to their source. He had to step across two leaking bodies on the way, a man and woman, stretched out nearly side by side across a corridor lined with more ghastly photographs—a counterpoint of murder then and murder now, all for the same demented motive.

Bolan found his first mark seconds later, kneeling in an alcove to his left, his back toward Bolan, peering through the wide slits in his ski mask, latex-covered hands inserting detonators in what could have been green blocks of clay, but wasn't.

"Yo, Adolf!"

Turning toward the unfamiliar voice, the bomber blinked once in surprise, then reached down for the Uzi resting on the floor, beside him. "Who the fu—?"

The Spectre slapped his unfinished question back between imploding teeth and bounced him off the wall before he slumped atop his C-4 charges. Bolan flinched involuntarily, half expecting them to blow, but nothing happened, and he left the corpse to brood its deadly eggs.

At least three more ahead of him, and Crouder had mentioned two or three around in back, presumably inside by now. He picked up his pace, noticed that the gunfire echoing somewhere ahead of him had slackened for a moment, then resumed with fewer shouts and screams as an accompaniment.

He pushed on past another body, twisted in a death sprawl, homing on a raging voice that sounded somehow furious and frightened, all at the same time. It shouted, "Up against the goddamned wall, you bastards! *Now!*"

A moment later, and he reached what seemed to be the main room of the center's Holocaust museum.

Aside from large photographs mounted on free-standing partitions, there were display cases containing dioramas, mannequins attired in the respective rags of prisoners and uniforms of keepers, wall-mounted displays of weapons, torture instruments and surgical equipment. At the center of the room, inside a shallow bowl-shaped base, a small gas flame burned steadily, emitting neither smoke nor sound.

Two ski-masked goons in denim coveralls were lining up roughly a dozen men and women on the east side of the room, prodding their captives, cursing them and jeering racist filth that sounded like some high-school parody of how a rough, tough fascist ought to sound. The third man—or the fourth, counting his late companion in the passageway—was busy with another C-4 plastic charge, away to Bolan's right, which put him in the northeast corner of the room.

And the soldier had a choice to make. If he took out the bomber first, his shots might trigger random firing by two thugs who, quite plainly, meant to execute the hostages they had collected. On the other hand, if he removed the shooters first, then number three might just have time to cap and fire his charges, bringing down a fair part of the building on their heads.

He finally decided that the only way to go was trying both at once, with just a dash of stealth to shave the odds, if that was even possible. His sense of urgency was powered by the knowledge that there had to be other members of the raiding party—two or three, at least—somewhere inside the center, maybe homing on this very gallery while Bolan stood and pondered possibilities.

So move, already!

Bolan used his left hand to extract the sound-suppressed Beretta from its shoulder rig, the thumb-break strap accommodating him. He kept the Spectre in his right hand, pictured how the play would have to go if it was going to succeed.

And if it went to hell, of course, there would be no way to predict what happened next, how many innocents would die.

He drew a bead with the Beretta, took the right-rear quadrant of the bomber's head off with a double tap that plucked him from an apelike crouch and slammed his wool-masked face against the wall. Again, no C-4 blast, and Bolan knew the dead man was beyond completing any critical connections with the wires and blasting caps.

He turned upon the last two gunners he could see, and found that neither one of them had noticed him as yet. A couple of the hostages had seen the bomber die, however, and they couldn't stop themselves from gaping at the new arrival who was either their deliverance or a grim embellishment to their worst nightmares.

One of the shooters leaned in close to a terrified woman, shouting in her face, "What the fuck are you looking at, bitch?" When she responded with a jerky nod, the bully in the ski mask cranked his head around, and Bolan could almost hear his jaw drop open in surprise.

"Shit! Barry! Trouble!"

Number two, who was obviously Barry, turned to

check out his partner and kept on turning until he was facing Bolan with an Uzi submachine gun in his hands.

Instead of challenging the stranger, Barry opened fire, his first rounds coming close enough that Bolan heard them buzzing past like hornets. He couldn't return full-auto fire without endangering the hostages. Instead, he ducked behind one of the free-standing partitions, converging streams of Uzi fire pursuing him. He hit the floor facedown and slid across its polished surface, clearing open space and finding flimsy cover in the shadow of a screenlike partition. The mounted photos depicted Nazi firing squads drawing down on women and children, their grainy images shredded a moment later by 9 mm Parabellum rounds.

They were firing too high, expecting Bolan to stand up and run. Instead, he wriggled on his belly to one corner of the shivering partition, hoping it wouldn't collapse on top of him before he found his target.

There!

One of the goons was open, moving, circling around to flank him. Bolan hit him twice with the Beretta, saw him lurch and stumble, plunge headfirst through the plate-glass of a display case, his face plowing up a scale model of Auschwitz.

The sole survivor panicked, turning back to face the hostages, intent on killing them, at least, if he couldn't bring down his unknown nemesis. Bolan rolled out from cover, cut the shooter's legs from under him with a short burst from the Spectre, dropping him away from the lineup of human targets, tracking his fall to put a burst dead center on the ski mask as he hit the floor.

Bolan was on his feet before the cringing hostages had time to take in what had happened. "Go out through the front," he ordered them. "Don't stop until you're on the far side of the street, and don't touch anything along the way. There may be some explosive charges that I missed."

"Wh-who...?" one of them stammered, working on a question.

"If you want to live," he told them all, "get out of here *right now!*"

They went without a backward glance, grateful to leave that place of death behind. The hunter saw them go, then turned and went in search of other prey.

"WE'RE SCREWED!" Sean Fletcher said, the grim recognition of failure striking home with the force of a punch to his solar plexus.

"What?" Biehl doubtless would have looked confused if Fletcher could have seen his face. The tone of his voice said it all.

"We're not alone," Fletcher replied. "That last piece wasn't an Uzi."

"You can tell that?"

"I can tell. You'll notice no one is returning fire."

"So what? You mean the other guys are...?"

"Hook up the C-4, and let's get out of here," he ordered, peering left and right as if he thought an ambush party might have crept up and surrounded them while they were talking.

"What, you want the stuff in here?"

"Just do it!"

"Sure, all right." Biehl headed for the nearest corner, found what had to be a load-bearing wall and started to unpack his plastique, blasting caps and timers. Fletcher drifted cautiously in the direction that the automatic fire had come from, picturing the first-floor layout from the drawings he had studied. The main part of the museum was straight ahead of him, more of it on the second floor, with offices, archives and storage on floors three through six. To bring the whole thing down, as planned, they would need more than just Biehl's charge, but there was nothing he could do about that now.

They would make do with what they had, inflict whatever damage they could with what remained of their supplies.

A goddamned ambush! That could only mean the Jews and/or police had been forewarned, and there was only one clear candidate for squealer of the century. The rotten bitch had followed through on her betrayal. If he ever had a chance to pay her back—

"So, Sean, long time no see."

He turned toward the familiar voice, and there she was, with a Kalashnikov aimed at his chest. Fletcher was tempted to start blazing with the Uzi, but he wasn't altogether sure that he could make it. He was wearing Kevlar underneath the coveralls—an edge his teammates didn't know about and didn't share—but even so, it only covered him between the shoulders and the waist. If Mary had the AK set for automatic fire, there was no telling whether she would take his head off, rip his legs apart or maybe miss him altogether.

"Hey, I know you!" Jerry Biehl was saying, turning from his work and rising to the limits of his five foot ten. ''You sold us out, you miserable—''

Mary shot him without thinking twice, Biehl fumbling with the Uzi on its shoulder strap when she squeezed off a burst that slammed him backward, feet all tangled up, even before his head and shoulders struck the wall behind him with resounding force.

Fletcher knew he would never have a better chance, and so he went for it, firing a short burst to confuse her, without bothering to aim or seriously hoping for a hit, much less a kill. At the same moment, he dodged to his left, seeking cover behind a stack of cardboard boxes filled with books or something. Decent cover, if he made it.

But he didn't.

Mary had more nerve than Fletcher gave her credit for, and she was better off the mark with the Kalashnikov than he had any reason to expect. She caught him with a burst that spun him in his tracks, like some ungainly figure skater. Fletcher's vest took most of it, except for one round that traced fire along the inside of his right biceps, but it still hurt like hell, as if he had been struck across the chest full force with something like an ax handle or baseball bat.

The good news was that since it hurt and he was struggling for breath, he had to still be alive. How long he would remain that way depended on his adversary's courage and his own reaction time. If she was quick enough to follow up, or he was too slow on response, then Fletcher knew he was as good as dead.

And that was no damned good at all.

He struggled to a crouch and came out firing, no

attempt to aim, spraying the room in front of him and offering a prayer to Wotan that he wouldn't run out of ammunition before he reached the door. He had a glimpse of Mary Krause recoiling from the Uzi, sprawling behind a stack of cartons, his bullets hacking cardboard and paper to tatters, heard the AK clattering behind him, felt the hot wind of its lethal breath before he stumbled past her, out of range, and hit the exit.

Sunlight stung his eyes, and he felt warm blood soaking through his sleeve. In front of him, his driver, Billy Thatcher, lay spread-eagle in a crimson pool, arms outflung as if he were trying to corral his own spilt blood. Fletcher leaped over him and threw himself into the driver's seat, knew that his luck was turning when he heard and felt the engine running. Shifting into gear and stamping down on the accelerator, Fletcher let momentum slam his door behind him, rubber burning as he powered out of there and left the other members of his team to die.

CHAPTER SEVEN

"So, what the hell was that about?" Bolan demanded after they had put the screaming sirens and the three-ring circus of downtown Los Angeles behind them.

"I was helping you," Marilyn Crouder replied.

"Helping *me?*" He didn't raise his voice, yet somehow she found his anger more threatening for the absence of high octaves and profanity, as if his pent-up feelings were a shaped charge with the timer running down. "You could have spooked them into setting off the charges."

"But I didn't," she reminded him.

"You could have gotten killed."

"And yet..."

"Dumb luck's the only reason you're alive right now," he said.

"I held my own," she stated.

"It didn't look that way to me."

"You had to be there."

"I was there," he retorted. "And I was supposed to be there on my own. Instead, I find you in the back room, stretched out on the floor—"

"You found me getting up, as I remember it."

"—and bullet strikes all over that pathetic excuse for cover."

"It worked out all right, I'd say."

"You would?"

"Damned right! We stopped them, took out all but one and saved the Sturnman Center. Plus—" she cast a sidelong glance toward the back seat, beneath which he had stashed Biehl's C-4 charge, without detonators "—you picked up a few new toys."

"One of them got away," Belasko said.

"One out of nine."

"The only one who counts," he said, as they drove south on Alameda, holding scrupulously to the speed limit. "He saw your face."

"Oh, no!" She feigned alarm. "You mean my cover's blown?"

"I *mean,* they might have let you slide, if you'd stayed out of it. Now, they'll be all the more determined to exact revenge."

"You obviously haven't read the psych profiles on these gorillas," Crouder replied. "Forgiveness is the third great no-no of their cult, right after being black or Jewish."

"Anyway, they'll be more anxious for some payback now, unless—"

"He recognized me," she cut in, anticipating his suggestion, brusquely putting it aside.

"Someone you knew, then."

It wasn't a question, but she felt compelled to answer anyway. "Sean Fletcher. I was never under him, in any sense, but we were casual acquaintances at Freedom Home."

"The Temple's chief enforcer," Bolan said. "Former Navy SEAL, busted for insubordination and af-filiation with the neo-Nazi fringe in 1995.''

"Okay, so you *have* done your homework." She was grudgingly impressed, and it was dawning on her that at least some portion of his anger stemmed from worry, fear that she could have been killed or wounded in the action at the Eli Sturnman Center. He was also pissed—and rightly so, she granted silently—that she had lied to him about remaining distant from the fight.

The radio was on, turned up just loud enough for them to pick up bits and pieces from the all-news network, following the racial violence in Watts and East L.A. Both miniriots seemed well on their way toward calming down, but everyone reporters interviewed, from looters and beat cops to the police chief and assistant mayor, was looking forward to potential mayhem in the streets after the sun went down.

"I really am all right," she told him, hoping it would help to cool things off between them. "All my parts are still attached and functioning quite nicely, thank you very much."

"Nobody has an inexhaustible reserve of luck," he said, eyes on the crawling lunchtime traffic that surrounded them.

"It helps if you have skill," she answered stiffly, more annoyed to find herself fishing for compliments than at Belasko for withholding them.

What did it matter if this stranger thought she was impulsive, rash or unprofessional? The odds were good that he would dump her after this, and she would never see or hear from him again.

Which should have made her jump for joy—or, at

the very least, experience a groundswell of relief. So why, then, did that prospect make her feel as if she would be missing out on something wild and wonderful? As if the termination of her brief and violent association with this man of mystery would leave an aching void behind?

"Where are we going?" she asked, more to distract herself than out of any yen for answers.

"Back to the hotel."

"Did you leave something there?"

He shook his head. "The room's paid up," he said. "We need to make reports—at least, I do—and there's no point in leaving town until I have a target destination."

Crouder was fully conscious of the fact that he'd said "I," not "we." Was he dissolving their tempestuous alliance after all?

The early radio reports described a shooting at the Eli Sturnman Center in downtown Los Angeles, with "several" casualties, and drew a speculative link between that incident and other hate crimes logged that morning in the city. L.A. reporters were no strangers to the lunatic fringe, and while they had no details yet, they had begun to make comparisons with other neo-Nazi crimes, most recently the shootings at a Jewish preschool, back in August 1999, and prior to that, a plot by teenage skinheads to provoke a racial holy war by means of arson, bombing and assassination.

"This could burn the Temple, once they start playing connect-the-dots," she said.

"I hope they don't," Bolan answered.

"What? Why not?"

"Because the farther they go underground, the deeper I'll have to dig to root them out. I like my targets visible, preferably cocksure and strutting their stuff."

"You think I ruined it," she said.

"We'll have to wait and see."

That "we" was slightly more encouraging, though Crouder couldn't afford to stake her hopes on it. She could no more apologize for what had happened at the Sturnman Center than she could produce a magic wand and turn herself into the President of the United States.

"I thought you needed help," she said at last. "Back there, I mean."

Bolan met her eyes and held them for a beat before he turned his focus back to traffic, red lights and pedestrians. "Okay," he said. "And I appreciate the thought, but you could just as easily have gotten killed."

"They didn't have—"

"By me, not them," he cut her off. His voice had dropped another octave, but retained its power to chill. "If I'd run into you, thinking you were outside, and if I hadn't recognized you at a glance—"

"You may as well stop if-ing," Crouder spoke up. "We're both all right, and I winged Fletcher on the run, I'm pretty sure."

"How badly?"

The woman considered it and shrugged. "I couldn't tell," she said, "but there were blood spots on the floor and sidewalk, where nobody else had any chance to bleed."

"I don't suppose he'd try to find a doctor?"

"Highly doubtful," she replied. "The Temple has its own medics, mostly ex-servicemen, a veterinarian or two. There used to be a guy who didn't make the cut in med school and decided he should blame the Jews for lousy grades. I don't believe that Sean would risk a hospital if he knew he was dying."

"So, he's gone."

"But not forgotten. If he doesn't bleed out—and I don't think he was hit that badly—then he's still got work to do. A nice long list of targets, waiting for the holy war to come along and knock them over."

"You believe they'll go ahead, after today?"

"Why not? Remember, Mike, you're dealing with fanatics, not some syndicate that's in it for the money. Every revolution calls for sacrifice. The Nordic Temple loves its martyrs."

"I suppose you have the list of targets, chronologically arranged," Bolan said.

She tapped her temple with an index finger. "Right up here," she answered him. "They wouldn't let me take a lot of notes or run off photocopies."

"That's all right," he said. "If you remember them, you'll have no problem writing out a list."

"As if."

"I don't have time for this," Bolan said. "I'm way past playing games."

"It's funny you should say that," she replied. "I wasn't playing from the start."

"You nearly got your—"

"Ass shot off back there?" she interrupted him, and winked. "Not even close, but thanks for noticing."

"You jeopardized the hostages, as well. It's dumb

luck that your playmates didn't set their plastic charges off or run in the opposite direction, toward the heart of the museum.''

"Where you were ready for them, I believe?"

"That's not—"

"The point? Okay, so maybe you'd explain what is the point, for those of us who can't quite work it out. We stopped the raid and saved the center, you saved all the hostages that anyone could hope to and we only lost one guy. One guy!"

"The leader of the team," Bolan said, "who can identify you, and who certainly will spread the word around their network."

"Here's a news flash—they already knew, okay? They knew I was a mole last night. That's why they were about to plant me in the woods, if you recall. It may have slipped your mind, being so trivial and all, but that was when you saved my ass."

"Enough about your ass, dammit! I have a job to do, and if you can't—or won't—supply the information that I need, you may as well head back to Washington."

It struck her then: he really *was* afraid she might be hurt—not in the sense that he would be concerned about a total stranger passing in the street, about to step in front of an approaching bus, but rather as a person whom he held in some regard.

It was a start.

It made her smile.

"You can forget about me going back to Washington," she said. "After today, Archer would most likely have me up on charges, anyway. I'm thinking maybe I should try a change of scene."

"That's not a bad idea," Bolan said. "Take off and find a beach where you can catch some rays. Just write me out that list before you go."

"Nice try, but no cigar," she told him, feeling suddenly, deliciously smug. "Looks like I'm in for the duration. So, are we still going back to the hotel...or what?"

Washington, D.C.

"I'VE GOT the news on here," Brognola said first thing when Bolan called. He thumbed the mute button on his remote control and let the jerky footage roll on silently. "Looks like a hot time in the old town, but I'd say LAPD has got a handle on it."

"I've been tracking what I can," Bolan replied. "No mention of the Nordic Temple yet on any of the news about the Sturnman Center."

"I wouldn't expect it, unless someone feels like leaking to the press. The word I get from out your way, the shooters carried no ID of any kind, nothing to any group or movement. Something may come back on them from fingerprints, but I'd be very much surprised if there was anything to put the Nordic Temple in the frame."

"What do you hear from ATF?" the Executioner asked.

"Nothing beyond the pledge of their cooperation 'to a point,'" the big Fed replied. "Is there a problem on that score?"

"My little helper got involved beyond her brief," Bolan said. "Now she wants to pull the plug unless she gets to play first string."

"Sounds like you hooked up with an Amazon," Brognola said. "She hasn't sliced one off, by any chance?"

"I'm thinking that the guys I'm after may prefer to handle that themselves."

"So kick her loose. Do what you have to do."

"She claims to have a list of targets for the trigger incidents. Her call was dead-on for the Sturnman Center, so I have to think the other information could be useful. Maybe critical."

"Sounds like a judgment call to me," Brognola said. "Just sitting here, I can imagine half a dozen ways to handle it, and I imagine that you're way ahead of me."

"I thought of reaching out to ATF, having this Archer guy she talks about pull rank."

"One way to go," Brognola agreed. "Of course, she may decide she's blown the job already, maybe looking at a little time. It couldn't get much worse if she was stricken with amnesia. Hell, most lawyers I can think of would insist on it."

"Or I could squeeze her," Bolan said.

"That sounds like fun," the big Fed quipped, knowing that cuddles weren't what Bolan had in mind, and knowing furthermore that he would no more rough up the lady than he would drop an infant from a highway overpass.

"What's new on your end?" Bolan asked him. "Anything?"

"Turns out this Stevens character stays on the move as much as possible. When he's not visiting the troops at one camp or another, seems he tools around the country in RVs, camps out, makes all his calls on pay phones. One of his buds used to call him 'the Wandering Jew.' Pissed him off, I imagine. The guy disappeared, anyway.''

"He's hard to track, then," Bolan said.

"The next thing to impossible. Hey, you remember the war wagon, right?''

"Vaguely.''

Brognola had to smile at that, despite himself. The war wagon had once been Bolan's mobile headquarters when he was on his own and running from the government, as well as from the Mafia. An RV that had been made over by a team of former NASA scientists to gather and transmit intelligence, as well as to kick ass with state-of-the-art weaponry, it had enabled Bolan to evade detection and wreak havoc with his enemies during the last months of his one-man war against the syndicate. Brognola had no reason to believe that Gary Stevens owned anything comparable, but the basic concept was the same: a moving target was more difficult to hit, particularly if you couldn't locate it in the first place.

"We've got wiretaps on the Temple's major stationary hangouts,'' the big Fed continued, ''so we have a shot at tracing any calls he makes to his subordinates as they come in, but by the time we backtrack to a phone booth in Des Moines or Birmingham, he's in the wind.''

"You may be on to something,'' Bolan said.

"Oh, yeah? Pray tell, what's that?''

"If he's a traveler, he might get off on watching from the sidelines while his soldiers do their thing.''

"You think he's in L.A.?''

"We'll know, if he makes any calls from the vicinity to numbers you've got covered. Even if he splits before he calls, there may be something in the conversation that's a tip-off.''

''Which, again,'' Hal said, ''would only tell us where he's been, not where he is.''

''Or maybe it could tell us where he *will* be next time out.''

''I wouldn't count on it,'' Brognola said. ''This guy may be a psycho, but he's still nobody's fool. We haven't picked up squat on the recordings, yet. A few names, maybe, and a ton of crap about the coming revolution or the racial holy war, whatever, but he doesn't spell out any plans or destinations.''

''He doesn't have to. If we peg him as a ringside watcher, all I have to do is pin down where his goons are heading next. His soldiers won't expect me to be waiting for them—neither will their boss.''

''You hope.'' Brognola had a sudden feeling of uneasiness, the kind he always got when Bolan was about to take some worse-than-average risk. ''They don't need Einstein on the payroll to place blame for the disruption in L.A. They've got to know your little friend is talking.''

''I've discussed that with her,'' Bolan said, ''and she believes they'll go ahead regardless. Call it arrogance, fanaticism, anything you want. She only has to be right once.''

''And if she's wrong across the board?''

''Then all I've lost is time,'' Bolan replied, ''which I'd be wasting anyway, trying to skull out some alternative scenario. This way, at least I have a shot.''

''You mean to say, they have a shot at you.''

''Don't tell me that surprises you.''

"Nothing surprises me," Brognola said, "but it does piss me off. I want to squash these roaches and move on to tracking someone who's at least on nodding terms with everyday reality."

"Like the Colombians? Maybe Hamas? The Russian Mafia?"

"You know. The usual."

"I'll see what I can do," Bolan replied, "but this may take a while."

"I was afraid of that."

"Which means that I should get my tail in gear and find out where we're going next."

"When you say 'we'…"

"She wants to do her bit," the Executioner explained. "It's not my place to put her on the bench. She knows the risks involved."

And so did Bolan, the big Fed thought, but kept it to himself. He knew that once Bolan had made his mind up on a subject, there was no point arguing about the dangers he would face if he proceeded with his plan. The soldier had seen it all, and he was still alive.

Unfortunately, there was no assurance that the same would still be true this time tomorrow afternoon.

"Okay," Brognola said. "You need me, I'll be here or at the house. Don't hesitate to call for transportation, hardware, anything at all."

"I won't."

"You may want to consider being careful also."

"It's my middle name."

"Yeah, right."

The line went dead without goodbyes. Brognola's admonition to take care was more than he had meant to say, and almost certainly a waste of breath. Bolan was never reckless, in the mold of wild-ass warriors who would put themselves at risk for the sheer hell of it. He never risked his life unless he felt a need to do so, and unless he saw at least a reasonable chance of pulling off the move he had in mind. The problem was that Bolan saw a need to place himself in jeopardy whenever and wherever innocents were threatened by the likes of Gary Stevens and his brownshirts. Bolan also had a reasonable chance of getting out alive in almost every situation he confronted. He was *that* good. And on the downside, there were times— too many of them, for Brognola's taste—he would offer up his own life in the place of someone else's, when it came to that.

Brognola never spoke the words aloud, but there had been occasions when he had questioned Bolan's judgment in that area. There was no point in arguing with Sergeant Mercy when he saw a need and rushed to fill it with his body, his lifeblood, but there were times when the big Fed came kissing-close to asking him, "Is this guy worth it, really?"

Not this time.

The Temple of the Nordic Covenant was everything Brognola hated in a clique of dwellers on the fringe. He wasn't black or Jewish, but it didn't matter. All he had to do was listen to the crazy bastards, see what they had done so far, and it was crystal clear they needed to be stopped in their tracks, with extreme prejudice. This wasn't just another handful of pathetic SS wanna-bes who swilled beer six nights a week and spent the sabbath picketing some local synagogue because it made them feel like members of

the Aryan elite, instead miserable losers scraping by
with dead-end jobs and IQs hovering around room
temperature.

These freaks were serious.

And while Brognola cherished no abiding doubts
that Bolan would derail their master plan—whatever
that turned out to be—he felt the old familiar fear that
his best friend might be consumed along the way,
claiming a Pyrrhic victory that left the world one hero
short.

God help the stragglers, if that fear was realized.
There would be no place on the globe for them to
hide: not in a bunker, not among their Nazi pals, not
even in the isolation wing of the new federal lockup
for the superfreaks at Terre Haute. Wherever the survivors dug a hole and tried to pull it in behind them,
Hal Brognola would be coming up behind them with
his trusty shovel and the full resources of the team at
Stony Man to root them out and make their final moments on the planet one long scream.

He checked his watch against the wall clock, saw
that he had gone too long without caffeine, rose from
behind his desk and moved out through his secretary's
office, toward the elevator and the cafeteria.

"Anybody calls for me, I'm in the pit," he said,
and left his secretary staring at the empty doorway
after he was gone.

Los Angeles

"So, WHAT'S the word?" Crouder asked, closing the
door to her motel room after him and double locking
it, as if she were afraid he might escape.

"You first," he said.

"I didn't call." She shrugged as Bolan turned to face her. "I mean, what's the point? I talk to Archer, he can either take a risk—which I have yet to see him do on anything related to his pension—or he yanks me in, maybe files charges, does whatever he can think of to cover himself. One thing I learned before I made it off probation is, it's always easier to get forgiveness than permission."

"Not always," the Executioner corrected her.

"Whatever. It's my neck. I'll take responsibility."

He let that pass and said, "My people tell me Stevens likes to take it on the road."

"They got that right. He's like a Nazi Charles Kuralt, without the folksy charm. It's almost funny, when you think about it."

"Why?"

"Well, hey, I mean, you've got this vast conspiracy that rules the world, except for isolated pockets of resistance, with the media, the FBI and CIA, the whole thing run by Gerhard's enemies, and he thinks he can fake them out by cruising up and down Route 66 like Mr. Tourist on vacation."

Bolan frowned. "It's worked so far."

"I see your point. So, what's the plan?"

"This cruising fetish made me wonder if he might want to watch his big plan come together, maybe catch a ringside seat and check it out."

"You're thinking that he's in L.A.?"

He shrugged. "Too late to move on that, regardless. Even if he stuck around after the fireworks, LAPD's not in any shape right now to stop and question every RV driver in the city, much less in the southern half of California.''

"So we look ahead and organize a welcoming committee for the next performance, right?'' Her smile was bright now, eager.

"If you still insist on coming with me,'' Bolan said.

"You're kidding, right?'' She laughed. "I wouldn't miss it for the world.''

He had expected Crouder to play it out—at least until the going got too rough and finally, irrevocably scared her off. The more he saw of her, however, Bolan questioned what would be required to manage that.

"Okay, then,'' he replied. "As soon as you give up the secondary target, we can check out of here, be on our way.''

"Relax,'' she said, drifting toward the bed. "We've got three days.''

"How's that?''

"The hits aren't going off like firecrackers. Gerhard gives his commandos time to breathe. In fact, the more I think about it—''

"What?''

"That may support your voyeurism theory,'' she replied. "He's giving himself time to get from here to there, before the next shoe drops.''

"And since we're planning to be there ahead of him...''

"No sweat,'' she said. "Why don't you trust me for a change?''

"I'm working on it,'' Bolan said. "The cryptic treatment doesn't help.''

"I wouldn't want you taking off and ditching me," she said, half-teasing.

"That won't happen," Bolan said. "You have my word."

"And I believe you," Crouder replied. "But I still need to pick some things up from my place before we go."

"Your place?"

"I've got a little house in Riverside," she said. "Well, ATF picks up the tab. It's where I hooked up with the Temple in the first place."

"And from there, you need...?"

"Just things," she said. Her left hand rose and carelessly undid the topmost button of her shirt. "I can't keep wearing the same thing, day after day. I mean, there's such a thing as hygiene, not to mention style."

Another button, and another.

"Listen, Marilyn—"

"I'm listening," she told him, stepping closer, with the shirt unbuttoned almost to her waist. He had already guessed that she wore nothing underneath it, and tan flesh confirmed his earlier surmise.

"This may not be the best idea you've had today," he said, standing his ground.

"You think it's worse than chasing Nazis all around the countryside?"

"It has potential risks."

"Relax," she urged again. "I promise not to bite...unless you ask me to."

"This isn't necessary," Bolan said.

"Speak for yourself."

"It's not part of the deal."

"Let's renegotiate."

"You don't want to do this," he told her.

"You're reading minds, now?"

"All right. *I* don't want to do this."

"Pants on fire," she said, and shot a glance below his waist. "Oh, my, they really are. Is that a Desert Eagle, or are you just glad to see me?"

As she spoke, she moved in closer, almost near enough for them to touch without the use of hands. She rolled one shoulder casually, and her shirt gaped open on that side, the fabric clinging to her breast, the turgid nipple on display. A half step closer, and the puckered exclamation point grazed Bolan's ribs.

"Excuse me," she said, almost whispering, head tilted back to let her meet his gaze. "I don't mean to invade your space."

"Feel free," he said, surrendering.

"I do." A more determined shrug, and suddenly her shirt was on the floor. She kicked it backward and away. "A penny for your thoughts."

"You wouldn't get your money's worth," he said.

"Liar. You're thinking that if we do this, you'll have to fret about me all the time, risking the mission and yourself. Of course, you always think about the mission first."

"You ought to be a psychic, friend," he said.

"But what you still don't get," she followed through, ignoring his remark, "is that I'm all grown up—"

"I'm getting that." His turn to interrupt.

"—and I can take care of myself. Unless, of course, I get all tense and frustrated, distracted. You know what I mean?'' Her fingers grazing, teasing him.

''I get your drift,'' he said.

''So, who's to say we shouldn't drift together for a while?''

To which his inner voice replied, Why not? As far as any worry for her safety was concerned, he had already been infected. She was on his mind, and would remain there for as long as she was part of Bolan's war—or he was part of hers. The moral issue didn't enter into it, and there was something to be said for taking comfort where you found it on the eve of mortal combat.

Taking his silence as assent, she started to unfasten Bolan's slacks. ''Let's get these off,'' she said. ''They don't look very comfortable.''

''I'm in your hands,'' he said.

''Almost.'' And then he was.

''What am I going to do with you?''

''I'll show you,'' Crouder replied.

CHAPTER EIGHT

"You're absolutely certain that this person was the same bitch who escaped from Freedom Home?"

Sean Fletcher nodded. "She was only ten or fifteen feet away. I'm sure."

"And yet she got away. Again. This time, *you* missed her...with an Uzi, I believe? What was that range, once more?"

"She had a weapon," Fletcher said. "She nearly killed me, dammit!"

Gerhard Steuben sensed the heat and color rising in his face. It felt like molten lava burbling up from underground, seeking a vent through which it could explode into the outer world. He clenched his teeth to keep it locked inside. A sudden pain began to throb behind his right eye, keeping time with Steuben's escalating pulse.

"You make excuses now," he hissed, the first escape of steam before the seismic blast. "Your teammates are all dead, your mission is a catastrophic failure, and this traitor has escaped from you a second time, but you return almost without a scratch. Tell me, Captain, why are you not lying in the morgue beside your men!"

The shriek came out of nowhere, Fletcher visibly recoiling from it, as if from a blow. Indeed, Steuben was leaning forward, his fists white knuckled at the end of jerking, trembling arms, as if it were all he could do to keep from lashing out at Fletcher physically. Lips drawn back from his teeth, eyes bulging like a wild man's, he poised on the verge of a perilous leap.

"Why aren't you dead, goddammit? How dare you return in failure, with excuses on your tongue? You could be shot for this, you miserable bastard!"

Suddenly, as if someone had punctured a balloon, his manic rage was spent, and Steuben slumped back in his chair, his heart pounding mightily against his sternum, the infernal headache fierce enough to make him nauseous.

Fletcher, who had witnessed such outbursts before, responded in a quiet and self-deprecating tone. "I'm sorry, Führer. In my own defense, I mention only that I thought it was important for the Temple to be notified about this traitor's actions. Clearly, she wasn't alone."

"And just as clearly," Steuben said, slouched in his chair, most of the fight gone out of him, "her helpers weren't ordinary federal agents. Not unless ZOG has abandoned any pretense of obeying statutory law."

"If not the Feds," Fletcher replied, "then who?"

"Ah, that's the question, isn't it? You were so certain that this bitch works for the FBI or some affiliated agency, that you've ignored the other possibilities."

"You mean Mossad?"

Steuben considered it. For years, he had predicted—and believed with all his heart—that Jew assassins would be sent to kill him in the precious final days. He had no way of knowing whether they would be dispatched from Tel Aviv or from Miami Beach, and it made no real difference to the end result. Their scheming masters meant to keep him from the treasure he had sought throughout his adult life, steal back the power he had wrested from their bloody hands.

But they wouldn't succeed.

In fact, they had already wasted too much time, had wasted so much ink and energy attempting to humiliate him, that he had been able to recruit and train an army for the holy war that was his destiny. They could destroy him now, today, and still not save themselves from the apocalypse to come.

Which didn't mean, of course, that Steuben meant to make it easy for them. He wasn't some eunuch Moses, sniveling and passively accepting exile from the promised land that he had fought so long and hard to win. Whatever Steuben's enemies desired to strip away from him, they would be required to take by force.

The only thing he owed them was contempt.

The only thing he meant to give them voluntarily was death.

And there were some for whom that death would be a blessing. They would beg and plead for it before their tab was paid in full.

"We must proceed on schedule to our ultimate objective," he informed Sean Fletcher, feeling some of the familiar strength returning to his limbs. It helped to mute his pounding headache slightly, but he knew it would take a double dose of drugs to clear his head—assuming anything could do the trick today.

"We will, Führer."

"But first, we must prevent this Jezebel from doing any further damage. She must be removed from circulation and interrogated. Find out what she knows and who she works for. That is critical."

"But, Führer—"

Steuben smiled through his delirium of pain. *"But Führer,"* he repeated, mocking Fletcher with his whine. "You are about to say you don't know where to find the bitch or how she can be traced. Correct?"

"Yes, sir."

"We may assume the name she used to join the Temple was a pseudonym," he said, "and she has almost certainly discarded it by now. But she didn't run back to Washington, New York, wherever such scum is recruited from the gutters. She requires a place to stay, a roof over her head. You follow me?"

"I...think so," Fletcher answered warily.

"I'll spell it out for you. This person had a place of residence when you recruited her."

"Führer, I didn't—"

"Silence!" The pain inside his head so pure that when he shouted, Steuben almost lost himself within its solar glare. "The application blank requires a home address and telephone. Notification of provisional acceptance would be sent by mail. If she hadn't received it, she wouldn't have been initiated, and we would be spared this tedious discussion. Are you with me now?"

"Yes, sir."

"You will retrieve the information from her application. Call headquarters east. Tell them I've cleared you to receive the data. Use the password 'Merlin' to confirm my order. It is changed at midnight, so you have no time to waste."

"No, sir."

"There is a possibility the address may be occupied by someone else today. How long has this bitch been among us?"

"Fifteen months, I think," Fletcher said.

Wotan, help him! Fifteen months of spying, eavesdropping on who knew what incriminating conversations, and it took a clumsy accident at last, to finally reveal the traitor in their midst. He had no memory of meeting her, but he had been to Freedom Home at least a dozen times within that period, resting, reviewing troop formations, laying plans with Fletcher for the coming war. Had he brushed shoulders with her, possibly been introduced, returned her smart salute?

He felt the anger rising in his throat and veins again, controlled it with a nearly superhuman force of will. Another outburst like the last one, and he thought his skull might detonate, frag Fletcher where he sat, with jagged bone fragments in place of shrapnel.

"When you've secured the address," he said, "find out who owns the property. If it's a rental, see the landlord—but discreetly. Badge him, bribe him if you have to, but do not expose yourself."

"No, sir."

"On the odd chance that it wasn't a rental, you can trace the deed and learn the owner's name. Someone somewhere knows something. All you have to do is find out who and what.''

"Yes, Führer, but—"

"You are about to say that time is running short before you are required to strike at your next target."

"Yes, sir."

"So it is," Steuben replied. "You have approximately two and one-half days to finish up this business and to get your troops in place. It should be no great challenge for an expert like yourself."

"No, sir. But…"

"Yes, Sean?" Switching on him, almost smiling, so that Fletcher nearly lost his train of thought.

"If she was in Los Angeles with shooters, then we must assume our other plans are known, as well. Eliminating her won't stop the others from continuing to meddle in our business."

"Maybe not," Steuben acknowledged, "but we won't know that for sure until you've done your job and rubbed her out, now, will we, Captain?"

"No, sir."

"Then, let's take first things first, shall we?"

"Yes, sir."

"You understand the greater timetable as well as I do, Captain. While specific targets are expendable, we have a schedule to observe. Our destiny depends on punctuality. You've heard me lecture on the reasons why the great reich failed to thrive."

"Yes, sir." Responding, even though it had not truly been a question. Every member of the Nordic Temple learned that vital lesson, going in.

"Delay! Procrastination!" Steuben snapped, repeating it for someone's benefit, perhaps his own.

"Confusion of the cosmic omens! Insubordination in the ranks! Excessive delegation of authority!"

"Yes, sir."

"Herr Hitler was a great example to us all, Captain. Unfortunately, there were times when he wasn't a *good* example. Still, his every action served a purpose, even if it lay in teaching us what errors to avoid."

"Yes, sir."

"I would be less than honest if I said you have not disappointed me. There's nothing to be gained from flattery and lies. Do you agree?"

"Yes, sir."

"Of course you do. And I believe you recognize your shortcomings, that you will make a strenuous attempt to overcome them."

"Yes, sir!"

"With your shield or on it, Captain Fletcher."

"Sir?" Confusion was written on the soldier's face.

"You really must find time to read more history," Steuben chided. "When the Spartan army went to war, the parents of each soldier told him to return home with his shield or on it. Cowards throw their shields away in battle, all the better to escape. A valiant soldier brings his shield home with him as a victor, or is carried on it by his comrades as a corpse."

"I understand, sir."

"Good. No more mistakes, Captain. You have much work to do. Dismissed."

Fletcher saluted, clicked his heels, turned sharply and closed the door behind him as he left. The Anaheim RV park was crowded, as always, with the mo-

tor homes of tourists bound for Disneyland, Knott's
Berry Farm and sundry lesser magnets for the herd.
Steuben had nearly bolted when he heard about the
failure of his troops to carry out their primary direc-
tive, but he had restrained himself, mastered his fear,
deciding that he had a better chance of running into
enemies if he was *on* the run, instead of sitting still
and merging with the landscape.

There was time enough for him to hit the road tomorrow, or the next day. Time enough to reach the
next mark well before his troops were in position and
prepared to strike.

For Fletcher's sake, he hoped they did not fail a
second time.

THE HACKER'S NAME was Theodore Marchand, although his handful of acquaintances was prone to call
him Teddy Mark. It was as good as anything, particularly since the names printed on musty documents
meant less and less to anyone on Earth as time went
by. Theo Marchand—or Teddy Mark—for all intents
and purposes, had nearly ceased to be. The entity that
had replaced him was a disembodied citizen of cyberspace.

Its name was Midnight Blue. Sometimes M.B. or
simply Blue to other cyberfolk, with no assumptions
as to gender, race or nationality. Such baggage was
superfluous in the miasmic realm where everybody
lied and no one seemed to care. Illusion had been
multiplied and magnified, made pseudo-flesh through
virtual reality programs. There were few limits to
what an expert and imaginative hacker could achieve
within the confines of his mind and monitor.

Which made it all the more uncomfortable now for Teddy Mark to leave his Midnight Blue persona on the shelf and venture out into the cold, cruel world of flesh and bone, asphalt and steel. It had been days since he had left his small apartment in West Hollywood. And he wouldn't be leaving now, in darkness, if one of his most valued—meaning fattest—clients hadn't earnestly insisted that the two of them go F2F.

He hated meeting face-to-face. What was the point of cruising flat-out down the information superhighway if you were repeatedly compelled to stop and talk to boring people in the flesh? What was the point of meeting anyone, in fact, when you could fight and fuck, pay bills and stalk your debtors, transport tons of cash and topple giant companies, all without rising from your keyboard?

If you weren't jacked in, you weren't alive.

The all-night diner chosen for their meeting was in neutral territory, which, to Teddy Mark, meant nearly anyplace outside a one-block radius of his apartment complex. Going out the door, he paused and made a desultory effort to remember his last shower, then the peevish little voice inside his head told him that if somebody demanded he go out in the middle of the night and F2F, he could be satisfied with what he got.

It sounded good in theory, but the truth was, Teddy Mark wasn't particularly keen on pissing off this customer. For one thing, he and those he had referred to Midnight Blue for sundry jobs were always flush with cash and weren't afraid to spend it. For another, Teddy had a general impression that these folks were into heavy shit, the kind that sometimes came back on an unsuspecting middleman and bit him in the ass if he was negligent.

So Teddy Mark was sweating more than usual by the time he reached the diner, hoofing it despite the hour, since his beat-up junker of a ride was in the shop and he refused to ride mass transit like a sardine in a can. Coming into the approach, he half expected Zyklon Bee—his contact's cyberhandle—to be waiting for him on the street outside, but there was no one loitering around beneath the vapor lamps.

Oh, well.

Since they had never met, he had proposed a recognition signal of some kind, but Zyklon Bee had said it wasn't necessary. ''I'll find you.'' The way he said it giving Teddy Marks the creeps.

And now, the more he thought about it, it began to piss him off. Jesus, it wasn't as if he wore a frigging uniform or something. Sure, he was a little overweight—no more than fifty, maybe sixty pounds, still several Happy Meals away from morbidly obese—and he wore black horn-rims with thick lenses, but so what? He hadn't worn a pocket protector since eighth grade, and he didn't even *own* a slide rule.

Never mind.

Teddy focused on the money, thinking he would have to use some of it on experimental antiperspirants. He could have used one at the moment, sweating like a prom queen getting set to lose her cherry to the captain of the football team.

Make that the whole damned football team.

He checked out the diner's patrons as he passed the windows facing on the street. Three of the fourteen booths were occupied, one by a pair of rapper types who definitely didn't fit the Zyklon Bee profile, the other two by white males in their twenties, maybe thirty-something. At the counter, spaced out well apart, as if they were afraid of cooties jumping ship, three older men were huddled over plates and coffee cups. There were no women in the place, unless the aging waitress counted, so he didn't bother sucking in his gut as he pushed through the door and made his way inside.

I'll find you.

Teddy Mark was standing near the register and feeling like a total idiot, when one of the solitary booth-sitters, all the way back on his left, raised a hand. Reluctantly, as if caught in some kind of tractor beam, he made his way the full length of the diner, nodding to the waitress as he passed. Arriving at the booth, he spent a moment checking out this stranger: blond, crew cut, athletic build, the tag end of an unidentifiable tattoo just peeking out beneath the short sleeve of a tight black T-shirt.

"Midnight Blue," the stranger said, not asking him.

"My friends just call me Blue."

That was a lie, of course. He had no friends of flesh and blood. In fact, if pressed, he could report with something close to pride that he had never really had a friend his whole life long.

"Well, Blue, I hope we're friends. Please, have a seat."

He sat, and felt the waitress at his elbow almost instantly.

"Hey, Teddy," she addressed him, snapping gum, hallucinating that she was some sweet young thing, instead of middle-aged and tragically surrendering to gravity.

"Hey, Joyce." Reading her plastic name tag to remind himself of the inconsequential name.

"What'll you have?"

He glanced at Zyklon Bee, an untouched beer in front of him. The stranger smiled without showing his teeth and said, "My treat."

"Okay. I'll have a root-beer float. Three scoops."

"Three scoops it is." Joyce snapped her gum again for emphasis and plodded back around the counter to prepare his float.

"So, Mr. Bee," he said. "Business too sensitive for telephones or modems, I believe it was?"

"It's not that big a deal," said Zyklon Bee, and Teddy knew that he was lying right away. "I need to run a check on someone, and I need it quickly, with a minimum of leakage."

"They have private eyes and credit agencies to do that sort of thing," Teddy replied.

"I don't need credit history, and I don't want a PI agency involved. I have a name, address, the various particulars."

"So, you know where this person lives?"

"Past tense. Last known address. I need to find out if she's likely to come back, or if there's any forwarding."

A woman. Teddy Mark had to restrain himself from smirking. Some sex thing that no one cared about except the man seated across from him, and he was summoned from the comfort of his home to chase some skirt around the country. Jesus.

Mollified at least in part by the arrival of his root-beer float, he sipped and said, "So, show me what you have."

An index card changed hands. Someone had typed out Mary Krause, together with a Riverside address and phone number. There was nothing in the nature of a physical description, but he didn't need one. He would never meet the woman, and in the places he would search for her in cyberspace, appearance was irrelevant. All human beings were reduced to numbers there. It was the one great equalizer, a realm where intellect truly, finally counted for more than brawn or beauty.

"There's some kind of rush on this, I take it," Teddy said.

"Sooner the better," Zyklon Bee replied. "Beyond thirty-six hours, though, I won't need it at all."

"I like a challenge, Mr. Bee."

"You mentioned five large as a fee."

"That's right."

"I'll let you have a thousand now, the rest upon delivery."

"I normally get half up front," Teddy reminded him.

"You normally don't have this kind of deadline," said the crew-cut blonde. "If you don't make it, by the way, I'll expect the thousand back."

"Now, wait a minute—"

"All or nothing, Blue. If you're not up to it…"

"Dream on. I'll get you what you need, if it exists."

"Meaning?"

"Some troglodytes are still stuck in the pen-and-ink age. If your lady's not jacked in, there's nothing

I can do. I don't go house to house and ring doorbells.''

"I could have guessed that," Zyklon Bee responded, glancing from the root-beer float, three-quarters gone, to Teddy's double chins.

The hacker didn't take offense—at least not visibly. "When I come up with something, can I reach you at the usual address?''

"For the advisory, but nothing else. Don't transmit any data.''

"So, you'll want another F2F." Teddy made no attempt to hide his frown.

"I'll send someone around to pick up the information.''

"What do you mean?''

"I mean, I'll send someone around to visit Theodore Marchand, aka Teddy Mark," the smiling blond replied, and rattled off the street address, apartment number, right down to the ZIP code. "Fair enough?''

"Suits me" was all that he could think of as he took the plain white envelope and tried to work his way out of the booth. "Thanks for the float.''

"My pleasure, Blue.''

He left the diner and walked home on rubber legs, afraid to turn and see if anyone was following. Why would they be? Christ, they already knew exactly where to find him, anytime they wanted to.

And who was "they?''

He didn't care. He'd do the job, collect the money and forget about the whole damned thing.

And maybe, if he had the energy, he would consider finding someplace new to live.

THEO MARCHAND DIDN'T need eighteen hours. He got back to Fletcher in a little under five, before the sun was truly up. Fletcher dispatched two of his men to get the information and retrieve his thousand dollars after they had dealt with Teddy Mark.

"Special instructions?" one of them had asked him, heading out the door.

"As clean as possible," he said. "No need to drag it out."

They regrouped within the hour, Fletcher's second meeting of the morning in a cheap café. He marveled at the fact that both of them—like every other greasy spoon in his experience—shared certain smells. Curiously, there was little variation even when the menus ran to ethnic dishes. One and all, they seemed to use the same stale cooking oil and cleaned up— when they cleaned at all—with the same sharp-smelling detergents.

Arriving ahead of the troops, he ordered coffee, black, and told the slinky jailbait waitress he would call her if he needed anything. His men arrived some moments later, squeezed into the booth across from him and handed him a slim manila envelope. Inside was a single-page computer printout. Mary Krause, according to the document, still claimed the same address in Riverside, no forwarding. It further told him that the rent was paid each month, in full, although the house had been unoccupied. The monthly checks had come from something called Investments Limited, which seemed to have no address other than a Bakersfield post-office box, but Midnight Blue had done some extra digging, and the last line of the document fairly leaped off the page: "Investments Limited identified as paper front shared commonly by FBI and ATF.''

"Did he keep this on disk?" Fletcher asked.

"We took care of it," one of his soldiers stated.

"Erased his hard drive," said the other, "and we've got his CDs and his floppies in the car, in case you want to look them over."

"Burn them," Fletcher ordered. "All of them."

"He's got some bitchin' games. I thought—"

"Don't think. Do as you're told."

"Yes, sir."

"I find out you've kept anything, you'll need the long arm of proctology before it sees the light of day."

"No problem, sir."

"Do that, first thing, then pick up Lester and Izzy. All of you go out to Riverside and camp on this address." He let them eye the printout long enough to memorize the number and the street, then folded it and put it in his pocket. "Don't be obvious about it, but be thorough. You remember who you're looking for?"

"We know her," one of them replied. "The bitch is history."

"Did I say that?" He glared at one and then the other, holding each man's eyes until he squirmed and glanced away, each muttering, "No, sir."

"What you *will* do," he told them, lowering his voice for emphasis, compelling both of them to lean across the table, drawing near, "is pick her up and take her to that place in San Diego. You know where I mean?"

"Yes, sir." A stereo duet.

"You're not to damage her in any way, except as necessary for immediate control. I hope that's crystal clear."

"Yes, sir!"

"It's not your job to punish anyone unless I say so," Fletcher said. "Meantime, I find so much as one unnecessary bruise, and I will rip you both new assholes. Got it?"

"Got it, sir!"

He sat back in the booth and raised his coffee cup again, then said, "What are you waiting for?"

The jailbait waitress took her time with Fletcher's bill, bending to show him all the cleavage she could muster without stripping on the spot. He thanked her, left two dollars on a six-bit tab and walked out feeling like a goddamned fool.

The young ones did it to him every time.

He nipped that train of thought in the bud and turned his focus back to Mary Krause—assuming that turned out to be her name. The late, lamented Midnight Blue had had no means of checking on an alias, without more detailed information than Sean Fletcher had been able to provide. No matter, though. When she was in his hands, he would have ample time and means to coax all kinds of secrets from her. By the time he finished, Fletcher would know everything there was to know about a certain lady working for the FBI or ATF.

He was already tired of speculating on how badly her betrayal might damage the Temple of the Nordic Covenant. In ordinary circumstances, if he had the final say, he would have scrubbed the missions they had scheduled, pulled back to await developments, regrouping just in case it turned into a last-ditch fight for life. His Führer didn't see it that way, though, and Fletcher knew that he would follow orders, even if they ultimately led him to his death.

No warrior was supposed to live forever, anyway. The best fate he could hope for, short of dying in bed at age ninety-eight, surrounded by new generations of Aryan offspring, was to give his life in combat for the race.

He didn't bother guessing as to whether Mary Krause worked for the FBI, the ATF or possibly some other agency controlled by ZOG. None of the agencies he was familiar with behaved as had the men who rescued Mary Krause from Freedom Home, much less the shooters at the Eli Sturnman Center in L.A. If either strike had been a full-dress federal operation, Fletcher would have been in jail by now, or staring back at countless strangers from ten thousand Wanted posters.

And if the shooters weren't FBI or ATF...then, what?

The flip side troubled Fletcher more than any thought of going underground and hiding from the Feds, because he had prepared himself for that, both mentally and physically. His soldiers knew the drill, exactly where to go and what to do if anything went seriously wrong. In the worst-case scenario, some of them were prepared to take off on their own, pursue the path of leaderless resistance as untouchable, undetectable rogues.

Unfortunately, Fletcher didn't know what kind of damned scenario he was involved in now. That was a problem that he meant to remedy, once he laid hands on Mary Krause. Before she screamed her final breath away, she would enlighten him, spare nothing in her recitation of the fine details.

And while he waited, Fletcher had to double-check the details for their next scheduled event. Allowing for the travel time, the schedule would be tight, but they could pull it off. Correction—they *would* pull it off. A race war had been brewing in America since the first slavers dropped their African cargo at Jamestown, almost four hundred years earlier. It was a miracle, in Fletcher's view, that it had been delayed this long. Of course, the lag time was explained by prophecy: this age had been selected by the gods to host the final conflict, when the last great Aryan apostle would step forward, shunning the mistakes of those who came before, and lead his army on to victory against the demons who had worked so long and hard to mongrelize the master race.

Sean Fletcher would be there beside him, Wotan willing, on the day of final victory. And if he fell along the way, he would receive his honors in Valhalla, sharing fellowship with others who had fought the good fight in their time: Himmler, Eichmann, Heydrich. It was a no-lose situation, any way he looked at it.

Which didn't mean, of course, that he could simply sit back on his laurels, coast and let the details take care of themselves. That kind of sloppy thinking had derailed the movement more than once, when victory was close enough to smell and taste. At Stalingrad, for instance. At Bastogne. When Bobby Matthews and The Order turned from liberating payrolls to the relatively ''safe'' and ''easy'' craft of counterfeiting, and performed the task so clumsily that all of them were either dead or waiting out their final years in federal prison cells.

No more repeating the mistakes of history. No more loose ends.

This time, he told himself, they would do it right.

CHAPTER NINE

"I promise, it would be a total waste of time. Go on and call your people or whatever, and I'll see you back here in about two hours, right?"

Belasko frowned and craned his neck to see around her, checking out the small, neat house. It was a block off Tyler Street, in Riverside, and they had made good time from the motel once they were dressed and packed. A bit too good, in fact, since Crouder would have enjoyed an instant replay of their intimate encounter, but she knew that time was flying past, and they had miles to go before they slept—together or apart.

"I ought to go inside with you and check it out," he said.

"Don't worry. Uncle Sugar keeps an eye out, when he's picking up the rent."

That wasn't strictly true, of course. She had no reason to believe that Archer would have detailed anyone to watch the house while she was living with the latter-day brownshirts at Freedom Home. Why would he? Man-hours were limited for active cases, as it was, and no field supervisor would have wasted money on surveillance of an empty house, particularly when there was no prospect of the effort leading to arrests and prosecution.

Still, she wasn't worried. Everything looked buttoned-down normal from the curb. Someone had kept the lawn trimmed, the hedges clipped, and there was no backlog of newspapers or junk mail on her doorstep. All the drapes were drawn, as she had left them when she walked out, nearly eighteen months before, and if the paint had faded slightly in her absence, she would have to blame the southern California climate, not the Temple of the Nordic Covenant.

"All right," he said at last. "Two hours, then. I make it 1900 hours."

"Ooh, I love it when you talk all military like."

"Don't start," he cautioned her.

"Heard that before." She resisted the impulse to kiss him as she opened her door and stepped out of the car.

She fished the keys out of her pocket as she stepped up to the door, and had a sudden flash that Archer might have changed the locks, a quick nod to security, once she went underground at Freedom Home.

Not likely, she decided, but if something of the sort had taken place, then she would simply make her way around to the back door and let herself in through the kitchen. Crouder was rusty when it came to picking locks, but it was just another simple motor skill, like riding a bike, or some other leisure activities that she could think of, if she wasn't anxious to avoid distractions.

She most definitely didn't want to concentrate on Mike Belasko at the moment, getting all steamed up about his kisses, his physique, the way he—

And then some.

Standing on the stoop, no porch light to alert her neighbors, Crouder glanced once in each direction, up and down the quiet street, before she tried the key. It fit the slot, turned in her grasp with just the slightest vestige of resistance. The door balked for a moment, slightly swollen in its frame and stiff from long disuse, but then she was inside.

The place smelled vaguely musty, as abandoned houses always did. There was no stench of rotten food, as she had cleaned out the refrigerator and the cupboards prior to leaving for her sojourn with the Nordic Temple. Make it dust, a trace of mildew and the smell of stale air trapped inside four walls for months on end, with no way to escape and precious little opportunity to circulate.

She tried the light switch by the door, uncertain as to whether Archer would have paid utilities, on top of rent, and smiled as lights came on around the modest living room. One of the bulbs blew out immediately, causing her to flinch, then she laughed out loud at her reaction.

She left the shopping bag that held her AK-74 on the coffee table, moving toward the answering machine that she had left behind so many months ago. The message counter showed three calls, and when she played them back, two were the tape-recorded spiels of automated telemarketers; the third was nothing but dead air.

"It's nice to know you missed me, people."

That was foolishness, of course. Aside from Archer and the goon squad at the Nordic Temple, no one else on Earth had any reason to be calling nonexistent

Mary Krause. The telemarketers picked numbers from a grab bag, and the silent call was a wrong number, more likely than not. In any case, it was no reason for concern.

She gave a passing thought to washing up—the shower she had taken with Belasko, back at the motel, had been delightful, but hadn't done much in terms of cleanliness—then told herself that it could wait until she saw how much time hasty packing would require. She had a suitcase waiting in the bedroom closet, ready to receive the extra clothes and underwear that she had left behind when she shipped out to Freedom Home. It wasn't all that much, in fact, but it was functional and would provide some badly missed variety.

As far as nightgowns went, she didn't own one, and didn't suppose she would be needing any, while her partnership with Belasko lasted.

Down, girl.

Force of habit made her check the kitchen, and it came as no surprise when she found nothing out of place. The empty fridge was humming softly, chilling nonexistent perishable foods. The ice cubes in her freezer trays would have evaporated since she filled them last, but since she wasn't mixing cocktails, that, too, was irrelevant.

She started toward the bedroom, thought about retrieving the Kalashnikov en route, but saw no reason for the wasted effort. She could pick it up on her way out, when she was packed and maybe showered, ready for the road.

She passed the bathroom, door half-open, leaving

it for last, and hesitated at the bedroom threshold, reaching for the light switch just inside. What was it?

Something...

An aroma? What *was* that, intruding on the empty rooms, too long unoccupied?

"Let there be light."

The voice came from behind her, and she whipped around to face its owner, saw him just emerging from the bathroom. Even with the light behind him, face in shadow, she could tell that he was trouble, with the close-cropped stubble on his scalp, the dull glint of a semiauto pistol in his hand. Its sound suppressor made the gun seem improbably large, like some kind of vaudeville weapon, where you pulled the trigger and a flag popped out, imprinted with the message Bang!

The bedroom lights came on behind her, showing her the shooter's face. He looked vaguely familiar, but she couldn't pin a name on him. Slowly, giving the man no reason to start shooting, Crouder half turned to find four crew-cut faces blocking her retreat. Each of the prowlers had a weapon showing, two of them with SMGs, all suppressed. Again, the faces were familiar, but she drew a blank on names, reflecting on the irony that all skinheads began to look alike after a while.

"You fellows make yourself at home," she said, pleased that she didn't hear a tremor in her voice. There would be time enough for that, no doubt, before she died.

"We'd like to, Mary," said the foremost of the quartet in her bedroom, "but we've got our orders. Party time's been put on hold. Maybe a little later, if you ask us nice and sweet, we can work something out.''

"Or maybe,'' she replied, "I could just gargle razor blades, and skip the freak show.''

"You can gargle *me*,'' one of the gunners sneered, "you little—''

"Shut the fuck up!'' their leader snapped. "We need to get her out of here.''

"What, just the five of you?''

"Smart bitch.'' The guy in charge looked past her, toward the goon blocking the hallway. "Lester.''

"Lester?" It was risky, taunting them, but Crouder had already decided she would rather take a bullet than submit to whatever interrogation methods Fletcher and his fellow fascists could devise. "I didn't know the Temple was recruiting from the gay community these days.''

Lester was scowling as he closed the gap between them, and she saw that in addition to his pistol, he was also holding something in his other hand. At first glance, it resembled a remote control for a TV or VCR, but then she saw the stubby gray electrodes that protruded from one end and recognized the stun gun.

"Overcompensating for a shortage are we, Lester?''

She was poised to launch a roundhouse kick at him, when someone grabbed her from behind and pinned her arms, the hard toe of someone's boots colliding with her shin and forcing her to clench her teeth around a gasp of pain.

The stun gun rushed to meet her, making contact with the outer swell of her left breast, and when the voltage hit her she convulsed, unconscious by the time restraining hands released her and she tumbled headlong into darkness streaked with comets' tails.

"I'M SICK OF ALL this waiting," Lester Burrage groused, sitting in darkness, with the silenced Beretta in his lap. "We should of taught that snotty bitch a lesson, right?"

"You're kind of late suggesting that," Rick Toler said. "I mean, you could of mentioned it to Zack before we put her in his car."

"Yeah, right." The jeering comment came from Skeeter Pangborn. "You see Lester telling Zack to hold his water while we make her pull the train? Save me a seat for that one, brother."

Burrage had half a dozen snappy retorts circling in his head, waiting for clearance from the tower, but he knew that any one of them might find its way to Zack, and that could land him in deep shit. Worse yet, if he was too damned insubordinate, word might get back to Fletcher, and he didn't want to think about *that* possibility at all.

"I'm saying that I hate this sitting on my ass, that's all," he grumbled in reply to his companions' gibes.

"Guy dropped her off," said Izzy Jakes. "Guy's comin' back."

"We don't know that."

"We know that Zack told us to wait," Toler said. "And that's Sean talking, just in case it slipped your mind. We wait."

"All right! Jesus!"

"You whine too much," Pangborn said. "I'm starting to think the bitch was right."

"Your mama didn't think so," Burrage said. At

least, there was no mortal risk inherent to insulting Skeeter Pangborn. They were both of equal rank, and Pangborn was a good four inches shorter, twenty-odd pounds lighter.

"Hey, what can I tell you?" Pangborn said. "My mama croaked in '92. I guess that makes you some kind of a necroflooziac."

"You know what, Skeeter—"

"Put a sock in it, the two of you." Rick Toler was in charge, once Zack bailed out to make delivery on Krause, and Burrage glared at Pangborn without saying any more. He was content to bide his time and wait.

What was it some guy said? Revenge was sweeter if you left it in the fridge, some shit like that. Let Skeeter think their little hassle was forgotten, that he had the best of it. Meanwhile, Burrage would nurse his grudge, devise some fitting payback to be sprung on Skeeter when he least expected it.

Les Burrage had the patience of a tree stump when it suited him. It simply didn't suit him at the moment, sitting in the dark, denied even a cigarette, and waiting for some guy who might not show his face for hours, if he came at all.

It had occurred to Burrage that the guy who dropped her off out front might have no connection whatsoever to the recent action in L.A., and might not be coming back regardless, after dropping her at home. Jew traitors needed rest sometimes, the same as anybody else. They could be sitting in the bitch's house all night and never see another living soul approach the door.

Burrage had voiced these personal concerns, albeit

with a fair degree of sham humility, before Zack left them in the lurch and took off with the woman. Zack hadn't thought much of it, clearly not enough to give up the stakeout and let them join him in preparing for the next big day. Instead, it was a cushy job for Zack, while Burrage and his buddies sat in darkness, killing time until they either fell asleep on watch or had to shoot it out with unknown troops of unknown strength.

It didn't strike Burrage as much of a plan, but then, what did he know? He wasn't officer material—he knew that much—but some plans had a fishy smell about them from the start. You didn't have to stand behind home plate to know that certain balls were really strikes, no matter what the frigging umpire said.

But he would wait, because to act in any other way was tantamount to mutiny, and he had seen what happened to rebellious soldiers in the Temple of the Nordic Covenant. Christ, it had taken him three days to get the burning smell out of his new fatigues, and he still heard the frenzied screams, sometimes, when he was on the brink of sleep.

"All right," he said to no one in particular. "You all heard me. I didn't challenge Zack. You're all my witnesses."

"Nobody said you challenged him," Toler said.

"Hell, no," Izzy Jakes stated. "You're still alive."

"So funny I forgot to laugh," Burrage grumbled, while the others chuckled at him, not hiding their mirth. "Look, I just think—"

"Headlights!" Toler snapped. "Shut up and take your places!"

Burrage scrambled from his chair at the dining-room table, clutching the Beretta so tightly in his fist that for a fleeting moment he was worried that it might pop free, like a cartoon bar of soap, and sail across the room. Self-consciously, now thankful for the darkness, Burrage clutched the piece in both hands as he moved to take his place.

Speaking of darkness, there was less of it to go around, as someone wheeled a car into the driveway, headlights shooting stray beams through gaps in the curtains, like something from a low-budget UFO movie. Instead of little green men, though, they were waiting for humans, more or less. Some kind of shooters, maybe Jew assassins from Mossad, maybe some kind of mongrels from the Federal Bureau of Integration.

Either way, there was a 98.5 percent probability of explosive confrontation in the next few moments, and Les Burrage only hoped that it would be a quick, clean kill. And that one of the stiffs his buddies ultimately hauled away wouldn't be his.

It would be such a frigging drag to die before the Day.

No LIGHTS WERE showing from the house as Bolan pulled into the driveway, switched his off and left the engine idling for another moment, checking out the night around him. Studying the dark and silent house, he told himself that Crouder had probably decided not to spook the neighbors, lighting up the place as if it were New Year's Eve, when there had been no one in residence for close to eighteen months. Another possible scenario—she could have turned the lights on while she packed and did whatever else she had to do before they hit the road, then might have switched them off again to wait for Bolan in the dark.

He had five minutes left to go on the two hours he had promised the woman, but he had nothing else to do, nowhere to go and kill the time. He had checked in with Hal Brognola and arranged for transportation to their next target, making it the big Fed's call as to whether he should tip off the locals and risk a huge snafu, or simply let the action run its course. There had been no late word from ATF about the shootings at the Eli Sturnman Center, much less Crouder's direct involvement, and he wondered if the agency was getting set to screen itself from any fallout, maybe leave her stranded in the crunch and hide behind a smooth wall of denial.

Bolan almost hoped they would. The last thing that he needed now was some enthusiastic SWAT team trying to beat his time.

Four minutes, and he didn't fancy sitting in the car until the final instant of the deadline. Taking one more cautious look around, he stepped out of the car and started toward the door. His jacket was unbuttoned for quicker access to the 93-R in its armpit holster if it came to that. He rang the bell, heard muffled chimes inside and waited. Rang again when no one answered.

What the hell?

His right hand slipped inside the open jacket, while his racing mind sought explanations for the deathly stillness of the house. How could she not have heard the doorbell? Bolan didn't know the floor plan of the house, but he suspected that if Crouder was in the shower, he should probably be able to pick up some distant sound of water running.

While he had set his mind on going in, the front door held no great appeal for him. Even without the porch light, it was too exposed to neighbors, passing motorists and lawmen on patrol. He took for granted that she would have locked the door as soon as it was closed behind her, and while Bolan carried both the gear and skill to pick that lock, it would be safer if he sought another means of entry.

Circling around the west side of the house, no fence to separate the backyard from the front, he drew his pistol, setting it for 3-round bursts before he thumbed the hammer back. With one round in the chamber and another twenty in the 93-R's magazine, he could fire seven times before reloading, and recipients of those Black Talon rounds would need a suit of body armor to protect them from a world of hurt.

He stopped and listened at a frosted bathroom window—still no light or sound—before he continued around back and found the small tract home's rear entrance. He guessed that it would put him in the kitchen, and this time he tried the knob, frowning as it turned easily, immediately, in his hand.

That was no good.

No good at all.

Still, whatever had happened in the past two hours, Bolan had to know, and there was no way to discover it by standing in the yard and beaming dour thoughts toward the house.

He gave the door a little of his weight, prepared to ease off if the hinges squealed, but there was no sound to betray him. Not that it would matter if a trap was waiting for him in the house. An ambush team would certainly have noted his approach, headlights and all.

They could have automatic weapons sighted on the
door, ready to cut him down before he crossed the
threshold.

Do it!

He gave the door a shove and lunged through in a
shoulder roll, noting the vinyl floor beneath him,
fetching up against the double doors of a refrigerator,
humming softly with the only sound of life that he
had yet detected from the house.

Until the shadows came alive and tried to kill him.

The sudden muzzle-flashes weren't entirely silent—few suppressors really were, and none remained
that way if they were used for any length of time—
but these were good enough to keep the neighbors out
of it, unless stray rounds flew out a window and
struck someone else's home. Bolan was busy ducking, sliding over dusty vinyl, trying to count flashes
in the early moments of the fight, but he could still
appreciate his adversaries' timing.

If they weren't exactly pros, they were the next-
best thing.

Which meant that Bolan had to be the *very* best, if
he intended to survive.

He didn't know what they expected from him,
maybe fire and thunder, but he answered silent death
with more of the same, firing from a prone position,
rolling swiftly to his right before they marked his
muzzle-flash, firing again. The only furniture around
him was a butcher's block on wheels, providing little
in the way of cover, but emitting squeaky noises when
he brushed against it and the casters carried it a foot
or so out of his way.

His faceless enemies, meanwhile, were tearing hell out of the kitchen, bullets striking the refrigerator, stove and cabinets, pocking the floor and walls, cracking a window somewhere overhead. Much more of that, and they would have the next-door neighbors on alert despite the sound suppressors.

His second burst apparently struck home, immediately answered by a muzzle-flash directed toward the ceiling and a thumping, grunting sound as someone hit the floor. His eyes were still adjusting to the deeper darkness of the home's interior, after the night outside, and Bolan couldn't tell if he had scored a kill. In fact, he wasn't even sure about the size of the opposing force, but they had clearly zeroed in on his only exit, and he didn't plan to leave without discovering what had become of Marilyn Crouder.

He marked another muzzle-flash, the spray of lead too close for comfort. This time, what he got back was a squeal of pain, some bitter cursing, and the rapid clomping of retreating footsteps.

Digging in with knees and elbows, Bolan traveled lizardlike across the kitchen floor, spent brass still warm beneath him as he crawled. There was a scuffling sound from somewhere up ahead, beyond the door that opened on a hallway, someone commanding, "Get back there and finish him, goddammit! If he gets away, it's *your* ass!"

They didn't need to worry, Bolan thought as he approached the doorway, rising to a crouch, lunging into the hallway, firing as he went.

The Executioner wasn't escaping.

He was carrying the battle to his enemies.

THE WOUND in Lester Burrage's shoulder hurt like hell, and he could barely move his left arm, felt it dangling uselessly against his side, ablaze with pain. In movies, guys were always taking shoulder hits as if they were nothing, sometimes fighting hand to hand with enemies despite the wound, as if it didn't even hurt. In fact, a solid shoulder wound could take a soldier out of action, leaving him one-handed if he didn't bleed to death, and Burrage could tell the world a thing or two about that white-hot, blinding pain.

Rick Toler ordered Burrage to go back to finish the guy.

Burrage was about to answer back, "I'm hit, you stupid prick," but as the words were forming in his mind, Toler's face imploded, spraying Les with something wet and warm.

Recoiling from the mess as Toler crumpled in a heap, Burrage plunged along the hallway in a shambling run, colliding with the wall and nearly passing out as new bolts of agony flared through his shoulder and torso. Jakes and Pangborn met him halfway to the living room, responding to the sounds of battle after no one tried their station at the front, and one of them bumped Burrage going past, driving him against the wall again.

Same agony, but doubled this time, forcing a helpless sob from his throat as his legs turned to pasta. He was falling, had perhaps a microsecond to adjust his posture, landing on his right side, rather than the wounded left, for all the good it did him. Even so, the jolt still felt as if a football lineman had collided with his wound. Burrage recognized the squealing girly voice as coming from himself, but even though he tried to bite it off, it was too late. The sound had already escaped, to echo through the house.

Burrage couldn't follow much of the battle from where he lay, twisted on the floor a few steps from the bathroom, rigid with pain. He was aware of throaty coughing sounds, the various suppressors, and of bullets striking plaster, wood, some of the furniture. At one point, he was panicked by a burst of automatic fire that stitched a ragged line of holes along the wall, perhaps a foot above his prostrate form, sprinkling his scalp and face with plaster dust. Some of it got in his eye, the left one, and it was incredible how much that hurt, considering the agony already flaring from his mangled shoulder.

"Fuck you, man!" somebody shouted. Was it Izzy Jakes? Burrage couldn't tell, between the ringing in his ears, the speaker's strange falsetto and the fierce—albeit muffled—sounds of combat. "Show yourse—" the man who might be Izzy Jakes started to demand, but he was cut off in midsyllable, the thump of a collapsing body serving as the final punctuation.

Someone sprinted down the hall in his direction, tripped on Burrage's feet and went sprawling on his face. Burrage couldn't see the runner's face, but there was no mistaking Skeeter Pangborn when he started cursing in that corn-pone voice of his, roundly denouncing everyone and everything from God to lowly mud people for his predicament. To Pangborn's credit, he recovered swiftly, and had somehow managed to retain his Uzi, though a moment earlier he had appeared more interested in bailing out than putting up a fight.

Now that he had no choice, Pangborn turned back

to face the unseen enemy, unloading with a burst that had to have used up half the Uzi's magazine. That wasn't how they had been taught to use an SMG, but Burrage, though barely lucid in his pain haze, reckoned that you had to make allowances for panic at a time like this.

A rain of hot brass from the Uzi pattered on his face, head, shoulder as he tried to squirm away and only bought himself more suffering for the attempt. Burrage didn't see the shots that finished Pangborn, but he heard them hit, three lethal punches, thrown so close together that no human boxer could have managed it.

Burrage closed his eyes and braced himself for still more pain as Pangborn toppled forward, but the tumbling body missed him by perhaps a foot. What *didn't* miss him was the Uzi, dropping onto his outstretched arm with bruising force.

He snapped his teeth around the squeal that tried to slip past his lips, contained and swallowed it alive. His own piece lost, he recognized the Uzi, pain or no, as his last hope for self-defense. Of course, he'd have to actually pick it up, then turn himself around somehow, locate a target, pray that the damned thing wasn't empty, after all.

His outstretched arm worked well enough to hook the Uzi closer, but it cost him pain, the interest paid in sweat and tears that further blurred his vision. With his neck cocked at an awkward angle, peering down the full length of his body, back in the direction he had come from, Burrage tried to pick out anything resembling a human target. He couldn't fire wildly in the dark, because he knew the Uzi had to be running low on ammo, and he still hadn't confirmed that Izzy Jakes was dead. It stood to reason, but until he could be positive...

Someone was moving toward him, gaining ground... The Uzi wasn't aimed, exactly, but he had the long suppressor braced across one of his knees. When he cut loose, the first rounds ought to strike his target in the legs, the last rounds rising as the Uzi kicked. He couldn't guarantee a kill, but any hit at all would be a kind of victory. With luck, perhaps his enemy might know the very pain that Burrage was suffering—or maybe worse.

Poetic justice.

Burrage was tightening his index finger on the Uzi's trigger, wondering if he should give some kind of warning first, maybe call Izzy's name, when something slammed into the SMG and ripped it from his grasp. There was another flash of blinding pain, almost as if he had plunged his hand into an acid bath. Burrage couldn't swallow the scream, this time, vaguely aware that blood was pumping from the tattered root of what was once his thumb.

The shooter stood above him for a moment, his face obscured in darkness. When he dropped into a crouch, the move reminded Burrage of an elevator going down. His mind went blank, as the muzzle of a still-warm pistol pressed into the flesh beneath his chin.

"Looks like you need first aid," the stranger said.

"I do," Burrage rapidly agreed. "I really do."

"Okay. But first, we need to have a little talk."

CHAPTER TEN

"You shouldn't get your hopes up, Lester," Bolan said after he had learned the wounded Nazi's name. That part was easy, skinhead Lester Burrage either hurting to the point where discipline went out the window, or perhaps enamored of the notion that the Nordic Temple's "racial holy war" entitled him to claim POW privileges under the Geneva Convention, offering no more than name, rank and serial number to his captors.

Unfortunately for the bleeding fascist, Bolan didn't recognize the conflict or the treaty, and he didn't give a damn about his captive's name. What Bolan wanted—what he meant to have, if it took every drop of Lester's blood to lubricate the burly bastard's tongue—was a complete and detailed explanation of what had happened to Marilyn Crouder and where he could find her, dead or alive.

"I want a lawyer," Burrage demanded.

"I want an island in the South Pacific. Get in line."

"Hey, man, I know my rights."

"You have no rights, Lester."

"Bullshit! You can't just come in here and—"

"Blow your friends away like they were targets in

a shooting gallery? Devote the next few hours to dissecting you if you don't tell me what I want to know? I think you'll find I can.''

''You have to take me in and book me, man. You have to call an ambulance and let me make a phone call. It's the Constitution, man!''

''Okay, I see your problem now,'' Bolan replied. ''You took a small knock on the head there, and you're starting to hallucinate that I'm some kind of cop. Does this look like a bust to you, bright boy? Has anything I've done or said so far given you any reason to believe I give a damn about your so-called rights?''

A light of sorts clicked on behind the skinhead's bleary eyes. ''Well, shit,'' he said. ''Who are you, man?''

''Who am I?'' Bolan smiled and shook his head. ''Now, that's insulting, Lester. You and your gorillas go to all this trouble just to meet me, and you don't know who I am? I tell you, Lester, I'm beginning to suspect Herr Steuben has a thing for morons.''

''Fuck you!''

The slap rocked Burrage's head and echoed through the still house like a pistol shot. It brought tears to the skinhead's eyes, a flush of angry crimson to his cheek, where Bolan's livid palm print took a while to fade.

''As I was saying, Lester, we can go the long way around on this, or you can make it easy on yourself. I know you're Mr. Macho Aryan and all, but you can spare yourself a world of grief by answering some simple questions.''

"I don't have to tell you anything," Burrage replied.

"That's where you're wrong. Before we're done here, you'll be begging me to let you tell about the first time you got laid and who the sheep belonged to, but you need to know that if we go that route, your chances of survival are...well, let's just say the odds are better that your half-assed Führer will be winning prizes from B'nai B'rith. You follow me?"

"I'm not afraid of you!"

"Please, Lester. You already proved you're stupid when you joined the Nordic Temple. Do you really want to go for suicidal?"

Silence, while the skinhead glared at him through pain-hazed eyes. He clenched the one fist over which he still had some control and set his tear-streaked face in an expression of defiance.

"Okay, then. Suits me," the Executioner remarked. "First thing, we need to make sure that you don't check out before I'm finished with you. Let's just stop the bleeding from that hand and shoulder, shall we?"

Bolan grabbed him by the wrist about his mangled hand and dragged the feebly struggling Nazi back along the hallway to the kitchen. There he switched on the ceiling lights, calculating that if all the shooting hadn't prompted neighbors to alert police by now, neither would lighting up a room that didn't face the street.

"We could apply a tourniquet above your elbow, for the hand," he told Burrage, "but I'm afraid we'll have to cauterize that shoulder wound. I don't have any anesthetic, but the good news is, we've got a stove and lots of cutlery."

He stood before the gas range, turned on the left-front burner, and listened to the blue flame hiss, shot through with darting streaks of orange. There was a wooden rack of knives between the stove top and the kitchen sink. He chose a chef's knife with a blade some thirteen inches long, at least two inches wide across the base. Half turning toward the skinhead stretched out on the floor, he showed Burrage the knife.

"It's not ideal, I grant you," Bolan said. "I'd prefer a soldering iron or a wood-burning set, but beggars can't be choosers. Let's make do with what we have, okay?"

That said, he turned back toward the stove and placed the long knife's handle on the silent right-front burner, so the first few inches of its blade were swaddled in the left-hand burner's steady flame. While he was waiting for the tempered steel to glow bright cherry-red, he rummaged through the kitchen drawers until he found a modest stash of towels and dishrags. Bolan took one of the dishrags, rolled it up into a ball and draped a towel across his shoulder as he walked back to his captive, crouching beside the Nazi.

"Open wide," he said.

Burrage defied him with clenched teeth until Bolan found a pressure point on his wounded hand and forced a gasp, quickly stifled with the dishrag. The soldier looped the towel around his prisoner's head, to hold the gag in place, and tied it off in back.

"Don't touch that, now," he warned. "Remember, you've got one thumb left. You'll have a chance to make all kinds of noise, as soon as I get through saving your worthless life."

The knife was turning pink, but Bolan left it on the fire awhile, painfully conscious of the fact that every moment wasted meant more jeopardy for Marilyn Crouder—unless, of course, she was already dead. He didn't think that was the case, though. Why would her assassins move the body if they meant to stay behind and mop up any visitors who came to call?

Bolan believed she was alive, which meant that she was marked for an interrogation or for some worse punishment than simple execution—probably for both. As long as she was breathing, he had a chance to rescue her, but first he had to find out where she had been taken by her kidnappers.

And there was only one man left alive for him to ask.

"Okay," he said at last, using a pot holder for insulation as he picked the glowing knife up off the stove, "let's stop those bleeders, shall we?"

Nazi Lester Burrage passed out fairly rapidly, a combination of his shock, the searing pain and Bolan kneeling on his chest, pinning his body to the floor. He cauterized the shoulder first, the dribbling stub of the man's thumb almost an afterthought. When he was done, he dropped the chef's knife in the sink, turning his full attention to the sight of an electric carving knife.

It was a cordless model, slotted into a recharger, which was plugged into the wall beside a toaster oven, on the far side of the sink. He picked it up and thumbed the button onto High, rewarded with a buzz and blur of motion.

Perfect.

Although he had exterminated literally thousands

of opponents, Bolan took no pleasure from inflicting pain. He didn't relish torture and had shied away from field interrogations on his Asian tours of duty, interrupting more than one rough session when he judged that the inquisitors were starting to enjoy themselves too much. It would have been a fatal error to believe that he was soft, though, that he would allow his sympathy for wounded enemies to leave a comrade in harm's way.

He found a glass, filled it with water from the tap and dumped it into Burrage's face. The Nazi came to slowly, twitching back to consciousness by stages, whimpering through his makeshift gag as the new pain kicked in from his cauterized wounds.

"Looks like you'll live," Bolan said, "if you're smart enough to tell me what I want to know."

"Mmfpl fugh!" the gagged man said.

"Hold on a second," Bolan said, and knelt beside him, revving the electric knife a time or two, while Burrage watched the whirring blade, wide-eyed. "Don't move, now."

It would have been a simple matter to untie the towel, but Bolan had a point to make. He slipped the cool blade of the carving knife between the fabric and his captive's cheek. When Bolan triggered it, the knife sheared through the towel in seconds flat, chafing the man's skin in the process.

"There, that's better," Bolan said as he removed the dishrag from his captive's mouth. "Now, shall we have that little chat?"

"I don't know anything," the Nazi told him stubbornly.

"In broad terms, I suspect that's very nearly true,"

the Executioner replied. "But you're in luck tonight, Les. All I need are some specific details of the operation that's already blown up in your face."

"Dream on."

"Wrong answer, Lester. This isn't my dream, but it could very well turn out to be your worst nightmare." He revved the carving knife again and held it close enough to Burrage's face that condensation from the Nazi's breath formed briefly on the dancing blade.

"Where did your people take the woman?" he asked.

"Kill me, and you'll never fucking find her," Burrage said, but he couldn't conceal the tremor in his voice.

"It makes no difference if you won't talk anyway," Bolan reminded him, "but I don't plan on killing you. Not for a good, long while. You're pretty husky, Lester. I suspect you could afford to lose a few pounds, here and there. Try shooting for that lean, mean, Aryan ideal. What do you say?"

Silence, but Bolan's prisoner was on the verge of hyperventilating, stoking up his courage, maybe hoping he could make himself black out before the carving knife met flesh.

"So, where's the woman?" Bolan asked.

"Prob'ly laying in a ditch, somewhere."

"Okay, it's your call, Les. How's this—you won't be shooting anybody after this, so you won't need that trigger finger. If you still feel like the strong and silent type, we'll go from there, and see what happens to your dream of playing the accordion at Nazi talent shows."

"You won't do this," the skinhead challenged him without conviction.

"No? I've killed three of your scumbag friends tonight, in case it slipped that powerhouse you call a mind. What's one more, fast or slow?"

No answer.

Bolan pinned the Nazi's left arm with his knee and grabbed the other blood-flecked wrist, above the wounded hand. He leaned across the supine prisoner and switched on the electric carving knife.

"This little piggy went to market, Lester. Say goodbye."

The blade had barely grazed his index finger, when the skinhead cried out, "No! Jesus! I'll tell you what you want to know, all right?"

"LONG TIME no see," Sean Fletcher said, circling the room until he came within her field of vision. "Why, it seems like hours, Mary. Shall I call you Mary?"

Marilyn Crouder had already decided that her best bet was to simply keep her mouth shut for as long as possible, instead of counterpunching verbally and playing smart-ass games that could betray her. She was already as good as dead; the only question now was whether she could reach that final exit ramp, somehow, before they broke her down and made her talk.

"Mary it is, then," Fletcher said, as if she had replied in the affirmative. "You're quite a woman, Mary, as we've seen. And in more ways than one."

Reminded of her nudity, the rigid wooden straight-backed chair to which she had been bound with duct tape, arms behind her, so her back was arched, torso presented to her captor's eyes, she fought against the feeling of embarrassment Fletcher was trying to achieve. She had been schooled in Basic Torture 101 before she took the undercover gig and knew the basic drill. With women, the interrogators normally compelled them to undress themselves, as Fletcher's bully boys had done to her, albeit with the help of cattle prods. Male victims, on the other hand, were usually stripped by force. It went back to the roots of so-called civilized psychology: forcing a woman to undress made her complicit in her own defilement, adding guilt to sheer embarrassment before the pain began; a man, meanwhile, got his first taste of helplessness when he was stripped by force, emasculated in effect, before the blades and the electrodes were applied.

"I'll give you this," Fletcher said. "You're no coward. I assumed that once you slipped away from us at Freedom Home, you'd run back to whoever hired you in the first place and report. No way would any brass with basic common sense return you to the firing line. So, when you showed up in L.A., you took me by surprise. Congratulations. That's no easy thing to do."

Her mind was spewing out sarcastic comments, force of habit dying hard, but Crouder refused to give them voice. The longer Fletcher paced and talked without that first, excruciating contact that was bound to come, the more time she would have to fortify herself against the pain.

She had already given up on any notion of escape. Naked, alone, bound hand and foot, surrounded by her enemies at some unknown location, in the middle of the night—her situation was as close to hopeless as it could be, short of death. And that was coming, too, of course. The only question in her mind was whether death would come in time to spare her from the worst of what Sean Fletcher and his playmates could devise to make her squeal.

Her silence might play into that, she had decided. If she kept it up, letting her captors' anger and frustration mount, and then unleashed one of her verbal barbs at the precisely perfect moment, maybe one of them would snap and kill her in a fit of rage, before the others could restrain him. It would be more difficult if Fletcher did the job alone, of course, but he was still a man, with all—or most—of the pathetic mortal weaknesses that term implied.

"The more I think about L.A., Mary," Fletcher was saying, "honestly, the more confused I am. I mean, you're obviously working for the government. Another bitch from ZOG who needs a major attitude adjustment, right? What I can't figure, though, is how your buddies operate. No uniforms, no warrants, no arrests, no TV vans. Two days, two hits, and you're the only member of the group we've even seen. So, what I have to ask myself, and what I'm asking you, is simply this—who do you work for, Mary?"

This, she knew, would set the tone for everything that followed. When she didn't answer him, Fletcher's reaction would determine how the rest of the interrogation would proceed. If he got angry and blew his top, the odds were good that he would slap, punch, kick her, maybe summon others to participate, and she would have a halfway decent chance of being knocked unconscious, maybe even comatose, before they got around to trying anything sophisticated. If he kept his cool, though, Crouder imagined that she could look forward to a grim, protracted tour of hell.

"The silent treatment," Fletcher said, frowning as he considered the appropriate response. Crouder saw a hint of angry color rising in his face, behind the year-round tan. "Have you considered that? The possibilities, I mean? Are you completely sure that's how you want to play this hand?"

Once again, a rush of snappy retorts came to mind. She could have done a stand-up show, right then and there, if only she could stand. Instead, she held eye contact with the man who would eventually give the order for her death, refusing to avert her eyes in fear.

It helped a little, Crouder discovered, if she thought of Belasko. Anyway, it helped at first, until she started wondering what had become of him. Even hog-tied, blindfolded, semiconscious, she was still aware that her abductors had left men to watch the house when she was carried off. They had been watching when Belasko dropped her off, and they would try to bag him when he came to pick her up.

Good luck, she thought, and almost smiled before reality kicked in.

She had no reason to believe that Belasko would let himself be captured. Something told her that would never happen, not unless he suffered some freak accident that left him helpless. No, the Temple goons would have to kill him, if he didn't kill them first, and that was where she lost her smile. Because despite his martial skills, the stunts that body could perform, Belasko was a man of flesh and blood, like any other. He could still be shot, stabbed, strangled—

killed, in short, like anybody else. It only took one
shot, correctly placed by skill, coincidence or sheer
dumb luck. A couple hundred grains of lead or cop-
per, and the job was done.

The thought of Belasko lying dead, blood spattered,
produced a sudden rush of hopelessness and fury, all
mixed together, that she almost launched into a tirade,
telling Fletcher what she thought of him. But what
would be the point? He didn't give a damn how anyone in civilized society regarded him, his soldiers or
the movement that they served. He was a freaking
lunatic, sadly able to perform the tasks for which he
had been trained with skill, efficiency and deadly
force.

"Okay, then," Fletcher said. "I hoped we might
be able to resolve this thing without a lot of mess.
My fault for thinking anyone who serves the Beast
could have a shred of common sense or decency."

She felt another outburst of sarcastic laughter coming on, and swallowed it before it could escape.

"I'd love to drag this out," he said when she made
no reply. "You and your pals have cost me eighteen
men. You have a lot to answer for. Unfortunately, as
you know, I have a schedule to keep, so I can't in-
dulge myself the way I'd like to. Still…"

She held his gaze and waited for the other shoe to
drop.

"After that business in L.A., at the Jewseum, it's
obvious that you've told someone of our plans."

She wished that was true, hating herself for taking
pleasure from Belasko first and holding back information on the next intended strike. He knew the general location, but she had been waiting to reveal the

rest of it, the crucial details, when he picked her up at home in Riverside.

"Nothing to say, Mary?" His tone was almost teasing now, with a malicious edge to it. "All right, then. Have it your way. Thomas? William?"

Crouder didn't recognize the two young men who answered Fletcher's call. One of them pushed a cart on rollers, one wheel wobbling, spinning on its axis as it squeaked its way around her chair and into view. She glanced at the array of instruments that had been spread out on the stainless-steel cart, then quickly looked away.

"It's not a pretty sight, is it?" Fletcher asked. "Did you ever see *Braveheart*, by any chance? Oh, well, you missed your chance. The disembowelment sequence was a showstopper."

Despite her nudity, the claustrophobic room was warm, verging on muggy. Still, Crouder was conscious of the goose bumps rising on her skin, silently cursing the uncontrollable expression of her fear.

"The problem with that kind of thing," Fletcher continued, "isn't just the mess, of course. It's the diminishing returns. I mean, for executions, fine. But for interrogation? Honestly, how is a subject going to confess his sins after you've ripped his lungs out? Still, there's something to be said for cutting tools. Don't you agree? Or electricity, selectively applied?"

Fletcher had palmed a stun gun from the cart and held it up appraisingly. When he depressed the trigger, minibolts of lighting crackled back and forth between the short electrodes. Crouder could smell a whiff of ozone in the air.

"Last chance to tell me what you know and buy yourself an easy out," he said.

Despite a sudden tremor in her muscles, Crouder still found the strength to shake her head in an emphatic negative.

"Okay. You want to know the truth? I was afraid you'd make it easy on yourself and spoil the fun." He passed the stun gun to the taller of his flunkies. "Here you go. Let's get to work."

IT WAS A SHAME to torch the house, but Bolan had no time to move the bodies, and he knew the place had not been Crouder's in any way that mattered. More than likely, if he knew the Feds, there would be fire insurance on the house, and someone at the ATF would pull all necessary strings to expedite the claim. In any case, it was the only way Bolan could think of to eradicate all evidentiary links between the missing woman and the four dead men he left behind.

There was no question of releasing Lester Burrage back into the wild, where he would certainly alert his fellow brownshirts to the latest threat as soon as he could reach a telephone. Aside from tipping Bolan's hand, that call would mean swift death for Crouder— assuming she wasn't already dead, of course.

Bolan had put a lid on that scenario as he constructed four incendiary bombs from household chemicals he found beneath the kitchen and the bathroom sinks. No timer was required; he simply had to let the compound simmer for a while—say, time enough for him to drive a mile or so before the mix went hot. It would be very hot indeed, within a few short moments after that, and by the time firefighters reached the scene, they would have four roasts and a gutted structure on their hands.

Burrage had talked his head off in the final moments of his life, disgorging scraps of information Bolan didn't want or need along with what he asked for, and the sum of it was filed away, cross-referenced in Bolan's mental filing cabinet. He had a fair idea of what Crouder would have told him, if she'd had the chance, about the Nordic Temple's second target for a "random" act of terrorism. He would have to see what he could do about that, too—alert Brognola and the team at Stony Man, if nothing else—but first he meant to see if it was possible to help the lady Fed.

He might already be too late, of course. He knew that the woman was tough, but taking down your adversaries in a firefight was one thing; standing up to torture, whether physical or psychological, was an entirely different game. The Special Forces and assorted other military units taught specific courses on resisting enemy interrogation, recognizing as they did that marksmanship and setting records on an obstacle course had nothing whatsoever to do with keeping your wits about you under torture.

Burrage hadn't known where the woman was being held. The last he'd seen of her, another Nazi named Zack Rogers had been driving off, the woman folded into his Camaro's trunk, while Burrage and the rest of the hit team remained behind to wait for Bolan to return. It steamed Bolan to think that they had been inside the house already, watching him, when he dropped Crouder out front. If he had gone inside with her, refused to be put off...

Stop that!

There was no profit to be made from playing would've-could've-should've. That part of the game was over, done with, gone. What Bolan had to do was to take advantage of the information that he *did* possess, use it to hurt the men who had abducted Crouder. Use it to kill them if he wasn't able to retrieve her, more or less intact.

Or even if he did.

However it went down from this point onward, one thing was already crystal clear in Bolan's mind. The Temple of the Nordic Covenant would have to go, regardless of the risk or what it cost him to achieve that goal. He had seen enough of them already to decide that they were dangerous beyond the built-in limitations of your average neo-Nazi clique, and what he'd learned from Lester Burrage only made things that much worse.

But Burrage had supplied him with a phone number, on top of the bad news, and if he caught a break, the number just might be enough—if not to rescue Crouder, at least to place him within striking distance of his enemies.

The Executioner would carry it from there.

The number wasn't local, but it wasn't out of state. A quick check with the operator, on his cellular, told Bolan that the area code matched Twentynine Palms, his road atlas locating the town of some twelve thousand people in south-central San Bernardino County, in the arid sprawl of the Mojave Desert. Bolan had no reason to believe that it was anything beyond a contact number, probably a cutout, but he started driving east from Riverside, closing the sixty-mile gap just in case.

Negotiation would be difficult, since Bolan had nothing to trade, but he had faced those odds before and walked away victorious. It was a relatively simple matter of applying pressure until something snapped among his enemies. The tricky parts were avoiding sudden death himself and pushing his adversaries to the brink without further endangering the prisoner.

In fact, though, Bolan knew that Crouder was already as good as dead if she remained in hostile hands. Once they had milked her dry of information, there was still the matter of her ''treason'' to be dealt with, and he understood that there could only be one sentence for betrayal of the Temple's secrets to outsiders. Caught up in their war against the Jews and ZOG, soldiers who served the man they knew as Gerhard Steuben were prepared to kill—or die—in the pursuit of their agenda.

Fine.

Bolan was hoping he could help them with the dying part.

But he would have to find them first.

A call was one thing, but he needed something more to capture their attention and convince them that he wasn't playing games. Taking out the hit team had been a start, but he couldn't trade corpses for a living prisoner. He needed something more to hold above the heads of Crouder's abductors, poised to strike them like the sword of God.

When it came to him, the Executioner couldn't help smiling. Crouder had spoken briefly of her first contact with members of the Nordic Temple, at an outpost not far from his present location. It would mean a short detour, a brief delay before he dialed the number he had memorized, but if it worked, it would pay off.

He didn't want to think about what Crouder might suffer during that lost time, and so he put it out of mind. Better to concentrate on his approach and get it right than be distracted in the crunch and wind up losing everything.

Unlike some other neo-Nazi sects, which staked out a specific part of the United States and tried to claim it for themselves, the Temple of the Nordic Covenant taught new disciples that they would inherit nothing less than Planet Earth itself. Therefore, the Temple's scope of operation wasn't limited to a particular locale. It had field offices around the country, scattered far and wide—around the world, in fact, as he had lately learned from Brognola and Crouder. As luck would have it, there was one nearby, in Hemet.

It was almost on his way.

He didn't know if anybody occupied the office after business hours, and he frankly didn't care. What Bolan needed, at the moment, was a little extra something to convince the Temple's kidnap team that he meant business, that he had the wherewithal to track them down and wipe them out if they did anything to anger him. A few more bodies couldn't hurt, but he would settle for an empty building if it was the best that he could do.

On top of the attacks in Washington, Los Angeles and Riverside, he thought his enemies would get the message. As to how they might respond, well, that was anybody's guess. Traditionally, Nazis tended toward retaliation, which was fine, as long as it gave Bolan any kind of fighting chance. A meet was all he needed, on the pretext of releasing Crouder. It didn't matter if his adversaries lied and set a trap, in fact, he would be counting on it.

Just as long as the woman was still alive.

He knew that her abduction wasn't his responsibility, his fault, but that did nothing to decrease his sense that he had to act to put it right.

And if he was too late for that, God help them all.

He took the Hemet turnoff, leaving Highway 60, southbound, planning as he drove. Bolan had all the gear he would require to do the job. He simply had to find his target, stay alert for any sign of lawmen on the prowl, as well as Nazis dozing on the premises.

Once it was clear, the only thing he had to do was strike a match.

CHAPTER ELEVEN

Sean Fletcher sipped his coffee, grimaced as it burned his tongue and set the steaming mug aside. Goddammit! Now whatever food he ate would taste like tinfoil for the next few days. The stinging of his blistered tongue combined with a dull ache behind his eyes, reminding Fletcher that his workday wasn't over yet. In fact, the way it looked, he would be lucky if he got to bed at all.

The bitch was stalling them, resisting the best efforts of his crack inquisitors. So far, instead of breaking down and spilling everything she knew, the only sounds that she had made were gasps and moans, with one particularly satisfying scream when Thomas—

"Sir?"

Fletcher was snapped out of his reverie, his headache coming back full force and echoing the pulse that kept time in his ears. He swiveled toward the voice and recognized the strapping young skinhead who filled the doorway, Larry Dixon, the long sleeves of his brown shirt covering the tattoos that festooned both arms.

"What is it?"

"Sir, you have a phone call."

"Who?"

"He didn't give a name, sir, but he said you've been expecting him."

That put a frown on Fletcher's face. He was expecting no one.

"How'd he get this number?" Fletcher asked, more to himself than to the young man in the doorway.

"It's the relay, sir. They patched him through."

"Oh, did they now?" Fletcher could feel the short hairs bristling on his nape. If this was who he thought it might be, then his night may not have been a total waste, despite the unexpected courage of their prisoner.

"You want me to, I'll blow him off, sir."

"No." Fletcher was on his feet and moving toward the doorway now. "I'll take it, Larry."

"Yes, sir. If you need me—"

"I know where to find you. Run along, now."

One room over, Fletcher found the telephone, picked up the receiver and listened to the hum of silence on the line.

"Who's this?" he asked without preliminaries.

"I'm the one you're looking for," a graveyard voice replied. "We missed each other in L.A. this afternoon. One of the boys you sent to pick me up in Riverside gave me your contact number."

"Ah."

"They won't be coming back, those four."

Fletcher knew better than to talk about such things with total strangers on a line that couldn't be secured. He let the comment pass, tried to blank out the increased tempo of the throbbing in his head.

"What do you want?" he asked.

The stranger answered with a question of his own. "You have a television where you are? Maybe a radio?"

"Don't tell me I'm about to win a prize?"

"Could be, if you've got fire insurance on your headquarters in Hemet."

Fletcher stiffened, closed his eyes against the thumping pain inside his skull. "I'm sure I don't know what you mean," he lied.

"Well, hey," the stranger said, "there could have been a mixup, I suppose. The sign outside of number 27, Third Street, advertised the Temple of the Nordic Covenant, but maybe the new tenants just forgot to take it down. You think?"

"I don't—"

"The two guys who were sleeping over didn't have a lot to say," the stranger told him. "They'll be saying even less from here on out."

"It sounds to me like you're confessing to a string of felonies," Fletcher replied.

"I would have called it a rehearsal for the main event," the caller said.

"Meaning?"

"One felon to another? You've got something that I want. You give it back to me, alive and functional, you just might buy yourself a little time."

"Assuming I knew what you meant, that wouldn't be much of a deal."

"It's all there is. Take it or leave it."

"And, again, since I have no idea what you're referring to—"

"How do you think Herr Steuben will react when

he finds out you had a chance to finish this and didn't grab it? I don't know the one-eyed bastard personally, but I hear his sense of humor's not his strong suit."

Fletcher's frown was edging into scowl potential. "It might be worth discussing this at greater length," he said, "if only to resolve your personal confusion."

Laughter on the other end, infuriating, confident. "Whatever. Just make sure you bring that item that was taken from me by mistake. And if it's broken, be prepared to take the consequences."

"I believe you'll find I always take the consequences for my actions," Fletcher said.

"That's good to know. I've had a bellyful of spineless Nazi weasels who can't pull their weight."

"You realize, of course, that if this is some kind of an elaborate entrapment scheme, it won't stand up in court?"

"I've never had much use for lawyers. Do we meet, or shall I send you a memento from the next office you used to have?"

Fletcher felt cornered, and the feeling rankled him, but he could see no way around it now. "A meeting, by all means," he said. "Shall I select the time and place?"

"Give it a shot. If I don't like it, we can go for best three out of five."

"How do you feel about the desert?"

"Depends on whether I remember sunblock."

"I was thinking of a meeting after dark."

"You have that kind of time to waste?" the caller asked.

A loud alarm bell sounded in the back of Fletcher's mind. "Why not?" he said. "Is there a rush?"

"Not on my end," the stranger said, allowing Fletcher to relax a bit. "It's just that if I think you're playing me, or if the extra time adds any damage whatsoever to the merchandise, I might do something you'll regret."

"I don't respond well to threats," Fletcher told him.

"Neither did your guys in Hemet. They were downright awkward, if you want to know the truth."

"I'm not."

"That's good. I'm hoping you're not stupid, either."

"No one's ever called me that." Not twice, he added silently.

"I guess we'll find out at the meet. Let's have the time and place."

"You know where Barstow is?"

"I've been there."

"Good. They've got a two-lane road that runs northeast of town, out toward the Tiefort Mountains and Fort Irwin Military Reservation. Once you hit the Army land, it's sealed off tight, but four, five miles before you get that far, there's another road that takes off to the east. You won't find it on many maps, but there's a sign, or used to be. Coyote Lake. I'll meet you there, if that's all right."

"Sounds fair enough."

He checked his watch. "Shall we say this same time tomorrow night?"

"Let's round it off and call it midnight."

"Fine. I'll see you then."

"Remember what I said about the merchandise,"

the caller said. "I'm keeping score. From this point on, whatever happens to it, happens to you."

The line went dead before he could respond, and Fletcher called upon a reservoir of will to let him cradle the receiver gently, instead of slamming it down with destructive force. The room was empty when he turned, door closed, as he had known it would be. None of his subordinates would dare disturb him when he wanted privacy.

"Larry?" When there was no immediate response, Fletcher stepped out into the hall and raised his voice. "Larry!"

"Yes, sir!"

The skinhead had been eating something, heavy on the garlic. He was swallowing a last bite as he came around the corner, stopping short and snapping to attention six or seven feet in front of Fletcher.

"Sir!" The ripe aroma wafting outward on his breath.

"How many men can we collect within the next six to eight hours?"

"Local men, sir?"

"*Any* men who know their way around a weapon and who aren't afraid of wet work."

Dixon thought about it for a moment. "Well, sir, with jets and all, you could have everybody in the States here by this afternoon. What's that, officially— three thousand? Maybe four?"

"It's not a damned parade," Fletcher replied. "Here's what I want from you. By noon tomorrow, I want thirty handpicked men—no, make it forty— armed and ready at the Hinkley farm."

"Ready for what, sir?"

"They'll be going up against the men who raided Freedom Home and fucked up our event this afternoon at the Jewseum. It's payback time."

"Yes, sir!"

"Get on the phone now. Use the locals if you can, but fly in anyone you think we absolutely need."

"I'm on it, sir." And he was gone, not even waiting for his quick stiff-armed salute to be returned.

Fletcher was sure his unknown enemy would try some underhanded trick, didn't suppose for one split second that the man would come alone. In fact, Fletcher was counting on duplicity, to help him stage a set-piece battle that would end this nameless threat once and for all.

And if the guy *was* dumb and arrogant enough to come alone, why, then, so much the better. With a force of forty men on hand, he could most likely be corralled, detained, interrogated. By the time Fletcher was finished with him, he would know all there was to know about Mary Krause, her associates and any threat remaining to the Temple of the Nordic Covenant.

Not that a threat would stop him from proceeding with the Führer's master plan.

It only made the game more dangerous, more interesting.

THE PAIN WOULD START to fade a bit, and then she felt an itch somewhere, a need to shift positions in the straight-backed chair, within the limits of her bonds. It all came rushing back, the raw sensations jumbled with her recent memories of threats and suffering, unanswered questions, mocking laughter.

Hurt, exhausted, naked underneath the rough wool blanket loosely draped around her shoulders, Crouder was fairly certain that she hadn't told them anything. She couldn't swear to it, of course. Between the stunning jolts of electricity, the pain of burns and alligator clamps, her mind had drifted toward the end. She thought she might have spoken, something more coherent than a squeal, but whether it had really happened—whether she was merely cursing Fletcher, or revealing something he could use—she couldn't say.

"You've got a friend."

The sound of Fletcher's voice, so close behind her, made her jerk and gasp, the blanket slipping from one shoulder. Crouder cursed the distraction that had kept her mind from registering sounds the bastard made when he came in.

"So, did you ever hear that song?" he asked her, circling around the chair to stand in front of her, frankly examining the portion of her body that the slipping blanket had revealed. "*You've Got a Friend,* I mean. I think it was recorded by Carole King, but then again, I could be wrong."

She didn't bother with the vain attempt to stare him down this time. Whatever Fletcher wanted, he would take. She was beyond withholding anything from him, except her voice.

"In any case," he said, "it seems that you *do* have a friend."

Crouder didn't need to feign confusion. She had no idea what Fletcher meant, and at the moment, she could hardly have cared less. Still, he appeared intent on filling in the blanks, and there was nothing she could do to shut him up.

"I just received a call from one of your associates," he said. "Which is a bit surprising in itself, you understand, considering the pains I've taken to prevent this number falling into the wrong hands."

Tough shit, she thought, and still refused to speak. But she was wondering what he meant by one of her "associates?" It seemed impossible that ATF—

And then it hit her.

Mike Belasko!

"You'll be delighted, I suppose, to learn that those who stayed behind to meet your friend in Riverside have gone to their reward. It seems that one of them lived long enough to pass on my private number without permission. It's distressing that I'll never have a chance to punish him for that myself, but I suppose he's learned his lesson."

Crouder could feel a cautious smile begin to twitch around the corners of her mouth, but she suppressed it. Anything that Fletcher wanted, anything he got from her, he had to take by force.

"Apparently, Sir Galahad is angry that we didn't ask permission first, before inviting you to come and play with your old friends. He wants you back—if not undamaged, then at least alive. He doesn't seem to take 'no' for an answer."

She had a mental image of Belasko, in a swirl of battle smoke, blue-eyed and dangerous. She wondered what he was prepared to do, what he had done already, in his effort to secure her freedom.

"You must have made quite an impression on this fellow," Fletcher said. He moved to stand beside her, on the right, and drew the blanket slowly from her shoulders, casting it aside, somewhere behind her. "I can see how that would happen, too. Don't get me wrong. In other circumstances, maybe, if you weren't a vile, Jew-loving traitor to your race—''

"Fuck you."

"She speaks!" Fletcher, apparently delighted, made her regret the breach of silence instantly. "And I appreciate the offer, honestly…but I'm afraid there won't be time right now. You see, I need to make arrangements for a party."

Lowering her eyes to focus on the concrete floor, she tried ignoring him again. It didn't work.

"You don't have much to wear for the festivities, I grant you, but it won't make any difference, since you're not the guest of honor this time. You're the bait. Besides, I never saw a party yet that suffered from a naked woman showing up."

She nearly missed the last part, focused as she was on the remark that had preceded it. *The bait.* There could be no misunderstanding Fletcher on that score. She was the lure to draw Belasko in and set him up for Fletcher's men to make the kill. It made no difference now that she hadn't betrayed him under torture. Just by living, breathing, she would serve her enemies.

A thought of suicide flashed through her mind, dismissed at once because she had no means at hand, and it would make no difference now, in any case. Belasko wouldn't know that she was dead, and he would walk into the trap, regardless. For her death to save him, Crouder would have to rewrite history, go back in time and force the goons to kill her when she found them in her house. That way, Belasko could have scratched her off his short list of distractions and moved on.

Moved on to what? She hadn't given him the details of the next strike yet. The city, yes, but nothing else. Goddammit! Her own stupid selfishness would ruin everything.

She closed her eyes to hide the scalding tears of shame, but Fletcher seemed to read her mind, at least in part. "Feel guilty, do we, love?" he taunted her. "That's understandable, of course. I mean, the damsel-in-distress routine, it almost never fails. Any Aryan would shrug it off, but these corrupt half-breeds, they smell a bitch in heat and can't resist."

She choked a sob back down and swallowed hard to keep it there. His words, the knowledge of Belasko's pending fate, hurt worse than anything that Fletcher's goons had done to her before.

Fletcher came back to stand in front of her, knees almost touching hers, reached down to grip a handful of her hair and drag her head back, forcing her to meet his gaze.

He smiled and said, "You know, on second thought, I do believe we might have time, at that."

THE MEET WOULD BE a trap, of course. There was no doubt of that in Bolan's mind. He could have hemmed and hawed about the time and place, but it wouldn't have made a difference in the end. His adversaries would be waiting for him, hungry for a kill, but they would also be uncertain as to how many opponents they would face, whom they were dealing with, what kind of hardware and resources were available to unknown enemies.

He would assume that they had broken Crouder by now, that she had told them everything she knew. It was a premature assumption, but he made a point of always being ready to confront worst-case scenarios. That way, the Executioner was seldom disappointed, and the rare occasions when he was were always pleasantly surprising.

He knew from Hal Brognola's files, and from what Crouder had told him, that the soldier he had spoken to—Sean Fletcher—was the Nordic Temple's top security officer and all-around enforcer, a one-time U.S. Navy SEAL, who had apparently been discharged for excessive violence—specifically, the shooting of civilians on a covert operation into Southeast Asia some years back. The evidence hadn't been clear enough to nail him on a murder charge, but Fletcher's ranting on the witness stand about some "Yellow Peril," coupled with results from psychological examinations ordered by the prosecution, was enough to bust him out of uniform.

Within six months of discharge, he had thrown his lot in with the Temple of the Nordic Covenant and had begun the swift rise through the ranks that placed him at the would-be Führer's side within another year. Details were vague on what he had to do to rise so far, so fast, but Crouder had remarked that he "knew where the bodies were buried," having planted most of them himself.

All right, then. Bolan knew that he was up against a well-trained and proficient killer, schooled in strategy, guerrilla warfare, black ops—all the things, in short, that Bolan had been taught to handle when he wore a green beret and drew a monthly paycheck from the Pentagon. If Fletcher had one glaring flaw, it was his pathological devotion to the Nordic Temple's racist nonsense and the mystic voodoo crap that went along with that.

And maybe, just a bit of egocentric overconfidence.

Bolan was guessing on that score, of course, but he was quite adept at reading voices even when he couldn't see the faces that they issued from. Sean Fletcher struck him as a man who liked to be in charge—so much so that he sometimes thought he was in charge, when circumstantial evidence might point the other way.

In this case, Fletcher was prepared to lay a trap for Bolan *and* whoever might accompany him to their midnight meeting. Fletcher had no way of knowing whether he would face one man or several dozen, but he had to have figured out from the negotiation process and the nature of the previous attacks that he wasn't facing immediate arrest by any normal agency.

The choice of killing grounds was problematic. Bolan didn't need a crystal ball to know that Fletcher would have people on the ground, concealed, well in advance of midnight's meeting. Based upon the strength of that defense, and its deployment, Bolan's rescue effort might range from severely difficult to physically impossible—unless he found himself an edge.

That meant arriving well before the other team, positioning himself where he could do the utmost damage with a minimum of risk. It also meant that he would be in place when Fletcher's troops arrived and started digging in, the built-in risk that they would stumble over Bolan in the process and precipitate a

firefight on the spot, thereby destroying any chance
he had of helping Crouder. Still, short of calling in
an air strike—which would risk the woman's life
along with those of her abductors—there was no alternative.

Before he made the drive out to Coyote Lake, Bolan had some last-minute specialty shopping to do.
He didn't fancy waiting for the local shops to open
in the morning, doing all the grunt work underneath
a broiling desert sun, uncertain as to when his enemies might put in an appearance—and some of the
gear he needed wasn't legally available to the civilian
trade in any case.

He called Brognola, caught the big Fed well before
he hit the sack and rattled off a list of what he needed
to achieve a telling measure of surprise. Brognola
read it back to him and promised that the items would
be waiting for him at Fort Irwin, north of Barstow,
once he had confirmed his bona fides with a compli-
cated password.

Satisfied that he wouldn't fall short through any
lack of hardware, Bolan drove through late-night
darkness, sorting out the puzzle pieces of his plan as
it took shape. Coyote Lake was on the map, although
the road accessing it wasn't. Fletcher hadn't specified
a meeting place, beyond the lake itself, but from the
map, Bolan calculated that the dry lake bed was some
two miles in length, perhaps a mile across the widest
point. It would be flat, of course, the kind of arid
ground that made dry lakes the perfect testing ground
for race cars, ideal landing strips for pilots hauling
contraband. The trick would be to find a point somewhere on the perimeter where he could hide himself

and scan the lake without being immediately sighted by his enemies.

The rest would be a mixture of technology, logistics and a healthy dash of luck. He could control the first two elements to some extent; as for the third, he'd simply have to keep his fingers crossed.

There was a chance, he knew, that Fletcher wouldn't show up for the meet himself, or that he might leave Crouder behind. For all Bolan knew, the woman could be dead, but given Fletcher's aversion to incriminating himself on an open line, there had been no way to elicit proof that she was still alive. He had to try, regardless, and if Crouder didn't show up for the Coyote Lake meeting—or if the Nazis brought a corpse—then he would try to capture someone from the hit team and squeeze his hostage for the information he required to bust their next move, and the next.

One prisoner would be enough. If Crouder was dead or absent from the meet, the rest of Fletcher's soldiers could prepare to kiss their Aryan asses goodbye.

And if he didn't make it out himself, what then? He had already told Brognola what he knew—specifically, that Gary Stevens's brownshirt goons planned "something big" for three days in the future, with the unknown target situated somewhere in Chicago. If he couldn't rescue Crouder, if Bolan lost it at Coyote Lake, it would be up to Brognola and Stony Man to somehow figure out the target, move in time to head off a catastrophe and clamp a lid on Gary Stevens so that he could do no more pernicious damage to society.

Bolan wasn't a fatalist, but he had seen enough of combat firsthand to know that anything could happen, any time. He had prepared himself, long years ago, for the near certainty that he wouldn't die of old age, in bed, surrounded by old friends and family.

And that was fine.

He simply didn't want his final hours on earth—be they this night, next month or twenty years from now—to be a wasted effort, capped by failure.

He would play this hand the way he always played them, betting high and living large.

ZACK ROGERS HAD expected greater difficulty in deployment of his soldiers on the dry flats that were once Coyote Lake. They had to hide somewhere, and no aboveground shelter could be camouflaged to match the landscape, meaning that his troops would have to dig. The bad news was, Coyote Lake had gone a year or more without a drop of rain, baked by the sun to a consistency approximating kiln-fired clay, with just enough loose dirt on top to raise a choking dust storm when the wind blew—which, apparently, was damned near all the time.

Rogers had taken one look at the place and known his men would never get their pits and trenches dug on time if they were left to do the job with picks and shovels. Even if they made the schedule, most of them would be laid up with sunstroke when he needed them the most. Hell, some of them might die before they even finished digging in.

The answer, when he found it, was simplicity itself. A member of the California Christian Knights—a Klan-type group with close ties to the Nordic Temple—lived in nearby Yermo, where they made a living digging ditches, wells, cesspools, whatever. Ninety minutes after Rogers called him, he was at Coyote Lake and revving up his backhoe, following Zack's lead on where to dig the gun pits for the best, most comprehensive field of fire.

The rest came down to camouflage and waiting. Tarps were staked out to conceal the pits, disguised with dirt, small stones, dry spiky brush and tumbleweeds. Beneath that cover, thirty soldiers baked in desert heat that entered triple digits well before the noon hour. Each man went under with a gallon jug of water and a second, empty jug for personal emergencies, reminded not to get the two mixed up while waiting in the dark. It was a trial, but they were handpicked volunteers, and they would simply have to tough it out.

The other ten, including Rogers, would be sitting out the afternoon and half the night at a motel in Barstow, waiting for the time when they were scheduled to take the woman out and see who came to fetch her. Rogers had suggested that they ice the traitor, take a female member of the Temple in her place, made up as a long-distance lookalike, but Fletcher had rejected the idea. Something about the "symmetry of justice," whatever that was supposed to mean. In any case, Rogers had been trained to follow orders, even when he didn't understand them fully, when he thought his own take on the situation might be better than the plan devised by his superiors.

Zack Rogers did as he was told.

Six hours now, and it was cooling off a bit outside, though you could still fry eggs and bacon on the pavement, where the day's heat lingered after simmering all day without a trace of shade. He hoped he had enough men left in fighting trim to do the job that they had been assigned out at Coyote Lake.

Rogers had never cared much for the desert as a battleground. Besides the heat, it offered little in the way of cover, lent itself more to stampedes of armored vehicles than to guerrilla warfare that he favored. Even simple waiting in the desert sapped a soldier's strength and nudged him closer to a state of dehydration, where he was completely useless to his unit, a potential casualty. But this was the assignment, and he wouldn't let the Temple down.

Fletcher's briefing had been sketchy to the point of being almost useless, for strategic purposes. Rogers knew that he was up against an enemy who might be affiliated in some unknown way with ATF, but who had broken every rule designed to govern federal law-enforcement agencies. He didn't know how many guns would be arrayed against his men, how they would arrive or whether they had air support on call. He took for granted that his own force might sustain some losses, but he hoped to minimize the damage by relying on surprise to give himself an edge.

The main thing Rogers knew was that the enemies he faced—or men closely affiliated with them—had already killed at least two dozen of his comrades from the Temple of the Nordic Covenant, had forced the Temple to evacuate its western headquarters at Freedom Home, and had aborted Fletcher's strike against the Eli Sturman Center in Los Angeles. For all these crimes against the Master Race, and for the arrogance that prompted them, Rogers meant to see them pay in blood.

He checked his watch against the wall clock, glanced disinterestedly at his female companion, trussed up on the bed, and started switching channels on the motel television set. There was an Arnold Schwarzenegger action film on HBO, incredible that such a well-built Austrian would choose to waste his talents on a lot of cinematic crap that always had him fighting for the so-called underdogs of a corrupt society. Passing the movie by, he skimmed through sports, some tepid situation comedies and stopped short on a news broadcast that caught his eye.

The camera was focused on the burned-out shell of what had been a storefront office, gutted, the facade blackened by smoke and fire. The sign out front, or what was left of it, identified the ruined structure as an office of the Te p e of he No dic Coven, sounding like some kind of tent for eunuch warlocks. Rogers didn't need to hear the voice-over to know that he was looking at the Nordic Temple's former headquarters in Hemet, sixty miles due south of where he sat. Two of his comrades—men he'd never met, but who had shared his racial destiny—had been assassinated there, perhaps by the same men whom he would meet tonight.

Rogers couldn't wait.

"Won't be long now," he told the woman as he switched off the television. She didn't answer him, of course; the gag prevented that. "Your friends took out my people, back in Riverside. Tonight, I get to teach them what a royal mistake that was."

He couldn't tell for sure, behind the gag that covered nearly half her face, but for a moment, Rogers could have sworn the bitch was smiling at him. Maybe it was something in her eyes, a glint of fear mistaken for amusement, but it made him hesitate.

Did she know something he was unaware of? Something he had overlooked, perhaps?

Bullshit.

A few more hours, and the dry earth of Coyote Lake would have its first bloodbath.

He only hoped that there would be enough to go around.

CHAPTER TWELVE

Bolan had watched the enemy deploy from his position at the southwest corner of the dry lake bed, where low and rocky hills provided him a marginal degree of cover. There was some question, when the Nordic Temple soldiers first arrived, if they would also fixate on the hills as a strategic vantage point, but they had gone for burrows, camouflaged with tarps, dry weeds and sand instead.

It would have been a killer set, if he wasn't aware of it beforehand, already in place and breathing down their sweaty necks. He could imagine the effect those troops would have if they were given the advantage of surprise, erupting from the very earth itself, like demon soldiers sprouted from a field of dragon's teeth.

More Nordic imagery, perhaps? No matter. He had seen them go to ground and waited with them, sweated with them in his hidey-hole, as the cruel sun inched its way across a nearly cloudless sky.

The Executioner was as prepared as he would ever be.

Beside him, standing on its bipod, was a Walther WA 2000 sniper rifle, chambered in Winchester .300

Magnum, fitted with an excellent Schmidt & Bender telescopic sight, a 2.5-to-10-power zoom. The Walther was a semiauto bullpup weapon, its 6-round magazine seated behind the contoured pistol grip, its twenty-three-inch free-floating barrel clamped to the frame fore and aft, fluted along its length to further resist vibration. Too expensive for general deployment in the field, the Rolls-Royce of sniper rifles was reserved for special missions, and Brognola had obtained this specimen for Bolan with a gentle tug on certain covert strings.

The big Fed had also arranged for the evening's pyrotechnics, including half a dozen mortar-style launchers for illumination rounds, which could be triggered by remote control, and three disposable LAW rocket tubes that lay beside Bolan's right leg in the niche where he sheltered, already extended and ready to fire.

Combine the hardware with the targets that the Nordic Temple had provided, burrowed in at ranges that varied from four hundred to six hundred yards, and Bolan was ready to rock.

All he needed now was a glimpse of Marilyn Crouder—or alternatively some reasonable confirmation of the fact that she wouldn't be coming, that he had been doubly double-crossed.

Patience.

It was a hunter's—and a sniper's—most important virtue, if the term *virtue* could truly be applied to stalking men. He thought about the moral aspect of his war from time to time, though not so much of late, those questions having been rehashed and fairly settled in his mind long years ago. These days, once

Bolan's targets had been singled out, identified and had presented their own case by words and deeds, proving themselves the kind of savages who threatened any civilized society, he concentrated on *how* rather than *why*.

Tonight, for instance.

As the sun dipped lower in the sky, fading from white-hot into incandescent red, then orange, finally dropping out of sight beyond the distant western mountains, Bolan scanned the killing ground below him with his infrared field glasses, making certain that his enemies weren't emerging from their holes. No movement yet, and he supposed that there had to be some signal, probably a code word flashed to them by radio, or maybe just the sound of gunfire crackling in the night.

Whatever they were waiting for, the game plan was about to change.

They were expecting someone else; that much was clear. Whether the neo-Nazis made good on their promise to deliver Crouder or not, they had to at least go through the motions, keep up the charade, until they had their target spotted, zeroed in. So far, Sean Fletcher and the rest couldn't be sure how many adversaries they were dealing with. Even if Crouder had told them everything she knew, it wasn't much. She had no idea who employed him, for example, and she couldn't swear that Bolan had no reinforcements at his beck and call.

So he was waiting, and the men dug in below were waiting, basting in their own sweat as they hunkered underground for someone to arrive and open the festivities. The MC might arrive by land or air. It made no difference to the end result, since Bolan had him covered, either way.

The trick, assuming Bolan's enemies brought Crouder along at all, would lie in sparing her once battle had been joined.

Bolan had counted thirty soldiers, give or take a couple, in the camouflaged foxholes. He guessed that when the officer in charge arrived, with or without his hostage, there would be at least a few more gunners riding with him—for appearances, if nothing else. Once Bolan had determined whether the lady Fed was with them, then he could make his move.

Six high-illumination rounds, the launchers keyed to different frequencies on his remote-control device, would turn midnight to blazing noon above Coyote Lake, only without the desert's brutal heat. Each round of artificial light was good for fifteen, maybe twenty seconds of illumination, during which he would be free to scope the human targets with his Walther, to waste their vehicles—at least three of them—with the powerful LAW rockets, made for killing tanks.

And all without damaging Marilyn Crouder.

If she was even at the meet.

There was a gap of four hours and fifty-one minutes between sundown and midnight. Bolan continued his vigil, thankful for the respite from a day of baking underneath his own camouflage tarp. By midnight, he knew, the desert would have worked its magic, the temperature drop transforming an oven into a cooler, but the rocks around him served double duty: having shaded him from the midday sun, they now retained heat to warm him through a chilly night.

And they warmed other predators, as well. An hour after sundown, Bolan heard a swift, insistent scratching on the rocks and saw a six-inch scorpion come scuttling toward him, pincers poised in front of it and questing in an endless search for prey. Using the black blade of his Ka-bar fighting knife, he stopped the venomous insect in its tracks and flicked it out of sight, beyond the rim of stones that formed a minor parapet in front of him.

Good hunting, brother.

Bolan waited, dining on granola bars and jerky, washing it down with water from one of his several canteens. It was 11:46 p.m. when he saw headlights in the distance, coming from the west two minutes more before they separated and became two vehicles, a minimotorcade rolling across the desert toward a rendezvous with death.

Whose death? he wondered, and immediately put the question out of mind. He had done everything he could in terms of preparation for the coming battle. It would soon become a test of skill, with more than just a dash of luck involved.

He lay and watched the headlights as they left pavement behind and started out into the middle of Coyote Lake, dust boiling up behind them, tinted crimson by their taillights as if they had set the arid land on fire. They had to have mapped it, Bolan realized, to keep from driving into one of the camouflaged foxholes and crushing the soldiers inside.

Not bad.

He tracked the cars with his binoculars until they reached a point roughly five hundred yards in front of him, surrounded by a broad horseshoe pattern of hidden dugouts. Then he shifted to the Walther and its zoom-lens sniper scope.

"Come on," he whispered to the desert night. "Let's get this over with."

"OKAY," ZACK ROGERS told his captive, "here we are." One-handed, he untied the blindfold she had worn throughout her final journey, a small, probably pointless concession to security, just in case something went wrong.

But what could go wrong?

He was surrounded by his soldiers, even if most of them were invisible. Four gunners with him in the Buick, five more in the second car and thirty buried in the darkness all around him, waiting for the signal that would bring them lurching into cool, crisp air and starlight, ready to confront the common enemy.

An enemy of which, as yet, there was no sign.

Zack Rogers checked his watch: 11:59 p.m., and nothing. "What time have you got up there?" he asked his men in the front seat.

"Midnight," the driver told him.

"I make it 12:01," the shotgun rider said.

"So, where the hell is he?"

Turning to Mary Krause, he dug an elbow in her ribs and said, "You think your boyfriend changed his mind? Maybe he thought about it and decided you aren't worth the trouble, after all."

"Could be," she said, surprising Rogers with her smile.

"Well, shit, we came this far," he said. "We may as well get out and stretch out legs."

Using his walkie-talkie, Rogers told the shooters in

the Cadillac behind him, "Everybody out. Act casual, but watch yourselves."

No one emerged from any of the hidden foxholes at his call of "everybody out." The soldiers waiting underground wouldn't emerge until they heard the trigger term "payday."

Rogers felt exposed as he stepped from the car. A part of it was his anticipation, triggering adrenaline, but there was something else at work, as well. It was the kind of someone's-watching feeling that he got sometimes when he was entering a danger situation. Still, there had been no sign of a vehicle along the highway, coming in, and there was nothing stirring on the dry lake bed that would suggest an enemy in hiding.

Anyway, where would he hide?

Where did your *soldiers hide?* a small voice asked him, nagging from a murky corner of his mind.

Not relevant, he answered silently. His soldiers would have been in place before the enemy arrived, assuming they had come to have a look around Coyote Lake in daylight. Half a dozen of his hidden troops had radios, and they would certainly have warned him if there was a trap in place.

He couldn't shake the feeling, though, and that angered him.

"Tick-tock," he told the handcuffed woman standing at his side, the fingers of his left hand digging deeply into her right biceps. "If this guy doesn't show within the next five minutes, you're dead meat."

She laughed at that. "Like you were going to release me, anyway. You really think I'm that dumb?"

"Dumb enough to let yourself get caught," he answered, tightening his grip until she winced in pain. "Say, how'd you like your time with Fletcher? Did he let you have some TLC?"

Her silence told him everything he had to know, let Rogers paste a strained smile on his own face, though it felt strange and transitory there.

"Jeff! Willie!" Rogers called out, addressing two of his men from the second car. They quick-stepped over to him, and he told them, "Take this bitch a few yards out and get her ready. Standard execution protocol. Fire on my order."

"Yes, sir!" the two voices said as one.

The shooters took her from him, one on either side, and marched her forty, fifty feet due south of where the Buick and the Caddy sat, nose to tail. One of them spoke to her and, when she ignored him, bent to whip the muzzle of his Uzi SMG across her legs, behind the knees. She folded, dropped into a kneeling posture with a grunt of pain, stiffening as the barrel pressed against her skull, behind one ear.

Better.

But where in holy hell was her relief?

Rogers had been assured that someone would show up to take the woman off his hands at the appointed hour. He'd been ordered to prepare the setup in advance, and it was done. The best mousetrap on Earth was no damned good, however, if the rodent never showed, never came close enough to even sniff the cheese.

Two minutes gone on Krause's deadline, and Rogers didn't care to wait for these anonymous hellraisers any longer. Fletcher had been suckered somehow, but that wasn't *his* fault. Rogers had his orders, and the final one instructed him to kill the woman, make her disappear. No matter what else happened at Coyote Lake, the scheming bitch was history.

"Heads up!" said Rogers to his pointmen as he eased his Glock 24 pistol from its holster, clutched in his right hand, while the left held his walkie-talkie in readiness, thumb covering the send button. "Dust her on three, my count," he ordered.

"Yes, sir."

"One!"

There was a crack or pop from somewhere in the darkness in front of him, beyond the shooters and their kneeling prisoner. Was that some kind of whistling sound that came along behind it, the distant sound of wind rush over a projectile?

"Two!"

The second cracking sound, somewhere above his head, was louder, like the detonation of a frag grenade, maybe a hundred yards away. A sudden flash of brilliant light made Rogers squint his eyes and curse, knowing immediately what it was, though he couldn't begin to guess where the illumination round had come from.

Before he could mouth the word "three," an astounding thing happened. As he stood over Mary Krause, Jeff's head exploded like a melon with a cherry bomb inside. Before the echo of the distant gunshot reached him, Willie also took a hit, somewhere between the chin and sternum, vaulting backward through a clumsy somersault that left him facedown in the dirt.

There was no time to think, Zack Rogers falling back on instinct as he raised the walkie-talkie to his lips and started shouting, "Payday! Up and at 'em, men! Pay-fucking-day!"

IT WAS LIKE something from a zombie movie on the late, late show, as soldiers from the Nordic Temple threw their camo tarps and tumbleweeds aside, leaping erect from their premature graves. Bathed in the ghostly light of his illumination round, without a target they could fix upon, some of them started firing blindly into darkness, the majority more disciplined, still looking for a mark before they wasted any rounds.

Between the sudden white-out and the WA 2000's flash-hider, Bolan knew it would take extraordinary eagle eyes to spot his sniper's nest. Using the time available before the first illumination round burned out, he shot the man who had clutched Crouder's arm as they emerged from the point car, saw him go down flopping like a headless chicken in the dirt.

Four rounds remained, having started with one in the chamber and six in the mag. He used the rest on skinhead gunners clustered near the cars before they had a chance to orient themselves and find cover. Reloading, Bolan set the Walther to one side, reached down along his flank and brought one of the three LAW rocket launchers to his shoulder.

Sighting quickly but effectively, he drew down on the point car, a Buick LeSabre, and sent his first armor-piercing rocket whistling downrange, above and to the right of the place where Crouder had fallen facedown, hands clasped behind her head, kissing the ground. Her prone position saved her as the Buick blew, shrapnel filling the air and striking several of the Nordic Temple gunners, while a rising fireball tinged the white light of his own illumination shell bloodred.

He ditched the empty rocket launcher, found one of its mates by touch and shouldered it. One of the so-called Aryans was in the driver's seat and twisting the ignition key as Bolan fired again, no time for Mr. X to put the Cadillac in gear, much less escape and save himself. The rocket struck its target broadside, detonating on impact with the passenger's door, imploding that steel-and-plastic barrier, slashing at the driver's corpse with fragments that ranged in size from needles to saucers, jolting the Caddy to port and killing its engine.

Better. Now his adversaries would be forced to flee on foot if they broke ranks. The flaming hulks also denied potential cover to his targets, since the soldiers of the master race couldn't get close enough to crouch and hide behind the shattered vehicles.

Firelight from burning cars helped spot his targets as he launched the third illumination round. He left the last LAW rocket launcher on its rocky shelf, returning to the WA 2000 sniper rifle for the moment, now that he was out of vehicles to kill. His first glance through the zoom lens showed him Crouder still lying on the hardpan, arms outflung, as if a bullet or shrapnel had cut her down. He told himself that she was faking, playing possum, hoping it was true, but he would only find out if and when he cleared the field of adversaries and was able to approach her for a closer look.

To business, then.

The milling shooters apparently still had no fix on

Bolan or his sniper's nest. At least half of them fired sporadically in various directions, and a few stray rounds came close enough to crack against the rocks ten feet or so above his hiding place. Between the firelight and illumination rounds, however, they had no luck spotting Bolan's muzzle-flashes, and the racket of their own guns instantly frustrated any vain attempt to track him by the echo of his shots across the dry lake bed.

He set them up and took them down, checking back with Crouder every few seconds to make sure she wasn't disturbed. The stillness of her form, no movement as of respiration visible when Bolan zoomed in on the body, troubled him. Still, there was nothing he could do except to keep the neo-Nazi thugs away from her as much as possible and finish clearing off the field.

He followed no apparent pattern, picking off a gunman here, another there, avoiding any systematic sweep that would have let observers calculate where he was firing from or where he would aim next. Here, Bolan dropped a young skinhead and left his flankers standing safe and sound if only for the moment. Over there, he caught two others huddled in discussion, kissing close, and spent one bullet on the two of them, their bodies dropping in a sprawl of tangled limbs.

And always, there were more.

Each 6-round magazine reduced the hostile numbers, but his mind was still divided, part of it focused on Crouder and keeping her alive.

If it wasn't too late already.

If he hadn't missed his chance.

MARILYN CROUDER LAY facedown in gritty dirt and wondered what the hell was happening. In two short days with Mike Belasko, she had already become accustomed to the sights and sounds of violent death, but this was something else entirely, nothing short of a pitched battle in the desert, underneath a ghostly crescent moon.

Had Belasko dredged up reinforcements from the agency that sponsored him? The one that he had yet to name? Or was there someone, something else involved?

The only thing that Crouder was sure of at the moment was that Archer and her buds from ATF weren't involved in what appeared to be a full-scale, no-holds-barred rescue attempt. There would have been loudspeakers blaring, endless warnings for the Nordic Temple goons to drop their weapons and surrender, but there had been nothing of that sort before the first two shots were fired, killing her would-be executioners.

At least one sniper, then, and maybe more. As for the cars burning behind her, warming the soles of her feet through her shoes, that little stunt had called for military hardware and the know-how to employ it. Such devices, likewise, weren't included in the standard ATF assault kit, nor was flattening a pair of private vehicles without regard to those inside the standard method of preventing felons from escaping.

Mike Belasko, then. And someone else?

It seemed to her that there was too much going on, too much confusion in the Nordic Temple ranks for one man to have caused it all. Of course, she didn't know where all these skinhead goons had come from,

either. There were three or four times more commandos than would fit into the pair of vehicles, and she
had glimpsed no other means of transportation as she
climbed out of the Buick.

Enough! she silently scolded herself. It made no
difference how the dead and dying men had reached
this place. The proper question was, how could she
get away from there without being shot?

So far, her chances weren't promising. She had an
urge to bolt and run, but Crouder had managed to
suppress it. As it was, she thought the Nazis might
mistake her for a corpse, or simply put her out of
mind while they were fighting for their own survival.
Up and moving, though, she made herself a stand-out
target in the firelight, with the bright flares overhead,
and she might also catch a bullet from her own rescuers, in the hectic cross fire.

So she had to stay put, she thought, and tried to
moderate her breathing, so the subtle rise and fall of
ribs and shoulders underneath her shirt wouldn't be
readily discerned. Crouder wished she had a weapon,
but obtaining one meant moving, and her one salva-
tion at the moment seemed to lie in playing dead.

She wasn't dead, though. If she had been, Crouder
wouldn't have been so frightened that she felt as if
she were about to jump out of her skin.

Three runners pounded toward her from her left.
She couldn't see them coming, since she had her eyes
closed, head turned in the opposite direction, but she
heard their combat boots impacting on the desert
floor. One of them passed within six inches of her
head; a second hurdled her, as if she were a fallen log
or other lifeless obstacle. The third man leaped across

her prostrate form, took two or three more loping strides, then grunted like a poleaxed hog and toppled over backward, landing squarely on her outstretched legs.

Crouder hoped that her reflexive jerk would be interpreted, by anyone who saw it, as an aftershock from impact of the sprawling corpse. She had no doubt the man stretched across her legs was dead, or that he weighed a freaking ton, for that matter. The sudden weight across her lower body made the situation worse, somehow; an element of claustrophobia was added to the mix, exacerbating helplessness and simple fear.

She wasn't pinned, exactly, in the sense that she couldn't worm out from underneath her burden and escape if she were so inclined. The dead man wasn't really that heavy. Whatever slim chance there had been of Crouder escaping unobserved, though, was completely lost when the dead goon collapsed across her legs. There was no way she could expect the others not to notice, even in the midst of battle, if one "corpse" began to thrash and struggle underneath another, trying to rise up and walk.

"Goddammit!"

Even as the words slipped out, she bit her tongue, felt tears of rage and terror brimming in her eyes. No one was close enough to hear her muffled curse, but it was still a lapse. She had to watch that. Jesus, what if her rescuers were defeated! What would happen then? The Nazis might remove their dead if there was time and opportunity. If they decided to leave Crouder where she had fallen, there was still a decent chance that they would roll her over, check for wounds, try to confirm that she was no more threat to any member of the master race.

In which case, she was truly dead.

She needed some means to defend herself—but what? And how?

It came to her as she was lying there, the sounds of gunfire echoing around her. There was no doubt that the hulk stretched out across her legs was armed. She couldn't turn to see what he was carrying, but if she took her time and exercised due caution, maybe she could *feel* how he was armed, perhaps relieve him of a pistol or grenade, even a knife, if that was all that she could reach.

Slowly, with a caution that was literally painful, muscles burning in her back and shoulder, Crouder began to inch her right arm backward, fingers spider-walking toward the corpse that pinned her.

A SNARLING FACE WAS framed in Bolan's sight for all of half a second, and he stroked the Walther's trigger, rode the recoil, watched the face implode, its owner toppling backward, out of frame.

How many left?

He had just fired the first round of his sixth full magazine. Three targets had required two shots apiece to finish them; two others, minimum, had fried when Bolan blew the Buick and the Caddy with his rockets. Starting with forty hostiles on the game board, call it ten still gunning for him if they hadn't fled into the night while he was mopping up their friends.

The problem now was finding them and making sure.

The Buick and the Cadillac had both burned since

the impact of Bolan's rockets and the secondary blasts from their respective fuel tanks. Much of their gasoline had burned instead of spreading, and the rest had soaked into the flat, parched ground, so he supposed there could be three or four live adversaries sheltering behind the blackened cars. The only way to know for sure would be to go down there and root them out. As for the rest—

A darting movement in his peripheral vision brought Bolan's head and weapon swiveling around in time to catch two runners on the move. He wasn't sure where they had come from; maybe they'd been playing dead, but they were up and moving now.

He launched his fifth illumination round, the next to last, and watched them freeze like rabbits in the headlights of a speeding pickup truck as it exploded overhead. He had the taller of the pair sighted before they broke the spell, squeezed off a round that drilled him through the sternum, taking out his heart, maybe a portion of one lung, and put him down.

The other neo-Nazi bolted, triggering a wild burst from his SMG, and running for his miserable life, boots raising little puffs of dust on impact with the ground.

A moving target was the worst for any shooter using telescopic sights. Unless the mark was moving toward the sniper or away from him in a straight line, the movement forced him to track and lead his quarry, blurring everything he saw. The higher a scope's intensity of magnification, the smaller its visual field— and the easier it was to miss or lose a target on the run.

The only way to save the situation, Bolan knew,

was to lift off the telescopic sight completely, spot his runner, quickly calculate the moving target's course, then sight down on a prospective point of impact. He accomplished all of that in something like three seconds, lining up the shot, sighting on empty air, hearing the numbers count down in his head as he began to squeeze the trigger.

Downrange, the runner seemed to stumble, as if tripped by some invisible obstruction in his path. He went down on his face, one arm twisted beneath him, while the other was flung above his head, and didn't rise again.

The renewed gunfire, after several moments of near silence on the killing field, sparked a new flurry of movement, three more targets rising from the "dead" and breaking off in various directions, while the Executioner spotted each one in turn and cut him down.

Five left below? Or had they fled? Had there been more than one man in each car, when Bolan's rockets turned them into blazing funeral pyres?

One way to know, and since he had to go down there for Crouder in any case, he might as well be done with it.

Before he left his roost, Bolan took one more look at the lady Fed through the sniper scope, noting that her position had changed. Her right arm, once outflung as if she had been crucified, was now tucked in against her flank, and there was something in her hand that had a metal glint about it, though he couldn't make out any details in the fading light from his illumination round.

He didn't fire the last flare as he rose, picked up the M-4 carbine from its place beside the last LAW rocket tube and started down the rocky hillside toward Coyote Lake. If there were really any wild coyotes in the neighborhood, and they hadn't been frightened off by all the sound and fury, they could slip back in, once he was gone, and have themselves a feast.

His treat, the warrior thought, then focused on the task at hand as he reached level ground and went to move among the dead. He had already found some of the neo-Nazis fond of playing corpses, and he checked each body as he passed it, looking for visible wounds. If there was none, he took the time to detour, treading heavily on wrists, fingers or ankles in an effort to elicit some reaction. Twice, when he still wasn't sure, he fired a single round into the back of crew-cut heads, thereby erasing any doubt.

"It's me," he said to Crouder from thirty feet away. "Stay where you are. Don't move." That said, he passed her by without a backward glance, circling the cars to see if they were hiding anyone from view.

He never knew whether the skinheads heard him coming, saw his shadow in the moonlight or if they were simply spooked from crouching in one place too long, surrounded by dead comrades. They broke from cover, scattering like quail from where they had concealed themselves behind the shattered cars. All five of them took off at once, one tripping in his haste, dropping to hands and knees.

He was the first to die, a 3-round burst from Bolan's carbine ripping through the left side of his face and skull, putting him down for the count. Two others hesitated in their headlong flight, turning to face him in the firelight with Kalashnikovs. He swept them with a burst that dumped both of them over backward, heads and shoulders striking hardpan well before their butts and boots came down.

The other two were simply running, and despite a fleeting urge to let them go, Bolan knew that he couldn't afford a lapse of maudlin sympathy. He raised the carbine to his shoulder, sighted down the barrel toward his first mark, squeezing off, then dropped the second in his tracks.

All done.

"Still me," he said to Crouder as he approached her from the left. "If that's a gun you're holding, please don't shoot."

"A gun!" she snorted as she pushed up on her elbows, showing him a dagger she had evidently lifted from the body sprawled atop her. "I should be so lucky!"

"Let me help you with this," he said, and stooped to roll the dead man off her legs. As the woman stood, he asked, "Are you all right?"

"I don't... Let's not... Can we just get away from here?"

"Sure thing," the Executioner replied.

She took an angry swipe at tears that glistened on her cheeks, staring past Bolan toward the blasted cars. "Hold on a second," she requested, moving toward a flaccid body he had dropped with one of his first rounds. He watched her crouch beside the supine corpse, draw back her knife and plunge it solidly into the dead man's chest.

"You piece of shit!" she sobbed. A moment later, she was on her feet and facing him. "Okay," she said, "we're done. You have some wheels, or do we have to walk?"

CHAPTER THIRTEEN

"I'm fine, Mike. Please, just take my word for it, okay?"

"You're not fine, Marilyn. You took a beating at the very least. You need some medical attention."

"No!" she snapped at him. "And what the hell is that supposed to mean—the very least?"

He sat back in his chair and held her gaze until she blushed and looked away. "It means you've been through hell," Bolan replied. "You may have injuries you're not even aware of at the moment."

"Oh, I'm perfectly aware," she said, but now her voice had sunken almost to a whisper. "All I really needed was a shower and the first-aid stuff you gave me. Really. Let it go, all right?"

"Not yet."

"I'm telling you—"

"I need to know what you told them," he interrupted her. "Before I make another move, I need to know if they'll be waiting for me."

"We," she told him. "Us. All right? Before *we* make another move, you need to know if they'll be waiting for *us.*"

"You want the truth?" he asked, and forged ahead

before she could respond. "I'm not convinced that you can handle any more of this."

"I'll handle anything they throw at us and pitch it right back in their goddamned faces!"

"What did you tell them, Marilyn?"

"I told them squat, all right? Name, rank and serial number, by the book." Her voice cracked then, and it was softer when she spoke again. "They would have broken me eventually, I suppose. They didn't get the chance, though. Some guy called and told Sean Fletcher he should let me go." Another pause, before she asked him, "Have I thanked you yet? I can't remember."

Bolan shrugged and said, "It doesn't matter."

"Yes, it does. To me."

"The main thing is—"

"Thank you."

"You're welcome," he replied.

"Okay." The bare trace of a smile.

"Now, then, you say they didn't ask about Chicago?"

"Not specifically," she said. "They asked me who I worked for, who you were—they saw you drop me off—and how I knew about the Sturnman Center. In reply to which, I told them zip. They also asked if I knew any more about their future plans, if I had passed more information on, that kind of thing. Chicago wasn't mentioned. I suppose they were afraid of spilling anything I didn't know already, even though they had to figure that I'd never have another chance to show and tell." Another hesitation. "Have I thanked you for my life?"

He smiled and nodded. "Yes, you have."

"Okay."

"So, what's your take?" he asked her. "Will they scrub Chicago after what went down tonight?"

She thought about that for a moment, frowning, finally shaking her head in a cautious negative. "I don't think so," she answered. "I can't be positive, of course, but it's the only card I'm holding at the moment. If they start to scramble targets now, we're screwed."

She had a point.

"All right," he said. "Then maybe you should tell me what it is they're after in Chicago, just in case they follow through."

"You've heard of FREE?" she asked. When Bolan gave no sign of recognition, she added, "The civil rights group?"

That rang a bell. "Oh, right. For Racial Equality Everywhere, something like that?"

"The very same. They haven't had too many headlines since the early seventies, so it's no wonder that they slipped your mind. Their big days were before my time—the freedom marches, fighting with the KKK and getting hosed by the police, all that. I saw a thing on the Discovery Channel."

"Right."

"Anyway, they have two anniversaries coming up—or, I should say, they've rolled two into one. The group was organized in 1961, so they're celebrating the big four-oh, and their first leader was killed ten years later, by some kind of car bomb. Apparently, the guys who blew him up were never caught, and FREE's using the anniversary to call for a new investigation of the case. And if you want the cynical version, to get some ink for themselves while they're at it.''

''And the ceremony's in Chicago?''

''Day after tomorrow. They're expecting some celebrities to make a showing, and I've heard a rumor that a certain liberal ex-president might have a few remarks. Whatever, there'll be TV cameras, a fairly decent crowd, all the free air time Steuben and his pet gorillas could hope for.''

''That's the day after tomorrow?''

''Right.''

''How do they plan to pull it off?'' he asked.

''I don't have any details,'' Crouder replied, ''but they've been looking forward to this since the meeting was announced, six months ago. You can imagine how this kind of thing would set them off, the things they say.''

''I'm more concerned with what they plan to do.''

''We're going to Chicago, though? I mean the two of us?''

''You think you're up to it?''

''Try me.''

It was against his better judgment, but he also knew that Crouder would find her way without him if he tried to cut her loose. To stop her, he would have to have Brognola take her into custody, and Hal would likely balk at snatching up an agent from the ATF, especially when that group and the team at Stony Man were trying to cooperate.

''I need to make some calls,'' he said, ''and see about our transportation. I imagine you should check in, too.''

''I guess.''

"Okay," he said, rising to leave the lady's motel room. "I'll see you in about an hour, ninety minutes, tops."

"I'll be here."

He was at the door, hand on the knob, when her voice stopped him. "Mike, wait. I just want to say, well, thanks again, all right?"

"My pleasure."

Out the door and waiting for the sharp sound as it locked behind him, automatically, he moved along the corridor, two doors, to reach his own. It was a fairly modern place, with plastic punch cards for the doors instead of standard keys. He gave his card a swipe and stepped inside, engaging the security bolt as soon as the door snicked shut.

He had a fair idea of what had happened to Crouder during her twenty-eight hours of captivity. That was to say, he had a fair idea of the mechanics, which was still light-years from understanding what the trauma felt like, what she saw when she looked in the mirror, how the shame—albeit wholly undeserved—came out of nowhere to envelop her. The anger was a natural reflex, and she could draw some slender solace from the fact that her tormentors had become a smorgasbord for buzzards, ants and beetles. Still, he knew, the private issues didn't simply fade away because the man or men responsible were taken out.

Bolan was tempted, even now, to pull whatever strings he could and have her taken off the case, but then he thought the job might be the only thing that let her keep it all together. If she were deprived of that, perhaps the only safety line remaining, once her dignity was stripped away, what would be left?

The flip side, obviously, was a risk that any private baggage she brought with her to Chicago might disrupt the mission, maybe fatally. If she was in a situation where she had to face the enemy and lost her cool—if she froze and couldn't act, or if her rage took over and she jumped in prematurely—then the whole damned thing could blow up in their faces. Bolan's life was riding on the line, along with hers. How many others would be jeopardized if anything went wrong?

It was a question Bolan couldn't answer, any more than he could honestly predict how Crouder would function when confronted with another delegation from the Temple of the Nordic Covenant. She might do fine…or, then again, she might blow up, collapse, go catatonic. He was gambling big by taking her along, but it was something Bolan felt he had to do.

How much of that was guilt on his part for his failure to prevent the kidnapping or to retrieve her earlier? If challenged on the point by anyone but Crouder, Bolan would have replied that he had done his best. He would have meant it, too, for whatever that might be worth.

And if the lady from the ATF had challenged him, what then?

He had no ready answer. How did you respond to someone who had served a stint in hell before their time? How did you say, "I did my best," and make it stick? What good, in fact, was Bolan's "best" in light of what she'd suffered and the memories that she might carry to her grave?

Forget about it!

Crouder was still alive, and that was more than

could be said for certain others who had taken part in Bolan's war, by choice or otherwise. He saw those other faces in his dreams sometimes, and even though the ghosts were friendly, never blaming him at all for what had happened, they still haunted him.

So many ghosts.

And if the shades of all the savages whom he had sent to their reward should gather to commemorate the act, how many would there be? Bolan did not keep score, but one of Hal Brognola's early Wanted posters, long ago, had placed the number at one thousand. Those were strictly mafiosi, tabulated midway through his one-man war against the Syndicate. How many more since then?

At least enough to fill a good-sized theater, he thought, but not enough for Yankee Stadium or Madison Square Garden. Plenty for a nice Day of the Dead parade, but not enough to march on Washington.

Get on with it.

He took the scrambler from his suitcase and attached it to the bedside telephone.

"ARCHER, IT'S ME."

"You made it out." Her supervisor's voice was hesitant, as if there were a hundred questions that he could not bring himself to ask. "Are you all right? Do you need anything?"

"I'll live," she said. "I need to know how far you'll cover us from here on out."

"We talked about this. You know the way things are with Congress, and—"

"The funny thing," she interrupted him, "is that I'm not *in* Congress at the moment, Archer. And the scum we're tracking doesn't take a three-month recess every spring. They don't just sit around and talk until they're all so fat on pork and graft that they can't get out of their chairs without some sweet young page to hold their hands.''

''I know that you're upset right now, but—''

''You *know*, Archer? *You* know? Explain that to me, would you, please? Because I'd love to hear your firsthand insight on the situation, all the way from Washington.''

''Okay, dumb choice of words. I'm sorry.''

''And you haven't answered me,'' she said.

''The question being…?''

''Don't play dumb.''

''All right. My answer is the same as when this whole thing started. You're playing with a team that doesn't only bend or break the rules, it throws them out the window. You're already way beyond the pale. There's absolutely nothing I can do for you officially, and precious little otherwise. I thought you understood that, going in.''

''I did,'' she told him. ''But I hoped you might have grown a pair. So much for wishful thinking.''

''Now, just wait a goddamned minute—''

She hung up on him, surprised by how much satisfaction she received from that small act. She had a mental image of her bridges burning, and was startled to discover that it didn't bother her tremendously. There would be other jobs, if she survived the next few days. And if she didn't, well, then, she wouldn't require a paycheck, anyway.

The sudden swell of laughter startled her. She really couldn't see a damned thing funny in her present situation, but she let it run its course, hearing the sharp note of hysteria, ignoring it, until the laughter suddenly dissolved into soul-wrenching sobs. She curled up on the bed, knees raised to meet her chest and wept into the cradle of her arms. It seemed to last for hours, but the digital alarm clock on the nightstand told her barely fifteen minutes had elapsed before the wave of grief swept past and left her huddled in its wake.

In place of pain, there was a great, numb, empty feeling, as if she had somehow managed to survive her own autopsy, hollowed out, stitched back together and embalmed. She wondered how long it would be before she felt again, for good or ill, and while a part of her was almost desperate to find out—thinking that she should follow Belasko to his room and seek the answer in his bed, right now, this minute—yet another part of her was sickened and revolted by the images it brought to mind.

Sean Fletcher.

He was still alive and well, presumably en route to meet his soldiers in the Windy City. More than likely, he had already dismissed her from his mind. He would be startled, angered, when he found out what had happened to his hit team in the desert, but that information might not reach him prior to H hour in Chicago. Meanwhile, Crouder retained the image of his leering face and focused all her hatred into it.

Stabbing his flunky, once the soldier was already dead, had been a small release of fury, but it barely made a dent in her abiding rage. She recognized the danger in allowing such emotions to control her actions, knew that Belasko was correct in questioning her own ability to function on the line.

And she would have to prove him wrong, at least until the moment when she had Sean Fletcher in her sights and she could send his worthless soul to hell.

The hitch in that scenario being that Marilyn, herself, did not believe in hell, heaven, Valhalla or the other trappings of the afterlife. She had seen too much suffering and inhumanity on Earth to put her faith in mythic deities who gave a damn about the fate of mortal men.

Which meant that taking out Fletcher would be the end, and she would have to make it count. For both of them.

Another shower's what she needed, she thought, and had her clothes off by the time she reached the bathroom, all beige paint and tile to match. She stole a quick glance at the mirror, noting sundry burns and bruises, but the wounds that counted were invisible. She carried them inside her, where no X ray could discover them, no doctor's healing art could ease the pain.

She had to do that for herself.

Crouder turned on the water as hot as she could stand it, flushing pink from neck to feet, as soon as she stepped underneath the stinging spray. She soaped herself and rinsed, went through the ritual twice more, and still didn't feel clean. At last, she stood beneath the shower with her head bowed, water drumming on her scalp and mingling with the tears that streaked her face. If asked, she couldn't have explained whether her tears were spawned by hatred, rage or shame. She wondered if there was enough soap and hot water in the world to make her soul feel clean again.

Or whether blood would help.

Something was telling her it couldn't hurt.

Archer had done no more or less than she expected of him, looking out for number one. He was a bureaucrat before he was a lawman, and to hell with all his talk about taking the bad guys off the street. When all was said and done, he was primarily concerned with budgets, paperwork, year-end reports and oversight committees that could hang his pension out to dry. It came as no surprise to Marilyn, and she suspected it wouldn't surprise Belasko, either.

Once again, she wondered what the shadow agency he served was all about. It scared her, in a way—the prospect of a sanctioned murder squad—but at the same time, in her present state of mind, it made perfect sense. The U.S. Constitution was a kind of miracle, no doubt about it, but it still had loopholes. It hadn't been written with the modern breed of predators in mind. George Washington and Thomas Jefferson could never have imagined dealing with an outfit like the Temple of the Nordic Covenant, the Russian Mafia or any of a thousand other criminal conspiracies that threatened the United States today. They hadn't known a thing about machine guns, much less the Islamikaze squads, truck bombs or suitcase nukes. How could the Bill of Rights apply to everyone, when there were savages abroad who dreamed of genocide and found those visions soothing to their twisted souls?

The shower's water had begun to cool, the drop in temperature drawing Crouder back, albeit reluctantly, from her most private thoughts. She turned it off and pulled a towel from the wall-mounted rack as she stepped from the steamy cubicle. Feeling neither clean nor particularly refreshed, she was at least thankful for the layer of condensation that covered the mirror, reducing her own reflection to a vague pink shape that moved disjointedly, as if behind a layer of frosted glass.

Time's wasting.

That, at least, was true enough. However she might feel, whatever she might wish had happened, nothing stopped the clock from running, nothing would postpone the scheduled strike against FREE's celebration in Chicago.

Not unless Steuben and Fletcher called it off.

And if they did...then what? She didn't have a clue what the next step should be. If they discarded their original schedule, started hitting targets at random, then she knew nothing of any further value to Belasko. He could bench her without qualms, without the fear that she would follow him or show up at the next appointed target on her own, a saucy wild card in the game.

She would be helpless. He would know it, and their common enemy was bound to know it, too.

The good news, if it could be called that, lay in Steuben's egomania and his conviction that the course of destiny was set by mystic powers far above his own or those of any federal agency. Steuben wasn't a money-grubbing "wizard" of some redneck Klan, who sold racism by the pound and always made a profit for himself. He was a true believer in the worst sense of the term, committed to destruction of his countless enemies at any cost.

Which meant, to Crouder, that he wouldn't scrub anything as long as he had troops and weapons readily accessible. He would proceed with the Chicago raid because, to him and those who served him, it was the fulfillment of an ancient prophecy, foretelling triumph for the Aryan combatants in a racial holy war.

Sean Fletcher would be there, she told herself.

He wouldn't miss it for the world.

"Neither would I," she whispered as she gingerly began to dress in freshly laundered clothes. "Neither would I."

"YOU'VE SEEN ME, right?" Brognola asked, his voice still rough around the edges, tinged with sleep. "I mean, you know how very much I need my beauty rest."

"Sorry," Bolan replied. "It couldn't wait. I'm turning on the scrambler...now."

The only difference in their conversation, once the compact box had been switched on, its green light glowing, was a certain hollowness that echoed on the line, as if they had a poor connection. Anyone who tried to intercept the call without a scrambler keyed to the same frequency, however, would hear nothing but metallic clicks and pops, completely indecipherable.

"Are we set?" Brognola asked.

"We're five by five."

"Okay. So, what's the what?"

"I made the pickup here, all right," Bolan replied,

still cryptic in his reference to Crouder's rescue, even with the scrambler engaged.

"That's good, right? Everything's okay?"

"I wouldn't go that far. She went through hell and doesn't want to talk about it. No surprise, I guess, but it still shows."

"She give you up?" Brognola's tone was sharper now, concerned.

"I asked her that," Bolan said. "She says no."

"Do you believe her?"

Bolan thought about that for a moment, finally replying, "Yes, I do."

"Okay. I never second-guess an operative on the ground."

"Since when?"

"Nobody likes a smartass," Brognola retorted. "Do you think she needs some R & R?"

"No go on that idea. Whatever happened to her overnight, she comes off twice as motivated as before. My guess would be she's tripping on revenge."

"So use it," the big Fed suggested. "Just don't let it take control, or it could blow up in your face."

"I'm well aware of that." It came out sounding testier than Bolan had intended, but Brognola didn't seem to notice.

"Is Chicago still the next stop on the hit parade?"

"Apparently. She seems convinced that Stevens and his crew won't deviate from their original intent, no matter what. If that's the case, I have a chance to damage them substantially. But if they change their plans—"

"You're left with zip. Right, I know," Brognola

said. "So, what's the action in Chicago, anyway? Do you have details yet?"

"An anniversary," the Executioner replied, and briefly summarized what Crouder had told him about FREE, its effort to recapture faded glory in a celebration of its history, staged for the television cameras.

"Sounds like a grade-A turkey shoot if they get through," Brognola said when he was finished. "Can I help you out with something in the way of backup? Is there any extra hardware that you need?"

"Unknown, so far," Bolan replied. "I haven't seen the kill zone yet. We'll need transportation, though. I'd like to be there well ahead of time, and driving doesn't cut it."

"I can handle that. Where are you?"

"Victorville."

"That's perfect. Just a few miles west, you've got George Air Force Base. I can pull some strings and book a hop from there to...um, let's see...the Great Lakes Naval Training Center, north Chicago. How's that?"

"Suits me," Bolan replied. "We'll need to have wheels waiting on the other end."

"Sure thing," Brognola said. "You want Chicago PD in on this? Maybe the Bureau? ATF?"

"Too many cooks. The lady's talking to her people, but I don't expect they'll want to get involved. My take is that a lot of flashing lights and uniforms will only make things worse. I'd rather do without the 'help' unless it really helps."

"Okay. Here's what I'll do—I'll call the FBI's Chicago field office and tip them off to something going down, no details. They can have the hostage rescue team on standby, just in case you need a little something extra.''

"Sounds fair." HRT was the Bureau's SWAT team, renamed in the image-conscious 1970s, after Hoover died and his abuses were revealed, to make the paramilitary squad sound more benign than Special Weapons And Tactics. Bolan knew it couldn't hurt to have the team available, as long as it didn't come barging in and put him on the spot. He also knew that if he needed armed assistance from the FBI, it would most likely be too little and too late for them to do him any good.

"Specifics on the target site?" Brognola asked.

"Not yet," Bolan replied. "She plays it close. Afraid I'll try to ditch her, I expect."

"Maybe you should."

"I thought about it," he admitted, "but I owe her something."

"That's a crock," Brognola told him, "and you know it."

Bolan let the judgment pass, adding, "Besides, she's pulled her weight so far. She knows her business. What I hope to do, this time, is keep her on the sidelines if I can."

"Hope springs eternal, right? And if she won't play ball?"

"I guess we'll see what happens," Bolan said.

"Well, hey…at least you've got a plan."

"Don't quit your day job," Bolan chided him. "Sarcastic humor's not your strong suit."

"Damn! And here I thought I might take over

when they finally wised up and pull the plug on Carrot Top.''

"Don't sweat it," Bolan said. "I'll make a deal with her. Push comes to shove, I can immobilize her when the time comes."

"If you want," the big Fed said, "I can have someone leave some mickeys in your ride. Maybe a little chloroform?"

"Nice subtlety," the Executioner replied. "I'll handle it."

"I'm thinking you might need some close liaison with the Bureau on this job," Brognola stated. "We've had some trouble with Chicago cutting corners, trying to pretend they didn't understand their orders, this and that."

"No, thanks. You show up out of nowhere, it will only make them jumpier. I'd rather have the HRT stand down than have the whole field office playing twenty questions, dragging in their street informants, trying to find out what's going on. One of them could get lucky, and the whole thing goes to hell."

"Oh, all right, then." Brognola feigned a pouty tone. "I never get to play."

"I've never seen a team that fields the coach."

"I've seen some that should have," Brognola replied.

"Not this time. Thanks, but no."

"Your call. I'd still appreciate a heads-up when you find out where the party's going to be held."

"I'll let you know as soon as I find out," the Executioner agreed. "Now, if we're finished, I've still got some packing left to do."

"One other thing. Should I have someone tip off the locals about Coyote Lake?"

"Don't bother," Bolan answered. "Someone always stumbles on the bodies, one way or another. As it is, the lag time plays to our advantage, keeps the black hats guessing, maybe even throws them off their game a little."

"You'll be sorry if a troop of Boy Scouts finds them," Brognola remarked.

"School days," Bolan reminded him. "If no one's found them by the time the smoke clears in Chicago, day after tomorrow, you can drop a coin to *USA Today,* for all I care."

"Okay," Brognola said. "I'll let you go and pack. Let's make your password for the air base 'predator.'"

"I'll touch base when we hit the Windy City," Bolan said, and lowered the receiver to its cradle.

Predator.

The code name fit both sides, although for different reasons. Bolan wasted no time dwelling on it or investing it with more significance than it deserved.

He started packing, hardware first, and then his personal effects, such as they were. The soldier traveled light, with more attention to his weapons and defensive capabilities than to his wardrobe, though he never would have been mistaken for a fashion victim. Bolan's interest in appearance was uniquely functional: it focused on his need to pass unnoticed, for the most part, without drawing any negative or unwanted attention to himself, but he could always manage a disguise or two, role camouflage, when the need arose.

He had a feeling that the need might well arise before he finished up his business in Chicago. Still without the critical details he would require to interdict the Nordic Temple's raid, he was already thinking through some possible scenarios, imagining what he would need.

And any way he looked at it, the play turned out the same.

Its final act was always marked by fire and blood.

CHAPTER FOURTEEN

Approaching Chicago from the south, on Interstate 57, Gerhard Steuben took the usual precautions. He wasn't a fugitive—not yet, at least—but he made a point of acting like one, covering his tracks, so that the moves were second nature to him now. When it was time for him to vanish underground, a time he knew was coming very soon, he would already have the routine memorized, rehearsed and polished to perfection.

"Watch the speed limit," he called out to his driver when he felt the RV starting to accelerate beyond the posted speed. Steuben was sensitive that way. He felt things more acutely than his fellow Aryans. It wasn't just the big things, either: racial pride, the call of destiny or when the weather was about to change. At times, he could predict when someone in his inner circle was about to come down with a cold, the flu, whatever. There were times when he swore that he could tell what they were thinking.

The phenomenon had startled him at first, before he realized that it was all a part of what he was becoming. Even though his people didn't know it yet, the man was changing. The spirit of a fallen hero had selected him as its new home, and it was working from the inside out, transforming him into the vehicle, the superman, it needed to complete its mission for the master race.

Predictably, some people said that he was crazy when he talked about such things. What did they know? Jew-lovers, he knew, or they were so damned blind they couldn't see how their America had been perverted into something that would drive the Founding Fathers to mass suicide if they could see it now. Some of his own men, he suspected, had to have doubts about his physical possession by the spirit of an SS captain—Gerhard Heinrich Steuben, who was killed in 1943 while trying to eradicate the godless Communists at Stalingrad—but they obeyed his orders just the same, and that was all that mattered for the moment.

True belief would follow when they saw how he had changed, what Gary Stevens had become.

The biggest question, in his own mind, was the matter of his missing eye. This day, he wore a plain glass eye to match the brown one on the right. It was a shame, he sometimes thought, that Dr. Mengele had never managed to perfect his formula for turning brown eyes blue. There was no hope for that in Steuben's lifetime, he supposed, although he owned a blue glass eye, as well—part of his perfectly unique collection—and was known to wear a tinted contact lens to match it, on occasion, when he spoke to full-dress rallies of the faithful. It was a conceit, he realized, but still, it helped to get him in the mood, strengthen his personal connection to the SS man within.

His bodyguard, relief driver and sometime chef

came back to check the RV's fridge for beer. "Yo, boss," he said, "do you want anything?"

Herr Steuben fixed him with a glare, his right eye even colder than the glassy left. "'Yo, boss'?" he mimicked, sneering it. "Is there a homeboy in the house?"

Instead of blushing, his subordinate went deathly pale. "No, sir!" he snapped, as he was rising to attention. "I apologize, sir."

"Blood is our honor, William. Yes?"

"Yes, sir!"

"Pollution of the blood is not a laughing matter. It means nothing less than the extermination of the master race by slow degrees."

"Yes, sir! I'm sorry, sir!"

"You are forgiven…this time."

"Thank you, sir!" William was hesitant to speak again, but finally he asked, "Do you want anything? A beer? A sandwich?"

Steuben shook his head. "No thank you, William."

"Right. Well, I'll just…go…then."

"Yes."

The brief exchange left him feeling better, looking forward to the next day's events. Los Angeles had been a bitter disappointment, even though his soldiers had succeeded in eliminating several Jews. The cost had been too high, with minimal rewards. On top of that, there was no word from Fletcher about his plan to deal with those responsible for the embarrassment. Chicago would redeem the movement, put his grand scheme back on track.

The long, straight run toward final victory.

He sometimes marveled at the ways in which mud

people tried to keep their hopeless causes in the headlines. FREE, for instance, had collapsed for all intents and purposes, after its leader had been blown to bits and the dues-paying members finally decided, ten years late, that singing hymns while Southern sheriffs beat them to the ground wasn't the most effective way to help their race. Some had defected to the Panthers or Black Liberation Army, taking up the gun briefly, before they were shot down or sent to prison; others simply drifted off into oblivion, as those with low IQs and short attention spans were wont to do. Now, after lying moribund for nearly two decades, FREE sought to grab the spotlight one more time, perhaps milk certain aging liberals for cash, by celebrating its defeat.

How very typical, Steuben thought.

Self-taught in history, eugenics and the other subjects vital to his mission, Steuben reckoned that the situation was, in fact, a microcosm of the weakness that would ultimately let his soldiers crush the mud people beneath their boots. Historians like Duke and Stoddard taught him that the mud races had never made a single contribution to society without the guiding, prodding hands of Aryans to assist them, speed them on their lazy way. These days, of course, in many U.S. schools, it was an article of faith that witless savages somehow invented everything from gunpowder and calculus to prehistoric aircraft, soaring through the vast skies over Africa. It would have been amusing, if white children hadn't been subjected to such rubbish in their classrooms, a catastrophe that caused Steuben's pulse to spike and lodged a throbbing pain behind his one good eye.

Chicago would relieve that headache for a little

while, at least. It would return, he knew from long experience, and wouldn't let him rest in peace at last, until his enemies were purged from everywhere that white men once held undisputed sway over the lesser breeds. The following day would be a start, a step in that direction, one more spark to light the fuse that would eventually detonate a worldwide racial holy war.

"It's coming," Steuben told himself.

When the time came, when the battle had been joined from California and New York to London and Berlin, Moscow, Johannesburg and Sydney, then he would emerge to claim his rightful place at the forefront of shock troops waging war against the Zionist conspiracy and the mud races it employed to do its dirty work. When Steuben dreamed at night, sometimes he saw himself leading an armored Panzer column into Tel Aviv, mowing down the rabbis and grinding them to mulch beneath his tank treads. Other beatific dreams involved the conquest of vast Asia, fabulously rich with natural resources and a reservoir of mindless slaves to do the digging, drilling, cutting, clearing.

On that day, once the earth's subhuman population had been cleansed and pacified, then all the mysteries that had eluded him in his troubled life would be resolved, his questions answered, his reward revealed.

Chicago was the launching pad, and he was just about to take the leap.

Sean Fletcher should be in the Windy City now, or else arriving very soon. He would have sent his troops ahead to meet with local members of the Nordic Temple and survey the target, polish any rough spots in their battle plan, preparing for tomorrow.

Steuben couldn't wait.

The next day, when he watched the news on television, parked in his RV a few miles from the action, he resolved that he would wear a special eye. Either the Iron Cross or the swastika; he wasn't certain which.

The better to see you with, my dear, he thought.

And smiled.

"YOU BLACK BABOONS are dead! You hear me? Dead, dead, dead!"

There was a click, and the Reverend Mr. Lewis Albright listened to the dial tone humming for a moment, frowning as he cradled the receiver. That made seven threats since dawn, close to three hundred since he had announced FREE's anniversary festivities six months earlier. The caller-ID box attached to Albright's telephone told him the call had come from somewhere out of area, which could have meant the wilds of darkest Mississippi, or a suburb fifteen minutes from his office on Pulaski Road.

One thing about the lunatics, he thought. He had no shortage of them in his own backyard.

The hate was nothing new, of course. Growing up black in the United States, Albright had known one aspect or another of it all his life. Growing up in Mississippi, in the days when White and Colored signs were found in almost every public building, he had learned that "separate but equal," as administered in Dixie, emphasized the *separate* but only paid lip service to the *equal*. He had joined FREE while attending segregated college classes, marched and went to jail with the Reverend Mr. Aaron Hayling— then FREE's leader, and the best-known leader of the movement after Dr. Martin Luther King. Between the civil rights laws and the new intransigence of Richard Nixon's Washington, the movement had seen bombers kill Hayling in 1971. With Dr. King already gone, there seemed to be no future for nonviolent protest in pursuit of racial equity.

Albright had moved north after Hayling was assassinated, trading on his marginal celebrity—a pale reflection of the martyr's glory—to obtain a pulpit in Chicago. Even there, the hate persisted: in the back rooms of police stations; with ragtag Nazis marching through the streets of Skokie to deny the Holocaust; in midnight raids by vandals who defaced the homes of African Americans, Islamic mosques and Jewish cemeteries. The announcement of a gathering to celebrate the anniversary of FREE and Reverend Hayling's death had brought them squirming out from underneath their rocks like the slimy invertebrates they were, and Albright had received more anonymous threats in the previous six months than in the past five years.

Was he afraid?

The question rankled him, but he was more unsettled by the answer: yes.

Outside of Mississippi in the 1960s, when the threats were very real indeed and members of the movement had been prone to disappear without a trace on moonless nights, Albright had found that most of those who called to vent their bigotry aloud, often in streams of nearly incoherent filth—were less inclined to act than those who kept the hatred bottled up inside. At least the callers had some outlet for their rage, using the telephone instead of building pipe bombs in the basement. Lately, though, the mood and temper of the haters in America had changed.

Albright couldn't explain it logically, since hate groups normally enjoyed their greatest affluence in periods of economic hardship, when the bitter unemployed sought scapegoats to explain their wretched lot in life. The 1990s, though, had been an era of prosperity, with unemployment and inflation figures at their lowest ebb in memory. Why was it, then, that neo-Nazi thugs, Klansmen and sundry bands of paramilitary "patriots" proliferated in the land?

Albright knew all the arguments—big government, high taxes, immigration, welfare, crime, abortion— and while all of them were clearly factors, he believed that the new millennium had much to do with it, as well. For nearly two decades, the racist fringe had couched its arguments increasingly in terms of an apocalyptic faith—or fear—of what would come to pass in Y2K. Now that the deadline had both come and gone, with no trace of catastrophe, the true believers were required to make adjustments and manipulate their prophecies, as Adventists had done in 1844, when Jesus failed to keep his date for the predicted Second Coming. Some groups had dissolved, apparently relieved that they wouldn't be facing down the Antichrist at Armageddon, but others were clearly angry, all dressed up with nowhere to go, determined that their effort and self-sacrifice wouldn't be wasted. If the last days had been put on hold, for some reason, then they would make the next-to-last days count.

Albright downplayed the threats he had received, kept many of them to himself, but he was conscious of the need for strict security precautions at the following day's gathering. Chicago PD had detailed six officers, all black, to help screen ticket holders and secure the Hotel Valentine, including banquet, conference and exhibition rooms. It wasn't much in terms of manpower, and after receiving the usual cold shoulder from the FBI, Albright had hired the cheapest rent-a-cops that he could find to make an even dozen guards.

Was it enough?

The bad part was that he would never know the answer to that question unless something went wrong—by which time, it would be too late.

He reckoned that Dr. Hayling had felt relatively secure on the morning he was killed. The Mississippi Klan and allied groups had been reduced to scattered remnants of their one-time strength, and from what Albright knew firsthand, the threats of death had tapered off to one or two a month, most of the callers windy drunks or troubled kids. So Hayling had relaxed, gone out to start his car one Sunday morning, and the world blew up in his face.

It troubled Albright that the men who killed his friend had never been identified. The shrunken hate groups had been widely infiltrated by that time—so thoroughly, in fact, that several Klans were actually led by FBI informants, most of their members drawing monthly checks from Uncle Sam to file reports on one another. It was almost comical—until that lethal bomb went off, and no one had a clue about who lit the fuse.

It had been years since Albright gave up fearing that the unknown bombers might return for him, but now, with so much bitter hate and violence in the land, he knew that anything was possible. The next day's celebration was his last, best hope to revive a movement that was virtually forgotten, if not positively moribund.

And to what end? Was it, as some had charged, a simple case of ego run amok on his part? Albright didn't like to think so—though, admittedly, he reveled in the planning and was pleased to see his name mentioned in the local press for something other than a one-line preview of next Sunday's sermon topic. If the movement didn't catch fire, if the celebration proved to be no more than a kind of nostalgic class reunion...well, then, what was wrong with that? Aging veterans hobbled off to Normandy each June to rehash their war stories. Why shouldn't the front-line soldiers of a longer, equally momentous struggle be allowed to reminisce and honor fallen comrades?

As long as no one joined the list, Albright thought, offering up a silent prayer. That done, he slid open his right-hand desk drawer and removed the Charter Arms Police Bulldog revolver that he kept there, loaded with five rounds of .44 Special hollowpoint ammunition.

He hoped he wouldn't need it.

And remembered that the Lord helped those who helped themselves.

MARILYN CROUDER STOOD on the runway and waited for Mike Belasko to finish retrieving his bags from the Air Force jet that had delivered them to north

Chicago. Another military installation, though she recognized from uniforms and signs that this one was a navy post. Off to the east, Lake Michigan lay vast and dark in front of her. Due north, Waukegan's lights seemed close enough to touch, while to the south, the great blaze of Chicagoland was bright enough to blot the stars out of the sky.

She was surprised to find herself imagining the great Chicago fire, more than a hundred years before, and wondering what it had looked like after sunset, with the city all in flames. If the Nordic Temple's goon squad kept its schedule, there would be another conflagration in the Windy City, though admittedly on a more modest scale. The death toll certainly shouldn't run into hundreds, if Belasko did his job effectively.

Whatever happened, though, the only death that truly interested Crouder would be Sean Fletcher's, and she hoped to cause that death herself.

Perhaps then she could sleep at night and face her image in the mirror, without having to relive what he had done to her.

"All set?"

Belasko's voice surprised her, nearly made her jump. She turned back from the dark expanse of lake to find him standing at her elbow, heavy-looking duffel bags in either hand, another slung across one shoulder. Two of them produced the muffled kind of shifting, clanking sounds a toolbox makes: his mobile arsenal. She wondered for an instant whether he had brought along the rifle she had liberated back at Freedom Home.

She hoped so. It would be more difficult to kill

Sean Fletcher if she had to tackle him with her Swiss army knife.

"As ready as I'll ever be," she told him, picking up her small suitcase, lighter than it appeared, because she had so few belongings left—two new outfits from Kmart, with an extra pair of sneakers and a thrown-together makeup kit with just enough of the essentials to keep her from looking like a street urchin.

"Car's back this way," Bolan said, and took the lead. She followed him across the tarmac, lacking energy to double-time or any need to walk beside him, rubbing shoulders. Any contact was repulsive at the moment. Something else she owed Sean Fletcher and intended to extract from him in mortal pain.

Their ride was yet another SUV—a Jeep Grand Cherokee this time, with room in back for all their bags, and then some. The keys were in the ignition as Bolan slid behind the wheel, and it occurred to her that military bases were perhaps the final sanctuary from the nation's glut of crime. A moment later, she recalled the "fatal vision" case and others like it, scrapping that illusion with the rest that her career in law enforcement had destroyed.

There was no sanctuary, no safe place in the United States. Perhaps no place on Earth. Did people rob and rape and kill each other in the Polynesian islands? In the tribes that eked a living from the Arctic tundra?

Jesus, what a world!

Of course, it was the only one they had.

"You really got rooms at the Hotel Valentine?" she asked, once they were off the base and rolling south on Green Bay Road bound for Chicago proper.

"They had a vacancy," Bolan said.

"That must have been some trick, between the weekend and the FREE convention."

"Let's just say I know a guy who knows a guy."

"Your guy must know a *lot* of guys, the way these military types roll over for you," Crouder observed.

"It's no big deal," he said. "We're all on the same side."

"I wonder, sometimes."

"Oh?"

"Forget it. I'm just feeling sorry for myself." When he made no reply to that, she said, "I hate to say it, but I'm also feeling kind of lagged. I know we have to scout the place and all, but I'll be more help to you later if I catch a nap as soon as we check in."

"No problem," he replied. "It shouldn't take much scouting, with the kill zone right downstairs."

Kill zone. A few days earlier, the phrase would have repulsed her, but now she found herself in full agreement, praying for the chance to bust a cap in Fletcher's ass.

"They'll have security in place," she said.

"I would imagine so."

Not long before, a fascist lone-wolf type had gone ballistic in Chicago, shooting several blacks and Jews before he fled to Indiana, killing as he went, finally committing suicide before he could be taken into custody. A few weeks later, yet another neo-Nazi freak had emulated the attacks in L.A. and Las Vegas, striking randomly at nonwhite citizens and Jewish centers. Since that time, there had been other incidents, most recently the Nordic Temple's budding reign of terror. It was rare, she knew, for any synagogue or civil rights group to hold meetings nowadays, without armed guards on hand to deal with any creeps who came out of the woodwork, looking for an easy mark.

"I guess there's no way you can tip them off that you're one of the good guys," Crouder remarked.

"And have them trust me?" Bolan was frowning as he shook his head. "I wouldn't think so. Anyway, they'd just tip the police or FBI."

Not long ago, she would have taken that as a good thing, but the new Marilyn Crouder shared her companion's aversion to involving law enforcement any more than absolutely necessary. They could have the scene when it was finished, take their photographs, pick up the pieces, but she didn't want a lot of suits or uniforms blocking her shot at Fletcher, if the bastard showed.

She didn't want him being taken in alive.

Crouder knew that she would never tell Archer about the rape, meaning no charges would be filed, and even if they managed to convict Fletcher on an epic list of charges, even if they sentenced him to die, the crime he had committed against her would go unpunished.

Unless she sought retribution for herself.

"So, when we get in," Bolan was saying, "you go up and hit the sheets, first thing. I'll stow my gear and have a look around, check out the various approaches, see what's what. They have some kind of brunch tomorrow at noon, to kick things off, and then the program runs till four o'clock. My guess would be, the shooters—if they're coming—will show up ahead of time, then wait until it seems like they have all the crowd they can expect. More targets that way. Hard to miss with automatic weapons."

"And supposing they just plant a bomb?" she asked. "What if it's in place, already counting down? They may not show at all. Just sit around a TV set, somewhere, and wait for the news flash."

"The FBI has people checking out the hotel as we speak," he said. "Bomb dogs and sniffers. If somebody left a package, they should find it."

"Let me guess," she said. "Your guy who knows a guy?"

"Something like that."

"Okay, we're set, then," she replied.

And silently, to gods unknown: *One shot. That's all I ask.*

SEAN FLETCHER LEFT the red-eye special carrying a gym bag that contained a change of clothing, an electric razor, toothbrush, toothpaste and a paperback novel. The novel was *Hunter*, a sequel to *The Turner Diaries*, which, in turn, was blamed by left-wing Jew-lovers around the country for inspiring the attack upon the Oklahoma City federal building back in 1995. Before that, it supposedly had spurred the martyrs of The Order to embark upon a string of bombings, robberies and executions aimed at ZOG.

Fletcher enjoyed the book, but he didn't believe it was responsible for any Aryan pursuing revolution in the flesh. Such theories failed to recognize the dedication of committed warriors like himself, who pledged their lives to dam the flood of filth that poured from Washington, Moscow and Tel Aviv to inundate the white man's world.

Fletcher required no book to tell him who his mortal adversaries were. His eyes and nose were all he needed to identity the enemy. If he had gone stone blind, he could have smelled them coming from a mile away.

Two comrades from the Nordic Temple waited for him midway down the airport concourse. They hadn't met Fletcher at the gate, because they both were carrying and couldn't pass the checkpoint to arrivals and departures without setting off alarms. One of them had an extra pistol he would pass to Fletcher once they cleared the terminal. Even at that hour, police were about, more travelers than Fletcher would have counted on. Trying to save a buck or two by flying with the freaks and ghouls.

Like him.

Unlike the airport terminal, which smelled of sweat and vague anxiety, the night was cool and clear outside. No stars were visible, of course—the city's all-night glare took care of that—but Fletcher didn't mind; after the hot, cramped quarters of his flight in coach, he even welcomed the pervasive smell of car and truck exhaust that tainted every breath. Chicago's famous wind was not in evidence just now, and that was fine, as well.

The next day, Fletcher and his troops would blow a measure of corruption from the city's streets themselves.

It was a fair hike to the parking garage, where his escorts had left their Plymouth Voyager SE minivan. He didn't comment on the choice of vehicles; it was irrelevant, as long as they had what was needed, when it mattered.

Fletcher had one leg up, stepping into the back seat, when one of the skinheads drew a pistol from underneath his Army-surplus jacket, saying, "This is for you." Fletcher tensed involuntarily, his paranoia far enough advanced that he could picture members of his own team turning traitor, plotting to assassinate him, but the young man simply held the weapon out to him, butt first.

"It's cocked and locked," he said. "We've got some holsters you can try out when we get back to the house."

"All right." Fletcher felt slightly foolish as the door shut behind him, and his two companions climbed into the seats up front, but he suppressed the feeling ruthlessly. Constant awareness was the price of leadership, particularly in a down-and-dirty revolution when your side was certifiably the underdog. There was no reason to believe that Mary Krause would be the last traitor to surface in the Temple of the Nordic Covenant, and it was evident that ZOG had shifted from a policy of spying and harassment in the courts to something darker and more devious.

The pistol Fletcher held was a .40-caliber Smith & Wesson Model 4006, the same piece that was standard issue for the FBI. With ten rounds in the magazine and one more in the chamber, it was ready to rock. Fletcher thumbed off the safety and left the hammer down, relying on the first-shot double-action mechanism to provide whatever speed he needed on the draw.

"You scope the target like I ordered?" Fletcher asked when they had cleared the cashier's booth to exit the garage.

"All done," the driver said while navigating toward the ramp that fed Highway 190, which in turn would take them to Chicago. "We've got floor plans, photos, uniforms, the whole nine yards. We did a dry run last weekend when the Shriners were in town. If it had been for real, they never would've known what hit them."

"Something tells me that the Shriners didn't put on much security," he said.

"Well, no. It was a dry run, like I said."

"This afternoon, it's wet," Fletcher replied. "We can expect Chicago's finest, maybe rent-a-cops or hotel dicks. Don't be surprised if they've got something more, on top of that."

"Like what?" the skinhead in the shotgun seat inquired.

"Like something that a dry run couldn't show you. Something that will take your head off if you give it half a chance."

"Is that what happened in L.A.?" the driver asked. From the expression in his eyes, reflected in the rearview mirror, he was sorry he had asked the question, even as he finished speaking.

"We were sold out in Los Angeles," Fletcher replied, keeping his cool. "There was a mole inside the Temple, and she knew enough to tip somebody off about the raid."

"A broad?" The front-seat passenger seemed outraged. "You said 'she'?"

"An enemy," Fletcher stated. "Did you think ZOG only uses Jews and blacks? Maybe all the Feds are white-bread preppie types in business suits?"

"No, sir," the chastened shotgun rider said.

"Are you two on the team that's going in this afternoon?"

"Yes, sir!" The driver sounded proud, psyched up.

"Then be damned sure you keep your eyes wide open all the time. The first time you take anything for granted, you're as good as dead. The one who kills you might turn out to be a wino on the street or a Korean maid. If you're not watching for it, you won't see it coming, and they own your ass."

"You think the Feds are wise to what we're doing, then?" The shotgun rider sounded nervous now.

"Always assume the worst and be prepared for anything," Fletcher replied.

"About that mole, sir," said the driver. "Is she still around?"

"I've taken care of that," he said.

But had he? It was going on five hours now, since Rogers and his men should have resolved the matter at Coyote Lake, and there was still no word. Granted, Fletcher had spent most of that time airborne, or shuffling in and out of airports. There was no way Rogers could have reached him to report the outcome, pro or con. For his own peace of mind, though, Fletcher had to know.

"I need to use a pay phone," he informed the driver. "Take the next off-ramp and find a service station, something."

"We've got telephones back at the house," the driver said.

"I don't believe I stuttered."

"No, sir. Next off-ramp. We're almost there."

He would feel better, once the clean sweep was confirmed by Rogers. But if something had gone wrong, then what?

Then they'd go ahead, as planned, he thought. And Wotan help any poor, dumb bastard who got in their way.

CHAPTER FIFTEEN

The Hotel Valentine wasn't the newest, flashiest or most luxurious hotel Chicago had to offer, but it had a certain air of slightly faded class, reminding Bolan of a bygone era modern yuppies probably didn't remember—that was, if they'd ever known about it in the first place.

He was up and dressed by 8:00 a.m., four hours' sleep enough to wipe the jet lag and the cobwebs from his mind. Another four, until the celebration was supposed to start downstairs, and that gave Bolan time to shower and consume the breakfast he had ordered from room service in advance. He dined alone and hoped that Crouder was still asleep in her room, two doors down the hall.

When he had cleaned his plate and brushed his teeth, Bolan prepared to meet his enemies. This wouldn't be a hit-and-git guerrilla action, so he left the blacksuit packed away. The suit he chose was charcoal-gray, conservative, nothing to make him stand out in a crowd. The jacket had been cut a half size larger than he normally required, to make allowance for the tailored Kevlar vest he wore beneath his shirt, along with any weapons he selected for the mission.

That would be the tricky part, he knew. Meeting his adversaries in a public venue, with civilian noncombatants all around, his choice of weapons was distinctly limited. No explosives or incendiaries, for a start. More to the point, Bolan knew that whatever automatic weapons he employed, he would be forced to handle them with utmost care.

Accordingly, he made his choices with efficiency and safety foremost in his mind. He wore the usual Beretta 93-R slung beneath his left arm, with a Heckler & Koch MP-5 K submachine gun tethered below his right. Both 9 mm weapons were set to fire 3-round bursts, providing maximum control, and the MP-5 K was also built for concealment, measuring a mere 12.8 inches overall, tipping the scales at barely six pounds, with a loaded magazine in place. Selective fire tamed the man-shredder's 800-rounds-per-minute cyclic rate, conserving ammunition at the same time it allowed a shooter to apply precision fire on target.

Bolan checked his watch again, after he slipped on his jacket: 8:45 a.m. He took a moment to repack his bags, closing the padlocks that secured each zipper. They could still be cut, of course, but he didn't expect a hotel maid to have much interest in the contents of three ordinary-looking duffel bags. Eventually, if he wasn't able to retrieve them, someone would remove the bags, defeat the locks and find the surplus arms and ammunition they contained, along with Bolan's other clothes and shaving gear. They would find nothing to identify the owner of the bags, much less to trace him back to Stony Man or Washington. If he didn't return to claim his things, it meant they were no further use to him.

He would be gone…or dead.

He took his key card with him, just in case he had the opportunity to come back for his things, but heard a grim finality in the click of the door as it locked automatically behind him. Passing Crouder's room on his way to the elevator, he paused to listen at the door, heard nothing to suggest that she was up and showering or watching television. That didn't mean she was still asleep, of course, but he allowed himself a moment's wishful thinking as he moved on down the hall.

Advance teams for the FREE convention had already moved the bulk of their materials into the Hotel Valentine sometime last night, and they were busy setting up when Bolan reached the level that contained the hotel's banquet hall and conference rooms. He didn't linger, noting several uniformed Chicago PD officers on hand, as well as an equal number of armed guards from some private security firm. They all wore side arms, the police with Kevlar vests beneath their powder-blue shirts, but they clearly weren't prepared for anything like the attack staged three days earlier, against the Eli Sturnman Center, in Los Angeles. How would they cope with gunmen bearing automatic weapons, high explosives and God knew what else in the way of armament?

Not well at all, he thought, and took the escalator down another floor before the uniforms took notice of him and decided they should ask his business, maybe pat him down for the heck of it.

He saw no evidence of any Feds in the hotel, although they could have been disguised as staff or guests. With that in mind, he eyeballed three employees chatting at the registration desk—too young. The hostess dawdling at the entry of the hotel's coffee shop was too glamorous by half, and the bell captain and doorman were both possibles, though neither had the federal "feel" about him. More likely, if Brognola had the local FBI on standby, they were staying out of sight, perhaps in some adjacent building or in vehicles dispersed around the neighborhood.

Bolan could only hope that when the time came, if they made it to the combat zone at all, the Feds wouldn't get in his way.

In any case, whether the hostage rescue team showed up or the Chicago officers and rent-a-cops were on their own when it went down, he ran a major risk of being caught in the cross fire—or, worse, being mistaken for one of the raiders himself. It was entirely probable, he knew, that one or more lawmen would try to take him down, in which case there was nothing he could do except to dodge their fire and try to keep from getting wasted by the good guys. There could be no question of returning fire, wounding or killing lawmen who were acting in performance of their duty. Bolan didn't play that game; he never had and never would.

Not even if it meant his death from not-so-friendly fire.

It was 9:20 a.m. by his watch, two minutes later by the large clock mounted on the hotel lobby's eastern wall. Call it two and a half hours remaining until the FREE convention was gaveled to order, probably at least an hour before the early bird attendees started straggling in. Their would-be killers, meanwhile, were almost certainly in place, or quickly getting there.

The bad news was that Bolan had no realistic chance of spotting them before they did some damage, most particularly if they were wise enough to divide their force for maximum effect.

The good news was they wouldn't strike silently, preferring maximum confusion for the targets it would offer and to increase chances of their getaway. Anywhere they struck in the hotel was readily accessible to Bolan, as long as he didn't allow the men in uniform to cut him off or take him down.

And there was nothing left for him to do but keep on drifting, picking up a free newspaper in the lobby, killing time and checking out arrivals and departures at the registration desk. He found a seat off to the west, well removed from the glide path between the hotel's entrance and the elevators, sat down with his paper opened to the local news and settled in to wait.

"YOU BELLHOPS, listen up," Sean Fletcher told the members of his strike team dressed in maroon blazers, each with the Hotel Valentine's logo embroidered on the breast pocket. "I want you to remember what you're here for and keep your stories straight. You're temps, laid on to handle any special traffic during the convention, right? If someone has you run their bags upstairs, whatever, do not under any circumstances cause a scene. If you have time, just do the frigging job and double-time back to the mezzanine."

"And if we don't have time?" one of them asked. "What then?"

"You know what then, Boyarski," Fletcher said.

"We move at 12:15 precisely, while the fat cats and their pet baboons are in the banquet hall, all misty-eyed about this guy who got wasted twenty years ago. They're sitting down, distracted, their attention's on the podium—we take them out. If anybody tries to interfere with that or keep you from assigned positions at H hour, you may use whatever force is necessary to remove the obstacle."

"All right!" Boyarski said.

"That does not mean you cap the manager at 12:02 for asking you to lug a bag upstairs, then stand around for thirteen minutes with your thumb up your ass, while the SWAT team moves in. Are we clear?"

Boyarski lost his smile and answered with the others when they snapped "Yes, sir!"

"All right, then. Keep your minds right and your times tight. Watches have been synchronized for a reason, people. Twelve-fifteen does *not* mean 12:14 or 12:16 and thirty seconds. Do you read me?"

"Yes, sir!" The thirteen voices answered as one.

"Okay, let's move!"

He didn't give them any extra time to check the compact submachine guns they were carrying, Ingrams and mini-Uzis selected for concealability, no sound suppressors to bulk them up or snag on clothing in a crunch. They also carried Army-issue frag grenades, spare magazines, approximately half with backup guns. The ten of them, including Fletcher, who didn't wear stolen hotel blazers were attired in normal, slightly upscale street clothes, nothing in the way of hunter's camouflage or any other garb that might attract undue attention.

They took two vans, with seven men each. Thirteen

of them had drawn straws to see which two would be left out, required to man the vehicles and miss all the fun, Fletcher alone exempt from that lottery, as leader of the hit team. Now, after a short run to the Hotel Valentine, one van dropped off the four "temps" in the alleyway out back before it moved on to a side street, disgorging Fletcher and his lone companion, a skinhead named Askew who had let his hair grow out for the occasion.

The other team was passing through the hotel's big revolving door as Fletcher and Askew rounded the corner, moving at a steady, though outwardly casual pace toward the entrance. Fletcher felt his mini-Uzi digging into the small of his back, where he carried it tucked inside the waistband of his slacks. He had it loaded with two magazines, clipped together in an L-shape, the spare protruding from below the weapon's pistol grip, parallel with its muzzle. Four more magazines filled Fletcher's pockets, and he had two frag grenades clipped to his belt, concealed beneath his navy blazer.

The hotel lobby wasn't jammed by any means, but it was filling with regular arrivals lined up for the registration counter, some who might belong to any one of three conventions being hosted at the Hotel Valentine that Saturday, employees in their trademark blazers and a UPS deliveryman. Two cops in uniform were standing well off to one side, a salt-and-pepper team, the black one muttering into a walkie-talkie, while his burly partner scoped out the lobby.

As Fletcher watched his people fanning out, proceeding toward the elevators, escalator and the service stairs, he wondered whether any of the various civil-

ians he could see were really undercover cops or
Feds. It troubled him that there was still no word
available from Rogers, and he wondered now if something had gone wrong. Two of his men were driving
from Los Angeles to Coyote Lake, disguised as quail
hunters, to have a look around. With his luck, it
would be too damned late to scrub the mission in
Chicago by the time they got out to the desert and
were able to report back anything they found.

He had already grappled with the obvious worst-
case scenario. Assuming Rogers blew it totally, that
Mary Krause somehow escaped and managed to contact authorities, what would it mean to the Chicago
mission? Did she even know a second strike was
planned after the Sturnman Center, much less its location, timing, target, all the rest of it? How could
she? he had asked himself repeatedly, and came up
blank for answers.

Screw it!

They were committed now, already had their heads
inside the lion's mouth, as it were. He had discussed
the problem with his Führer, hours earlier, and had
been ordered to proceed. After the fuck-up in Los
Angeles, at the Jewseum, Fletcher was determined not
to fail a second time.

He moved off toward the escalator, Askew following, their target on the mezzanine. Passing the two
policemen, Fletcher flashed a grin and nodded toward
the black cop with the radio. He got the barest nod
back in return, the cop—a sergeant, Fletcher saw,
with smaller hash marks showing ten years' service
on his sleeve—dismissing him as he would any other
honky businessman. Whatever their mission, perhaps

as simple as keeping an eye out for thieves at a fair-sized convention hotel, the officers apparently saw nothing wrong with Fletcher or his sidekick, as they passed within arm's reach.

So far so good.

He stepped onto the escalator, Askew right behind him, resting one hand casually on the rubber handrail, feeling the machinery's vibration through his hand and arm. It felt as if the hotel were alive, a dozing giant, Fletcher no more than an insect, crawling on its skin.

Make that a spider, seeking prey. He was about to find a whole roomful of fat black beetles, waiting for him. They had turned out for a banquet, never realizing *they* were on the menu.

Fletcher and his soldiers were about to ring the dinner bell.

IT SEEMED to Lewis Albright, working on a head count from the dais, that the crowd was somewhat larger than anticipated. That had to be illusion, though, he told himself, because the seating for the banquet was presold, no walk-ins off the street, no places set unless a diner was expected. What he calculated, then, was that they weren't suffering the normal dropout rate of those who purchased tickets for events and then decided, for whatever reason, not to show.

It pleased him that the names of FREE and the Reverend Mr. Aaron Hayling still had drawing power, even after all these years. Albright didn't delude himself that anyone aside from certain friends and relatives were here for *him,* surrendering their Saturday because Lewis Albright was delivering the keynote speech. Fat chance of that, he thought. But they would hear him, all the same, and some of them would almost certainly write checks to help finance FREE's next campaign in Congress, seeking passage of a civil rights bill for the new millennium, to pick up where the old-time victories of Hayling, King and others had left off so long ago.

The banquet hall was nearly filled, a hum of conversation filling the high-ceilinged room. They were already running late, but that was typical for almost any gathering, more particularly those more affluent and privileged individuals to whom the rules of punctuality and common courtesy didn't apply in equal measure.

Never mind that now, he told himself, and smiled. Once they were seated, they were his. A captive audience. Their overpriced baked chicken and steamed vegetables wouldn't be served until Albright had finished speaking to them, reminiscing of the bad old days and slipping in his sales pitch, toward the end.

They could jabber all they wanted. He was about to pick their pockets, and he wanted them in a good mood when he made the touch.

He gave them five more minutes, saw the eighty tables nearly full, with seven diners each at most of them, before he stepped up to the podium, reached out and scratched the microphone a few times with the thick nail of his index finger. Testing. Instantly, the scraping sound was amplified, bounced back to Albright from the far wall, sounding like some kind of giant carnivore gnawing bones.

"Good afternoon, my friends," he said into the

microphone. There was a high, sharp squeal of feed-
back, swiftly vanquished as the hotel's sound man
fiddled with knobs on the unit's control panel, away
to Albright's left. "It's good to see so many people
here on this fine day, to celebrate FREE's anniversary
and to commemorate the passing of a great man I was
privileged to call my friend."

Albright had printed out his speech on a computer,
as he did with every Sunday sermon he delivered, but
he found the notes almost superfluous, as he continued speaking of his old friend Aaron Hayling, and the
movement they had helped to lead.

"It still surprises me, sometimes—and I'll admit it
saddens me a bit, as well—when I'm reminded that
the monumental freedom struggle of the 1960s has
been relegated to the status of a few short paragraphs,
perhaps only a footnote, in the textbooks that our children study when they're learning history in school. I
can assure you that it felt more like a banner headline
back in those days, when the actual events were starting to unfold. We had some days when there was
cause to wonder whether we would all survive. And
some of us, as you all know, didn't survive the struggle, after all."

That brought a murmur from the audience, a lady
here and there already dabbing at her eyes. He had
them, Albright thought, and he was only warming up.
Wait till he started rattling the ceiling tiles.

"But time moves on," he said, "and sometimes
heroes are forgotten, their sacrifice taken for granted
by new generations, with new problems. It remains a
challenge for each one of us to see that heroes *shall
not* be forgotten by our children and grandchildren.

More important, though, it falls to each and every one of us to see that problems we thought were vanquished long ago do not return and rear their ugly heads again to blight the days of those young ones we love so much.''

He got a lonely "Amen!" from the audience on that one, coming from somewhere in back, a woman's voice. It pleased him, but before he could proceed, Albright was conscious of a sudden movement at the double doors, directly opposite the podium at which he stood.

A young white man had poked his head in through the door, and just as quickly stepped back out again, ducked to his left, the speaker's right, and out of sight. A heartbeat later, while Albright was still distracted, two arms whipped around the doorjamb, one on each side, and Albright saw dark egg-shaped objects tumbling through the air into the dining room.

Before he had a chance to recognize them, much less understand exactly what was happening, he heard the loud, unmistakable sounds of gunfire—automatic weapons—from somewhere close by, outside the banquet hall.

"Ladies and gentlemen—"

But Albright got no further with his warning, for the hand grenades exploded then, and turned the dining room into a scene from hell.

MARILYN CROUDER didn't seek out Belasko; in fact, she had deliberately avoided running into him. She knew what he would say about her personal involvement, her emotions getting in the way, the risk that she would either freeze when it was time to act, or else that she would run amok.

All true.

She recognized the risks herself, and knew that she could no more stand aside, remain aloof while Fletcher's gunmen made their move, than she could stand beside a swimming pool and watch a drowning child go down for the last time. She had a duty to perform, and she would see it through, regardless of the cost.

If Sean Fletcher should cross her path, and she was favored with an opportunity to blow out his frigging brains, that was simply icing on the cake.

She had been watching through the peephole in her door when Belasko passed, paused momentarily outside her room and then moved on to go downstairs and scout the battleground. She had delayed another twenty-seven minutes prior to following, until she could no longer stand the tension without screaming, maybe smashing something.

As it was, the only hotel property she had destroyed was one bath towel, which she had cut in strips to make an awkward sling for her Kalashnikov. Because she dared not walk around the busy hotel with the weapon in a shopping bag, and since she couldn't wear a simple sling across her chest, where it would instantly be visible, she made two separate slings of terry cloth instead. One looped around her left shoulder, securing the automatic rifle's pistol grip. The other went around her right shoulder, its longer free end tied off to the weapon's barrel, so the AK hung across her back diagonally with the muzzle poking into her right buttock. Barely covered by the longest, loosest jacket she possessed, it was the best arrangement that she could come up with in the circumstances. If and when the shooting started, she would have to ditch the jacket first, then shrug off the rifle as if it were a backpack.

If she wasn't grabbed by the police or shot by one of Fletcher's goons while that was going on, the lady Fed believed she had a fighting chance.

Downstairs, she lurked as much as possible, watching out for Belasko and for any members of the Nordic Temple she might recognize, sidestepping the police and rent-a-cops she met, keeping her back against a wall whenever feasible, avoiding situations where she would be followed, prompting anyone to speculate about the lumpy shape beneath her jacket. In between her circuits of the second floor and mezzanine, she ducked into the ladies' room and found herself an empty stall, to kill time and protect herself from undue scrutiny. Each time she left the rest room, Crouder expected to feel handcuffs close around her wrists, but if the cops in evidence took any notice of her, they dismissed her just as quickly.

She glimpsed Belasko half a dozen times, retreating in each instance, seemingly unnoticed. She couldn't keep that up for long, if trouble started, but by then it wouldn't matter. There was no way he could stop in the midst of a firefight and order her back to her room, like a child.

She was changing her pattern, descending from the second floor to the mezzanine via the service stairs—a risk, if Belasko should take the same path, but too late to reconsider now—when she heard sounds of gunfire from her destination on the floor below. At least two automatic weapons, firing staggered bursts, and while the noise was muffled by the concrete walls surrounding her, she also heard the high-pitched sound of screams.

A moment later, Crouder still frozen on the stairs, and she was jarred out of her immobility by two loud, rapid-fire explosions. Hand grenades? Some kind of flash bangs? She didn't believe the blasts were strong enough to indicate C-4 in use, though it was still a possibility if Fletcher's men were using small, shaped charges.

One way to find out.

Halfway down the final flight of stairs, she paused to strip off her jacket, then grappled with the twin slings that secured her rifle, nearly toppling over in the process as she lost her balance. Grabbing at the nearer banister, she kept herself from falling, cursed the fleeting seconds it required to free the crude slings from her AK and to put her jacket on again. Concealment in a pinch—not much, but better than nothing. Chambering a live round as she jolted down the last few stairs, she reached the access door and pulled it open, leaning out to take a look around.

The first thing that she saw was people running pell-mell for the exits, two of them beelining for the doorway where she stood, until they saw the rifle in her hands and veered off in a panic, sprinting with their hands raised in a hopeless gesture of surrender, even as they fled. Next, Crouder made out a scattering of bodies, two of them in uniforms that marked them as police.

Most of the racket was emerging from the banquet hall, its doors still open, though the lulling echoes of a speaker at the podium had been replaced by screams and sounds of mortal combat.

"This must be the place," she told herself, and moved in that direction, running hard, as if her life depended on it.

BOLAN HAD BEEN riding on the escalator when the first shots echoed from the mezzanine above. In front of him, a stylish couple clutched each other, gasping, then reversed directions, trying to descend against the upward motion of the moving staircase.

Bolan stood aside to let them pass, then vaulted up the last few steps to reach the mezzanine, his MP-5 K submachine gun already in hand. At first, despite a general scene of panic—or because of it—he could narrow down no more than the general direction of the sounds of gunfire. When the hand grenades went off, there was no longer any doubt in Bolan's mind. The crowd inside the banquet hall was under fire.

So much for watching out for skinheads in the hotel lobby. Bolan's enemies had slipped past him as easily as if he had been blind, deaf and unconscious, all at once. He didn't know how they had managed it, and that no longer mattered. Battle had been joined, and he could already make out the prostrate forms of fallen casualties. What mattered now was cutting short the raid before the butcher's bill got any higher.

Checking out the mezzanine for uniforms, he saw two fallen officers among the other dead and wounded, several yards in front of him. Neither had drawn his side arm from its holster, indicating that they had been shot as a preventive measure when the hit team was prepared to make its move.

How many guns? He counted three, by the erratic spacing of their bursts, but after that, the sounds all ran together in chaotic counterpoint. A third grenade blast rocked the mezzanine, and Bolan hated to imagine what the banquet hall had to look like, turned into a veritable slaughter pen.

His first sight of the raiders came a moment later, Bolan almost to the open doorway that would put him in the banquet hall. A young white man, dressed in one of the hotel's trademark blazers, stepped outside to scan the mezzanine, then raised a small machine pistol and fired a burst in the direction of some fleeing noncombatants.

Bolan saw his chance and took it, squeezing off a 3-round burst that slugged his target backward, ripping through his face and throat, the shooter unaware that Death had found him as his long legs buckled and he slithered to the floor.

He reached the doorway, pressed his back against the wall and risked a glance into the banquet room. He had a jumbled view of tables lying on their sides, chairs cast about in all directions as their occupants had bolted or fallen, tablecloths tangled and strewed about the floor where running feet had dragged them, resembling streamers from some giant ticker-tape parade.

Shooters were strafing the room from several positions, raking the tables and dais, their probing rounds evoking squeals and screams from targets wounded or hiding. Bolan counted four, five guns, and was about to start subtracting from that number when another SMG cut loose immediately to his left, the gunner in a hotel blazer, backing toward the open doorway.

As he got there, squeezing off another burst, the guy half turned toward Bolan, calling out a name. Rick? Dick? It hardly mattered. He was clearly looking for the gunner Bolan had already iced, and it was only common courtesy to hook him up.

The Executioner's left hand shot out and snagged the gunman by his collar, dragged him backward through the open doorway, ankles cut from underneath him by a sweeping kick as Bolan flung him headlong to the floor. He never had a chance to rise again, the 3-round burst from Bolan's MP-5 K hammering his skull to bloody pulp as he lay facedown on the carpet.

Two for two, and Bolan knew he couldn't count on any others coming to the door, obliging him that way. He had to go in after them before the slaughter in the banquet hall got any worse, and he still had no way of knowing whether there were other members of the Nordic Temple hit team still at large in the hotel. For all he knew—

Forget that, now. He had to take one objective at a time.

The front-line warrior's maxim: if you tried to see the big picture, imagining a whole campaign—even a major battle, end to end—the chances were extremely good that you would never live to fight another day. Whatever strategists and politicians say, war was extremely personal for soldiers in the trenches. Soldiers fought to stay alive, to help their friends, perhaps to seize a finite piece of ground, but when the guns were going off, most had no more concept of sweeping, long-range victories than they did of pulsars or quantum mechanics.

Bolan risked another glance around the doorjamb and saw nothing to suggest that either of his two kills had been missed, as yet. The shooters that were left, all five of them, were still intent on killing every person they could see inside the banquet hall.

He was about to offer them another target, when he had a sudden thought, stripped off his jacket, stepped back to his second kill and wrestled off the hotel blazer. It was small on Bolan, binding slightly in the armpits, but he wasn't going to a fashion show. He pointedly ignored the feel of warm blood on his neck, from where the collar had been spattered when its owner lost his head. If that was all the blood that stained his flesh today, he would be lucky, and then some.

Ready at last, he turned and ducked into the charnel house.

CHAPTER SIXTEEN

Why was he still alive?

The question wasn't new to Lewis Albright. He had asked the same thing of himself repeatedly throughout his years of struggle: after confrontations with the KKK and Southern sheriff's deputies; after his youngest son was killed in Operation Desert Storm; after he beat the cancer, five years, seven months and thirteen days ago. And since he never had an answer handy when he asked the question, Albright fell back on the reason he had learned in childhood, coming up through Sunday school in Mississippi: God had to have a reason of His own.

From where he lay, cheek pressed against the polished wooden surface of the dais, Albright had a field of vision covering perhaps one-quarter of the banquet hall. The podium blocked any view of what lay to his left, but he could see the carnage straight ahead and to his right, at least until the point where his eyeballs began to roll back in their sockets. Playing dead, aware that he was totally exposed to several gunmen as they raked the room from different sides, he dared not move his head, much less get up on hands and knees to have a better look around.

This was the end, he thought. It had to be. And just as soon as he had formed the thought, another voice inside his head responded, *Not unless I will it so.*

He was hallucinating now. Terrific. Hearing voices, while a bunch of redneck peckerwoods were shooting up his best contributors, the last hope he and FREE would ever have of moving back toward center state, or at least keeping a seat on the movement band wagon.

Selfish pride, the deep voice in his head proclaimed.

"Goeth before a fall," he whispered in response.

Oh, God! Had one of the assassins seen his lips move? Suddenly, a stream of bullets raked and rocked the podium, causing his eyes to flicker shut, before he realized that even that small movement could betray him.

They had tried to kill him at the very start, but he was only grazed, a burning, leaking wound beneath his left arm, gouged between two ribs. It hurt like hell, but he had suffered and survived much worse: a broken jaw that cost him three teeth, on the freedom rides; bomb shrapnel in his thigh and buttocks, from the time the Klan blew up FREE's headquarters in Oxford, Mississippi; broken ribs, when he was bounced along the sidewalk by the stream from a fire hose, in Birmingham; dogs bites, same day, from when they claimed he was "resisting arrest."

Staring off across the smoky room of capsized chairs and tables, scattered bodies—some of them still breathing, others past all that—he felt an anger building up inside him that was anything but saintly. Albright wished he had a rifle, shotgun, anything at all, with which he could return fire and inflict some damage on the men responsible for all this carnage. Stop them—or distract them, at the very least—and in so doing, give at least a few of the survivors in his audience a chance to get away.

He wanted to be brave, courageous like his martyred friend whom they had come to honor, but the years had taken something out of him, and it was more than simply physical. He had the strength to rise and run, create some kind of a diversion for the others, but he lacked the will, the courage such a move required.

His eyes were focused on the open doors directly opposite, watching as one of the killers stepped outside and fired a burst off to his left, at someone Albright couldn't see. Immediately, there were more shots, barely audible with all the racket in the banquet room, but these cut down the gunman, dropping him as if he were a sack of someone's dirty laundry sprawling on the floor.

Police!

There was a time in Albright's life when uniforms had made him nervous, sometimes even terrified, but that had been another time, another place. This day, nothing would make him happier than to behold a righteous SWAT team bulling through the doorway, mopping up his enemies.

But nothing happened.

No, that wasn't right. A white face poked around the corner of the doorjamb, scanned the banquet hall with narrowed eyes, then ducked out of sight again. No uniform that he could see, but what did that mean? He had only seen the face and glimpsed a portion of one shoulder. In the circumstances, he could easily have been mistaken.

Wild rounds struck the wall above him, making Albright flinch involuntarily, but none of the assassins seemed to notice. Yet another of them drifted toward the doorway, firing as he went. When he got there, he turned and shouted something, words inaudible to Albright: calling to the dead man, maybe, without knowing he was down and out.

And then, a most extraordinary thing occurred.

Before the preacher's startled eyes, an arm reached through the doorway, grabbed the gunman by his neck or collar, snatched him through and out of sight. Another sound of gunfire, almost lost amid the rest, and Albright knew that he was gone.

He scanned the room again, trying to spot survivors, but the people who hadn't been hit so far were lying low, just as he was, trusting immobility to save them if nothing else could. It stood to reason that the shooters were aware of passing time, the risk of being cornered by police responding to a shooting call.

Where *were* the cops? The security guards he had hired?

Something told him he wouldn't be seeing them enter the banquet hall anytime soon.

Someone was coming through the doorway, though, the new arrival decked out in one of the Hotel Valentine's maroon blazers. Both dead gunners had been similarly garbed, and while this wasn't one of them, a sudden flash of insight told Albright that one of them had worn that jacket very recently.

The new arrival had some kind of fancy-looking weapon in his hand—not large, but plenty lethal if the net results were anything to judge by. He was edging toward the nearest shooter on his left, cautious but closing in to striking range.

How long before one of the others spotted him and realized that something had gone wrong? What if they turned on him as one and killed him where he stood? What would become of Albright's few surviving donors, then?

Diversion's what he needed.

Despite his nearly paralyzing fear, the logic of the thought couldn't be denied. He had to do *something*.

With the decision made, nothing to do but act upon it or submit to abject cowardice and try to save himself, he rose to hands and knees, then lurched erect, and shouted to the nearest of his enemies, "Yo, whitey! Over here! Black power's gonna get your momma!"

Blinking at Albright through a haze of rage and battle smoke, the shooter swung his piece around and sprayed the stage, joined by at least one other, to create converging streams of fire.

He'd done it now, Albright thought, ducking behind the podium until it started taking hits, then vaulting to his feet again and diving headlong off the dais to the polished vinyl floor.

BOLAN WAS STARTLED when the black man came alive on stage and started shouting at the gunman nearest to him, drawing fire from two sides as he turned and made his leap to something less than safety, but he didn't let it slow him. With any luck, the strange diversion might just be the edge he needed to survive the next few minutes, maybe even to emerge victorious.

No time to waste.

The shooter twenty feet or so in front of him wasn't distracted by the action on the stage. He fired another burst across the room, chipping at toppled furniture, then dropped his Ingram's empty magazine and reached inside his jacket—not a hotel blazer, Bolan noted—for another. Bolan hit him with a 3-round burst that spun him sideways, left him facing toward the MP-5 K's muzzle, where a second burst erupted, stitching holes across his chest, and put him down.

Twelve rounds expended so far, meaning that he still had eighteen left before reloading. Six more bursts. Enough to clear the room of enemies, if he was lucky, but the odds and angles were against him pulling off that kind of trick.

Focus. One target at a time. Let the long view take care of itself.

In fact, his other three opponents were ranged across the far side of the banquet room, including two whose weapons were directed toward the stage and their elusive target of a moment earlier. The distance wasn't all *that* far, perhaps no more than thirty-five or forty feet, and while that put them well within the MP-5 K's killing range, he didn't choose to fight a duel across the prostrate bodies of the dead, wounded and some who might be still unscathed.

He doubled back in the direction he had come from, past the open doorway, glancing through it as he passed and wondering how much time still remained before police arrived in force. The calls to 911 had certainly gone out by now, and units would be

rolling. The hotel was situated roughly two miles
south of city hall, a little closer to the Federal Building, if Brognola had the FBI on call. Six minutes,
maybe seven, eight before the first units arrived.

Which meant that he was swiftly running out of
time.

None of his surviving adversaries resembled Sean
Fletcher. Bolan wondered briefly if the Nordic Temple's chief enforcer had been spooked by the encounter in Los Angeles, or whether he had learned about
the slaughter at Coyote Lake. Would either be enough
to put him off participating in an action he had
planned and trained for, promising his Führer optimal
results? If he was somewhere in the Hotel Valentine,
but not ringside to join the turkey shoot, where *was*
he?

Bolan derailed that train of thought and concentrated on his nearest enemy. The man had seen him
now, apparently mistook him for an ally until Bolan's
swift approach caused him to reconsider. Blinking,
squinting through a pair of wire-rimmed spectacles,
the shooter jerked back, startled, when he couldn't
recognize the new arrival's face. Uncertain as to
whether this armed stranger represented some extreme hotel-security response, or maybe something
else entirely, the young man recoiled and swung his
SMG around to cut the runner down.

Bolan was faster by a fraction of a second, triggering a burst that caught his target in the throat and
upper chest. Death wasn't instantaneous, as he had
hoped, but the explosive impact of his Parabellum
rounds, combined with spurting blood that filled the
neo-Nazi's throat, threw off his aim as he depressed

the trigger of his mini-Uzi, spraying walls and ceiling as he toppled backward and collapsed.

He was still twitching as the Executioner stepped over him, but he was out of it for all intents and purposes, his eyes already glazed with the advance of death. Dismissing him, Bolan was halfway to the next man on his hit parade when that one turned around and saw him coming, shouted out a warning to his comrade and cut loose with his MAC-10.

The Ingram's greatest strength *and* weakness was its awesome rate of fire, twelve hundred rounds per minute, give or take. It was a dreadful killer at close range, but it devoured a 32-round magazine in something like a second and a half. It was for that reason that Bolan's adversary found himself confronting his unknown assailant with an empty gun, the grim expression on his face revealing that he knew there would be no time to reload.

There wasn't.

Bolan shot him on the run, a tight group to the center of his chest that blew him backward, feet up in the air as shoulders hit the deck. He thrashed around a little, bleeding out internally.

The sixth and final gunner in the banquet hall had used his comrade's dying time to feed his mini-Uzi with a brand-new magazine. He had it up and running, firing off a burst toward Bolan that was just a trifle high, the Parabellum rounds crackling briskly overhead. Bolan ducked, returned fire, but his target was moving, two rounds wasted, while the third plucked at the neo-Nazi's sleeve.

It was enough to stagger him, apparently, but not enough to make him drop his SMG. Still firing, he retreated toward a nearby table that had been flipped over on its side when the shooting started. It was pocked with holes and streaked with blood, no major cover there, but Bolan didn't feel like letting his opponent go to ground, even behind the flimsiest of shelter.

Standing firm and lining up the shot, he stroked the MP-5 K's trigger twice, the six rounds drilling home in two fair patterns, either one enough to drop the guy, their combined lethal force irresistible. He slumped, legs folding under him, and went down loosely in a boneless sprawl.

What next?

A glance around the banquet room told Bolan there was nothing he could do to help the dead or wounded; they would simply have to wait for the police and paramedics to arrive. Meanwhile, whatever time remained to him was better used in finding out if there were any other shooters lurking in the Hotel Valentine—and, if so, what they were doing with themselves.

Ears cocked for any sound of sirens, knowing he probably wouldn't hear them on the mezzanine, Bolan moved out to search for other prey.

IT WAS A FLUKE that Marilyn Crouder encountered Fletcher and his men at all. She had come close to following Belasko as he rushed the shooters in the banquet hall, but then she had decided that her unexpected entry might distract him, even get him killed. A kind of reverse chivalry kicked in at that point, and she decided that to help him, she would have to find another means of access to the battlefield.

But how?

She ran on past the open doorway to the banquet hall, fleet-footed, glancing in there briefly as she passed, seeing enough to make her cringe. It was a slaughter, blood and bodies everywhere, the guns still hammering away. Two dead men lay outside the door, still clutching automatic weapons in their hands, one wearing a hotel staff blazer, the other in shirtsleeves. Mike Belasko had already disappeared inside the killing room, but a familiar-looking sport coat caught her eye, lying beside the door, a rumpled mess.

Now, what the hell…?

Before the answer had a chance to click, she ducked into an empty conference room next door, but found no means of access through the folding wall that screened it from the banquet hall.

"Dammit!"

She knew there was at least one other door that served the banquet room, somewhere behind the dais that had been set up along the north wall. How to reach it? Moving farther east, she found a corridor and turned left into it, still running, reckless in her speed. In front of her, some fifty feet ahead, a bland employees-only door was swinging shut.

Since no one stood between her and the door, Crouder knew that someone had to have passed through in the opposite direction, just ahead of her. Most likely, it would be a staff member, or possibly a guest who had escaped the carnage on the mezzanine.

But then again….

No matter who it was, pure logic told her that to find the access door she sought, into the banquet hall, she had to go this way. White knuckling the Kalashnikov, she slowed her pace and eased up to the door, reached out her left hand toward the knob, feeling relief and grim anxiety all mixed together as it turned without resistance in her grasp.

Unlocked.

The door opened in her direction, one more hassle, but she did her best and threw it open, rushed through in a crouch, both hands now locked around the assault rifle. Another empty hallway yawned at her, the echoes of the battle going on next door filling her ears. She moved along the hallway, picking up the pace, wishing the shooters in the banquet hall would take a breather, let her hear if there was anyone ahead of her, either concealed or moving off at speed.

Another door in front of her, no subtle movement this time. It was steel, again restricted to employees only, but she doubted whether it would stop an armor-piercing round if someone less than friendly waited for her on the other side.

One way to tell.

This time, the door opened away from her, a pressure bar to open it. She took a chance, kept both hands on the rifle, leveled, as she stepped up to the door and gave the bar a solid jolt with her right foot. The door flew back to meet its low, floor-mounted stop with a resounding clang. There was no room behind it for a shooter to conceal himself, but she saw someone at the end of a short hall that led her farther north, just disappearing up a flight of service stairs.

Was that a weapon dangling from his hand?

She had a choice to make. A left turn would bring her up behind the dais in the banquet room, potentially in time and in a fair position to assist Belasko. On the other hand, if she *had* seen a weapon in the fleeing stranger's fist, it meant he had to be one of the Nordic Temple's raiders. No policeman worthy of his badge and paycheck would avoid the bloody chaos reigning in the banquet room. Whatever else the running man might be, she would have bet her life that he wasn't a cop.

Fletcher?

From what she'd seen, the man bore no resemblance to him, but if Fletcher had accompanied his raiders to the Hotel Valentine, and if he wasn't busy dueling Belasko in the banquet hall, there was at least an outside chance that one of his escaping thugs might lead her to the chief. If nothing else, perhaps she could prevent one of the bastards from escaping, maybe raising hell with other guests in the hotel.

The service stairs led upward, toward a dozen floors of rooms, most of them occupied.

That made her mind up for her, and she moved more quickly as she neared the stairs, though still with caution. Halfway up, she heard the sound of muffled voices from above and proceeded from there more carefully, on tiptoe, easing toward the sound. An access door stood open on the third-floor landing, voices emanating from the hallway just beyond.

"We haven't got much time," a too familiar voice was saying. "While the other guys are mopping up downstairs, I want you fanning out along this floor and raising all the hell you can. We're looking at five minutes, max, so make it count."

Without a conscious thought behind the move, she scaled the final steps, barged through the door and found herself confronted by six men, all armed, Sean Fletcher standing in their midst.

"I think you've raised enough hell for today," she said, and opened fire with the Kalashnikov.

THE TIME CONSTRAINT was eating at Sean Fletcher as he led his second group of soldiers past the banquet hall, leaving the first team to mop up the survivors gathered there. It would have been a waste to throw in six more guns when they could wreak more havoc elsewhere in the building, make the Hotel Valentine, its owners and the whole damned city sorry as could be that they had ever played host to a so-called civil rights convention in Chicago.

It was time to kick some ass, and at that moment, Fletcher didn't care what color ass it was—black, white or yellow, Jew or Gentile—just as long as he could drive his message home and make it stick. When they looked back upon this day, ZOG's mindless tools would weep and gnash their teeth.

Until somebody came along and put them out of their misery.

Five soldiers trailed him down a hallway next door to the banquet hall, flinching as bullets rattled off the wall immediately to their left, then through one doorway, then another, finally ascending concrete stairs to reach the floor where guest rooms started and the hotel's conference facilities were left behind.

On three, he took a moment to remind them of their orders, hardening their young hearts to the slaughter that had to follow. Killing was a part of war, and noncombatants often suffered more than fighting men. It was a fact of life—and death—that Aryan warriors had to learn to accept before the great cleansing began.

"We haven't got much time," he told them. "While the other guys are mopping up downstairs, I want you fanning out along this floor and raising all the hell you can. We're looking at five minutes, max, so make it count."

The words had barely left his lips before a female voice distracted him. "I think you've raised enough hell for today," it said.

He turned in the direction of the sound, his soldiers following. Before them, framed in the doorway granting access to the service stairs, stood Mary Krause, with a Kalashnikov assault rifle. Fletcher was groping for a comeback when she opened fire.

Ironically, the first rounds from her AK hammered Reggie Stanko, who had brought up the rear, and who should certainly have known that she was following them. Stitched across the chest, he made a canine sort of woofing noise as he was airborne, just before he slammed into the wall and folded, leaving crimson streaks behind him, on the wallpaper, as he slid to the floor.

The tag end of the burst that finished Stanko clipped Joe Bauer's shoulder, spinning him and dropping him to one knee with a startled gasp of pain. He bounced right back, though, lurching to his feet, unloading on the traitor with his Ingram SMG, while Fletcher and the rest of them did likewise, firing on the run, in search of cover that didn't exist.

As it turned out, they didn't need it. Krause saw five submachine guns swinging into target acquisition, something close to point-blank range, and even with the shooters dodging, weaving, it was obvious that some of them would score decisive hits. Retreating through the doorway, even as she fired another burst and cut Joe Bauer's legs from under him, she disappeared from sight as several dozen slugs tore up the doorjamb and surrounding wall.

"Get after her!" Fletcher snapped at his commandos. "That's the bitch who sold us out! I want her dead!"

The three of them were off and running, pounding down the stairs in hot pursuit, as Fletcher turned to check on Bauer. He was still alive, but with a shoulder and both femurs shattered, he was clearly in no shape to travel.

"Sorry, Joe," said Fletcher as he raised his mini-Uzi.

"Wait!"

A 3-round burst tore through the open mouth and finished it, Fletcher already racing down the service stairs before the echo of those final shots had died away.

Police were on their way by now, he realized, and found it didn't matter. Mary Krause had managed to escape from him three times, and Fletcher was determined that her run of luck would end, right here and now, no matter what it cost to take her down.

THE FAINT ECHOES of gunfire came from somewhere overhead. That much was clear to Bolan, and he knew that small-arms fire would probably have been inaudible more than a single floor below the source of noise. That meant the shooters were on three—if not directly overhead, then near enough for sound to carry through the hotel's floor and walls.

Or down the built-in echo chamber of a staircase.

He was moving briskly toward the steel, beige-painted door marked Stairs when he heard footsteps clatter on the other side, someone descending in a rush. He stepped to one side, back against the wall and sighted down the barrel of his SMG as Marilyn Crouder burst through the door.

She recognized him just in time to lower her Kalashnikov, instead of firing from the hip, breathless and flushed as she approached him.

"Fletcher...three, four others...right behind me!"

Bolan didn't have to ask if she was sure. The sound of footsteps rapidly descending was repeated from behind the access door, and from the racket, Bolan knew that several persons were approaching, reckless in their haste.

"Is that thing loaded?" he had time to ask.

She answered with a jerky nod. "Three-quarters of a clip, at least."

"Okay, then," Bolan said, a final glance around confirming that the service corridor offered nowhere to hide. "We're short on cover here."

"Let's get it done," she said, and brought the rifle to her shoulder, index finger curled around the trigger.

"Right."

The access door burst open, framing one man, others crowding close behind him. From the shocked expression on his face, the shooter hadn't counted on resistance, much less meeting two guns in the corridor.

Twin bursts of automatic fire ripped through the

leader of the pack and pitched him backward, toppling his flankers in confusion. Before Bolan and Crouder could make it a clean sweep, the steel door swung shut, deflecting the last of their rounds.

"What now?" she inquired.

It was a worthwhile question, and an urgent one. The odds were fifty-fifty that their adversaries—the survivors—would be crouched behind that door, prepared to cut down anyone who opened it. The other possibility, however, was that they would make a break for it, using the momentary lull in combat to escape from the hotel.

Bolan, for one, wasn't prepared to let them get away that easily.

"I think—"

The door edged open, interrupting him, and he was braced to fire the MP-5 K when a pale hand darted through the opening, flipped something round and olive drab in their direction, then retreated as the door swung shut.

"Grenade!" The cry came from Crouder, in case he hadn't recognized the lethal sphere as it came wobbling toward them, bouncing on the carpet.

Bolan swept the lady off her feet, Kalashnikov and all, and carried her for three long strides along the hall before he dropped her, covering her supine body with his own.

The standard fragmentation grenade has a five- or six-second fuse. The kill radius varies by model and size of the explosive charge within, but one law of physics remains constant: most of the destructive force from any explosive charge that detonates on flat, open ground goes upward.

In this case, while the explosion nearly deafened Bolan, and he felt the heat, sensed jagged shards of shrapnel passing overhead, he suffered no serious damage.

The problem came in disentangling himself from Crouder and rising to his feet again, before their enemies could follow up on the grenade. Still in a crouch and pivoting to face the source of danger, Bolan saw the door swing open and disgorge a pair of gunmen, firing as they came.

They overcompensated in the smoky haze of the explosion, firing higher than they might have with an unobstructed field of vision. Even with his ears still ringing, Bolan heard the rattle of their submachine guns and imagined he could see the bullets slicing channels through the smoke. Crouching, he hit the gunners with a rising zigzag burst and gave them everything remaining in the MP-5 K's magazine, watching them dance as they were ventilated, staggered, taken down.

And he was reaching for a fresh clip when a 3-round burst struck Bolan in the chest, dead center, slamming him backward and stealing his breath. Despite the Kevlar vest that saved his life, the stunning blow still made his ribs and sternum throb with pain. He knew that he had dropped the submachine gun's magazine and fumbled for it on the carpet, came up empty, groping for another in his pocket as the precious seconds ticked away.

"One down." The voice was familiar from their conversation on the telephone, in California. "Now it's your turn, bitch."

Crouder's answer came from the Kalashnikov, firing until the slide locked open on an empty chamber. Bolan, by that time, had managed to retrieve another magazine and load his SMG, but Crouder didn't require his help this time. Some ten or fifteen feet away, a third gunman lay crumpled near the other two, Sean Fletcher barely recognizable from photographs on file at Stony Man. He blew a crimson bubble, one last breath escaping from his ruptured lungs before his muscles slackened and were still.

"Are you all right?"

"Aside from feeling like somebody danced the tango on my chest," he said, "I'm fine."

"That's all of them," Crouder told him. "If there were any more, they'd be on top of us by now."

"Drivers?"

She shrugged. "They won't stay long enough for the police to collar them. We shouldn't either, I suppose."

He could hear sirens now, sounding more distant than they were, in fact. It would be dicey, getting out, if they had sealed off the hotel.

"What should we do?"

"We're paying guests," he said. "I'd recommend we get back to our rooms, ASAP, and get cleaned up. You have much practice playing dumb?"

"You must be kidding," Crouder replied, flashing the first smile he had seen since her abduction. "You're forgetting that I work for Uncle Sam?"

Touché.

They started for the elevator, Bolan pleasantly surprised when Crouder reached out and took his hand.

CHAPTER SEVENTEEN

"The man came out of nowhere, is exactly what he did. First thing, these others came in shooting, throwing bombs. I'm tellin' you, it felt like Armageddon, no mistake. Then comes another man, and he was dressed just like the others, in a hotel jacket, but they tell me now he wasn't anybody from their staff or from security."

Below the black man's animated face, subtitles advertised WXBN News, from Chicago, and identified the speaker as the Reverend Mr. Lewis Albright, president of FREE. Fed up with the report and all the other bad news he had listened to the past few hours, Gerhard Steuben pressed the mute button on his remote control, silencing the minister while leaving his face on-screen, lips moving in a silent litany.

"'The man came out of nowhere,'" Steuben mimicked, furious. "These men *always* come from nowhere, interfering with my soldiers. Filthy bastards!"

On the television screen, two paramedics bore a sheet-covered stretcher from an exit of the Hotel Valentine, an inset photograph of Sean Fletcher suddenly superimposed on the scene. Steuben quickly turned the sound back on.

"—etcher, a one-time U.S. Navy SEAL, discharged in 1995 for insubordination and affiliation with a neo-Nazi cult identified by federal agents as the Temple of the Nordic Covenant. It is unknown, at this time, whether his companions in the raid against the Hotel Valentine were also members of the cult, or whether—"

Steuben killed the sound again, then switched the set off altogether. He had seen enough—too much, in fact. A knot was forming in his stomach, and he had a sour taste in his mouth.

It was the first time that the Temple had been publicly identified with any of the actions he had ordered. Fletcher's notoriety had never been a problem in the past, as long as he remained at large and wasn't linked to a specific incident. Now he was dead—apparently from sheer damned carelessness—and in his passing he had left the Nordic Temple vulnerable to its enemies as it had never been before.

This was enough to spark a whole new round of state and federal investigations, or to bring the ones already under way out of the closet, into daylight. It was probable—no, make that *guaranteed*—that Steuben would himself be sought to testify before grand juries, possibly Congressional investigators. Watchdog groups that thrived on litigation, like that Morris Dees outfit in Alabama, would be lining up to file lawsuits for wrongful death and any other charge that they could think of, if the Temple as a group could be connected to the slaughter at the Hotel Valentine. And if the scavengers looked deep enough, what would prevent them drawing links between Chicago and the recent mayhem in Los Angeles?

"Nothing," he muttered to himself. "Nothing at all."

His own face might be on the television, even now, but he didn't care to see it if it was. Prepared as he believed himself to be for going underground, having already severed ties with what most people would have called the "normal" world around him, he was still surprised—disheartened, even—by the speed with which the move had now been forced upon him by his enemies. There was a sense of having lost control, immediately followed by a deep, abiding rage directed toward his panoply of foes—the Jews, mud people, Communists and intellectuals, the whole damned scurvy crew.

Steuben controlled his brooding anger with a force of sheer, indomitable will. If ZOG and its affiliates were anxious for a war, he would most certainly oblige them, but on his own terms, and in his own good time. While they were picking over Fletcher's bones, trying to pin names on the other warriors they had slaughtered and connect the Nordic Temple to the raid with evidence required for even ZOG's charade of "justice" in the courts, he would be busily at work, fomenting his own racial holy war.

The time was now, and his response wouldn't be limited to the Jewnited States. How could it be, when Aryans around the world were counting on him, mobilizing to defend their racial heritage, reclaim the world that once was theirs?

His enemies had no idea what they had done. No doubt, they thought that he was on the ropes, or soon would be. Perhaps they hoped he would surrender or decamp to Mexico like Louis Beam, only to be re-

turned in handcuffs and humiliation, treated as a gro-
tesque laughingstock. But even Beam, a fighter in his
day, had beaten ZOG, winning acquittal in the Arkansas sedition trial. Steuben, this time around, would
go one better and defeat his scheming adversaries on
the battlefield, bypassing their pathetic legal system.

He wouldn't submit, and he wouldn't repeat the
various mistakes of those who went before him, from
the Third Reich to the battered and defunct Fifth Era
KKK. Steuben had learned from those mistakes, unlike some hopeless fools who still believed that they
could work within the system or petition Congress to
create their own white bastion somewhere in the
Rocky Mountains.

Idiots!

They should have known, as he did, that the enemy
would never yield until he felt the pistol at his head,
the blade against his throat. Even in that extremity,
he would be scheming, double-dealing, trying des-
perately to play for time. Steuben wasn't prepared to
grant that time, however. He would show no mercy,
take no prisoners—unless, of course, they could be
used to his advantage, for some profit to the master
race.

"Is my time now," he said, unconscious of the fact
that he had said the words aloud.

"How's that, sir?" asked his bodyguard, standing
before the Winnebago's packed refrigerator, lifting
out a can of beer.

"Nothing," Stevens replied.

"Okay. Sorry."

He heard the can pop as the man retreated to his

place beside the driver, low-pitched conversation from that quarter only momentarily distracting him.

They were rolling south on Highway 57, nearing Kankakee, but they wouldn't be stopping there unless the RV needed fuel. They would proceed beyond Champaign-Urbana, on to Effingham, and there join Highway 70, westbound into St. Louis. Steuben had ordained the course, and he saw no reason to change it, even as the new plan took shape in his mind.

St. Louis would be perfect for a jumping-off point. If the FBI was looking for him—and he had no doubt it was, or soon would be—the agents would have forty-eight of the Jewnited States to choose from, fanning out across the map. If they assumed that he had been in Illinois, to supervise the action in Chicago, then his natural escape route would lie northward, through Wisconsin, into Canada. The Bureau lacked sufficient eyes to watch all major airports in the country, though it *could* alert customs and immigration officers, even the local law, if necessary.

Still, it wouldn't be enough.

He was prepared to leave, had been for months, in fact. He carried German, Austrian and Dutch passports, as well as materials for the disguises that allowed him to put on the faces shown in those three different photographs. Obsessed with learning German since his high-school days, he was fluent in the language of his forefathers.

All Steuben needed was an airline ticket, and he was history. The age of Gerhard Steuben would begin, and no one in the world would ever truly be the same again.

He rose to join his driver and his bodyguard up

front. It was a rare event, and both of them wore questioning expressions on their faces, though they kept their mouths shut.

"When we get closer to St. Louis," Steuben said, "watch out for rental agencies. We need another vehicle before we check into the airport."

"Are we flying somewhere, boss?" the driver asked.

"Indeed we are," the Führer of the Nordic Temple said. "We're going home."

"SO," HAL BROGNOLA SAID, once he had switched on the scrambler, "I guess you've seen the news about Chicago."

"Bits and pieces," Bolan answered.

"They're saying nineteen dead, for sure, not counting Fletcher and his crew. At least another twenty-three are in the hospital, and some of them will probably check out."

"It was a mess, no doubt about it," Bolan said.

"Could have been worse, though, I suppose," Brognola granted. "Still, the heat from this one isn't going to blow over in a day or two. Word has it, all four networks are cranking out special reports on hate groups in America, and Albright's shopping for a publisher to pick up his memoirs before this thing cools down. We've got the same old racket on the Hill—investigate the Nazis, pass new hate-crime laws. As if some bastard facing twenty counts of murder in the first degree would give a damn about an extra five years tacked on for his attitude."

"I should have stopped them going in," Bolan said.

"No way you could do that," Brognola replied. "You didn't know who you were looking for, how many there would be. You damned sure didn't know they'd come in dressed as members of the staff. Chicago PD let them pass, and they had four, five times as many pairs of eyes as you did on the scene."

"Still," Bolan said.

"Still nothing. Our job now is to run Stevens down before he pulls another trick out of his hat."

"Speaking of tricks," Bolan replied, "if you can tell me where he is, that wouldn't be a bad one."

"Funny you should ask," Brognola said.

"You've got a lead?"

"At least. Last night, three men with German passports booked a flight out of St. Louis to Berlin. Nobody thought a thing about it at the time, and they were off the ground before we got a whiff that anything was funny on the deal, but I'm convinced it was Herr Steuben and a couple of his goons."

"How's that?" Bolan asked.

"First thing," Brognola said, "would have to be the brilliant choice of names. Our subject's passport called him Gerhard Steuffel—close enough to Steuben for my money, if you figure he was running just a tad short on imagination, or else overdosed on arrogance. Airport surveillance videos confirm that Steuffel doesn't look a thing like Stevens—not unless you take away the gray hair, glasses, mustache and goatee, in which case he's a perfect match. His bookends changed their names on paper, but they didn't bother with disguises. I suppose they didn't think their mugs would be on file."

"And are they?" Bolan asked.

"One is. He's Joshua Padilla, and he made a point of sounding off when he was booked for battery, in '92, that it's Italian, not a 'greaser' name."

"Who did he batter?"

"He saw an interracial couple at a movie, in L.A. A Korean man, white girl. It pissed him off enough to throw his Coke and popcorn in their faces, slap the woman and start pounding on the man. He was sixteen and got probation from the juvey court, conditional on his avoidance of contact with other skinheads in the neighborhood."

"I'd say it didn't take."

"Not much," Brognola said. "Fact is, he ran away from home, dropped out of sight until last year, when someone from the Klanwatch outfit snapped his picture at a public rally of the Nordic Temple, down in Arkansas. They reached out to LAPD, but no one was inclined to extradite—statute of limitations, time elapsed, expenses—take your pick."

"They were relieved to see him go."

"I'd say."

"And now he's going international."

"Looks like," Brognola said.

"I guess I'm going to Berlin."

"Will that be one or two?"

Bolan was silent for a moment, pondering, before he said, "I can't imagine that she'd be much use to me in Germany."

"I really couldn't say. It's off her range, for sure."

"What do you hear from ATF?"

"'No comment' sums it up," Brognola said. "They're never going to admit that one of theirs was mixed up in what happened yesterday, or in Los Angeles. After the Waco thing, and all the other bad PR they've had to live with, it would be the kiss of death.''

"You're telling me she's out, or what?''

"I'm telling you that no one out of ATF has squat to say, to me or to the press. Your friend may have a better chance of getting through, for what it's worth. One thing's for sure, though—even with the badge, she's got no legal weight to throw around in Germany, or anywhere outside the States, for that matter.''

"I get it,'' Bolan said. "It would be helpful if there was someone available to meet me on the other end, maybe help out with targets in the area.''

"I'll see what I can do,'' Brognola said. "You want me to arrange the flight?''

"No, I'll take care of it,'' the Executioner replied. "I'll want to book on a civilian airline, just in case somebody's watching.''

"Right. You never know.'' Brognola was reminded of the fact members of the Nordic Temple and some other neo-Nazi groups had been uncovered in the U.S. military, both at home and overseas. They were inevitably processed out as soon as they had been identified, but it was foolish to assume that every active fascist in all branches of the service had been weeded out. In fact, if one believed the FBI, their numbers had been growing, right along with thefts of military hardware and explosives.

"I'd better go and get my act together, then,'' Bolan said.

"Right. Touch base when you get over there. With any luck, I'll have a contact on the line by then.''

"Okay. I'll see you."

"Yeah."

As he returned the handset to its cradle, the big Fed's mind was already running down the list of agencies he could consult in seeking backup for the big guy's play on German soil. Unfortunately, since the battleground would be a foreign one—and Bolan's target was already maximum high-profile in the States—he couldn't ask the FBI or DEA, and ATF was clearly out, the brass intent on covering their butts while time remained.

Who else would have an agent he could trust working Berlin or the vicinity, with knowledge of the neo-Nazi underground.

A light clicked on inside Brognola's head, and he leaned over toward the intercom.

"Kelly?"

"Yes, sir?" his secretary answered from the outer office.

"I need to have a word with Moshe Levin, chief of cultural affairs at the Israeli embassy."

"I'M SORRY, Agent Crouder. Mr. Archer still hasn't returned from that lunch meeting." Sitting half a continent away, the secretary didn't sound the least bit sorry.

"Really." It was not a question; nothing in her tone betrayed belief.

"I'm sorry, no." The lie again. "But he does have your number there. I'm sure he'll call as soon as possible, when he returns."

"I'm sure."

She hung up on the secretary without going through

the usual amenities. It was a lame riposte, at best, but short of screaming at the woman, cursing her for following her orders, there was nothing else for Crouder to do, no other way for her to register the feeling of disgust.

Archer had hung her out to dry.

She wondered for a moment whether he was filing charges, then decided that if such had been the case, he would have spoken to her, tried to reel her in. Besides, if any charges were preferred, the ATF would suffer big-time from the worst PR nightmare in its traumatic recent history. The Waco siege and Ruby Ridge would pale to insignificance beside the tabloid handling of an ATF agent participating in— what was it, now, two dozen homicides? And all without the slightest effort to arrest or prosecute the heavies, much less any legal paperwork to cover her admittedly bizarre activities.

If *that* went public, then it would be Archer's ass on fire, along with hers, and he had more to lose, careerwise, in the weird, backstabbing world of bureaucratic office politics. He might not go to jail, but he could definitely wave bye-bye to any pension, benefits or future work in any field vaguely resembling law enforcement. If he was quick enough to take advantage of his notoriety, he might find a publisher to do his memoirs, put the best spin on it that he could, a kind of Ollie North arrangement.

But it wouldn't fly.

If her involvement in the L.A. and Chicago killings while on active duty with the ATF went public, Archer's great career would be as good as dead. And he would leave with nothing.

Zip.

It made more sense, therefore, for him to stall her, wait until the heat died down a bit, then find some way to ease her out. He might not fire her—which would, after all, require at least some vestige of an explanation, and which might provoke retaliation on her part, exposure of his own involvement in the dirty game—but there was nothing to prevent him exercising his discretion, shipping her off to the least-desirable field posting he could find. A slow office, perhaps, where nothing ever happened and the aging misfits shuffled papers all day long, just putting in their time. Or maybe he would find a little something more exciting, like a high-risk detail where she stood an even chance of being shot and killed before she got angry enough to quit and hawk her story to the media.

Bad options everywhere she looked.

And yet there was a certain freedom also in the knowledge that she had been set adrift, however temporarily. She had a sense that there were options open to her now, as there hadn't been since she graduated from the ATF academy ten years before. It hadn't been a wasted decade; no such thought had ever crossed her mind, but if that phase of Crouder's existence was about to end, at least she could take solace in the fact that there were still places to go and things to do.

People to kill.

They had checked out of the hotel as soon as the police downstairs would let them go. A tight-faced manager confirmed that they were paying guests, a homicide detective frowned at their ID, and they were out of there. It wasn't far to Joliet, just far enough for safety's sake, and Belasko had booked them two rooms at the local motel. No sooner were the bags lugged in, than he had left her on her own to go and make some calls.

More than an hour, now—two brush-offs from the secretary in D.C. to show for it—and he hadn't returned.

Crouder knew one thing with perfect clarity, before they even talked about it—Belasko wouldn't let Gary Stevens slip away, if there was anything that he could do to stop it. And considering what she had seen him do so far, the resources he seemed to have available and constantly on call, she had no doubt that he would give the tin-pot Führer a run for his deutsche marks.

But would it be enough?

Stevens was certifiably insane, of course. Beyond the standard lust for power and prestige, he honestly believed the mystic Wotan-and-Valhalla crap he preached to his disciples; really thought there was a perfect race of pure, unsullied Aryans residing somewhere near the center of Earth; truly believed that he—and he alone—could light the fuse for an apocalyptic racial holy war that would engulf the planet, burn off all the human chaff that didn't meet the standards for slave labor, and install the master race as rulers of the whole shebang, with "Gerhard Steuben" at the pinnacle of power.

He was crazy, right…but also crafty, slick and *very* dangerous. He had a private army, relatively small and scattered over several continents, but lethal even in small doses, bankrolled by a shadowy cabal of neo-fascist businessmen, some right-wing criminals, the

odd sheikh here and there. Stevens could never fight
the Third World War himself, but he and his com-
patriots could wreak sufficient havoc that the world
would rue the night his parents did the wild thing in
Poughkeepsie, back in '52.

If Crouder could stop that, any part of it, she felt
compelled to try. And if Belasko tried to brush her
off, refused to let her tag along for the remainder of
the game, then she would do it on her own somehow.
She suddenly had free time on her hands, some
money in the bank that she could use until it went
into the red, and hard-won knowledge of the Nordic
Temple that might be enough, with any luck, to bring
her through alive and more or less intact.

A little late for that, she thought, and felt hot, bitter
tears. Crouder blinked them back. There was no time
for breaking down and getting weepy. Not with a
campaign to plan.

The knock, though long awaited, made her jump.
She took the AK with her, checked the peephole and
stood back to let Belasko in. He didn't seem surprised
to see the automatic rifle in her hand.

"Stevens has gone to Germany," he told her.

"Ah." She took a leap and wondered whether there
was any safety net below. "When do we leave?"

"What did your people say?" he asked her in reply.

"My supervisor's taking meetings every time I call
him. If I didn't have such super self-esteem, I'd feel
downright unloved."

"It could be worse," Bolan replied, without undue
elaboration.

"I considered that," she said, "but I don't think
they can afford to charge me. If somebody blew the

whistle, that would be a different story, but the only witnesses who can connect me to felonious behavior, so far, have a previous appointment with the county medical examiner.''

''I wasn't thinking jail,'' he said.

''Oh, right.'' She lost the strained smile she had worn a moment earlier and broke eye contact. ''They've already done the worst that they can do, and Fletcher paid the price this afternoon.''

''The worst?'' he challenged her. ''You don't have much imagination.''

''It's a matter of priorities,'' she answered, locking eyes with him again. ''Your 'worst' and mine don't necessarily conform.''

''Okay,'' he granted, ''but you're still alive.''

''That was their second big mistake.''

''Why give them any further chances to correct it?'' Bolan asked.

''Because they won't roll over and play dead, all right? The assholes took a beating in L.A., and kept on coming. We just kicked their ass again, but they scored more hits than they took. Nothing will stop them from proceeding with their plans. You get it? Nothing.''

''I may have a trick or two still up my sleeve,'' he said.

''You want to chase this pack of animals around the world like you were playing tag? How long do you expect your luck to hold? Who lacks imagination now?''

She had a point, of course—the same one Bolan had to deal with every time he took the field against another enemy.

"I called in sick," he said, "the day in basic training when they taught us how to quit."

"So, it's okay for you to bet the killer odds, but not for me?"

"You had some fallback options in the States," Bolan said, "even if they haven't really tested out. You start to operate outside the country, with the brass already looking for a reason to come down on you, and you can kiss your badge goodbye."

"I'll never have another chance to use it, anyway," she said.

"You can't be sure of that."

"I know these people," she informed him. "Archer, in particular. The only time he isn't looking out for number one, is when he stops to hand somebody else a load of number two. The guy's afraid of me, of what one careless word could do to his career. If he can't bury me alive in some jerkwater field office, he'll drop me into every high-risk situation he can find, until I either pull the pin or buy the farm."

"You make him sound more like Saddam Hussein than Mr. Clean."

"He's clean enough, in terms of staying off the pad and doing what he's told by anyone with higher rank, but his subordinates exist to serve his interest, just as much as to enforce the law. He's got a quick hand with the knife, if you're not facing him."

"Sounds like you may be better off without that job," Bolan replied.

"I'm way ahead of you," she said. "And I was thinking, maybe we could try some kind of lateral transfer. I'd say I've proved myself. What do you think?"

"I'm not a talent scout," he told her, "and so far, you've managed to ignore your orders both times we engaged the enemy."

"The second time was personal," she told him, standing with her chin high, bright defiance in her eyes. "I needed Fletcher for myself. Besides, I saved your life back there, if you recall."

"And nearly lost your own, three times," he said, "not counting the predicament I found you in at Freedom Home."

"That's finished now," she said. "Besides, if I was really on your team, we'd have the whole chain-of-command thing going on."

"And that would make a difference?"

"You bet your life," she said.

"I would be betting *yours.*"

"You're going to need backup over there."

"It's being taken care of," Bolan said.

"Oh, yeah? By whom, if I may be so bold?"

"I won't know till I check in on the other side," he said. "Not ATF."

"Could be GSG-9," she said, referring to the German counter terrorist police.

"I'll find out soon enough."

"Of course, you won't know who to trust in Germany, with all those sons and grandsons of the reich hanging around. At least, you won't know till your ass is on the line." She frowned and added, "I, for one, would hate to see it get shot off."

"Don't tell me you're an expert on who's who in German politics and law enforcement?"

"I could write a nice fat book about the things I learned while I was hanging with the Nordic Temple,'' she replied. ''In fact, I probably *will* write one, when they're in the bag. Meanwhile, I know some overseas connections, some of them by name, others by code and references to occupations, offices, that sort of thing. Beyond that, I've refined my sense of smell for Nazis. I can pick out some who might slip by you in a pinch.''

''You get that from the Psychic Friends?'' he asked.

''Try eighteen months in Nazi never-never land,'' she said. ''I lived with these psycho bastards twenty-four, seven. You spend that much time staring evil in the face, you get to see behind the mask it wears.''

''And what if something happens to you over there?''

She flashed another smile. ''You mean to say, what happens if I get *my* ass shot off?''

He nodded. ''Stranger things have happened.''

''Then, if you have time and you feel like it, find the bastard. Square it up.''

''Don't you have people you'd rather spend time with? Contact?''

''You're talking family?'' she asked. ''I don't have any, that I know of. Ditto on friends, unless you count the guys at work. I don't, these days. No one to miss me, see? No lawsuits, nothing in the way of liability.''

''It wouldn't matter,'' Bolan said, ignoring her description of the loneliness that was a feature of his world, as well. ''Who would they sue?''

''So, there you are.''

''It's still a bad idea,'' he said.

''You don't like that scenario? Try this one—you go on without me, and I catch the next flight to Berlin myself, alone.''

"You'd rather sabotage the game than miss the final gun?" he asked.

"What sabotage?" she countered. "Hell, you may not find a thing, with your anonymous connection over there. He may lead you around in circles, if he doesn't set you up. I may be left to do the whole damned thing myself."

"You think so, do you?"

"Stranger things have happened, like you said."

"If we do this," he told her, "then we're allies, nothing more. We're not a couple, and I'm not your bodyguard. The job comes first."

There was the barest hint of disappointment in her frown as she replied, "I wouldn't have it any other way."

Reluctantly, he said, "All right. Let's try it on for size."

Her smile was dazzling. "Like I said before, when do we leave?"

*   *   *   *   *

*The heart-stopping action
continues in SuperBolan 79,*
POWER OF THE LANCE,
the second book of
THE TYRANNY FILES
coming in July 2001.